THE GUNNER
AT THE ACADEMY

THE GUNNER
AT THE ACADEMY

BY

HAROLD R THOMSON

www.penmorepress.com

ISBN: 978-1-957851-67-9(EBOOK)
ISBN: 978-1-957851-68-6(Paperback)
BISAC Subject Headings:

FIC014000FICTION / Historical
FIC032000FICTION / War & Military
FIC002000FICTION / Action

Editor: Chris Wozney

Book Cover:
Emilija Rakić PR Emily's World of Design
Acknowledgments to the Artist for the book cover :

Captain Sillery's Company, 7th Battalion Royal Artillery at the Battle of Talavera, 27-28 July 1809. By David Rowlands

Please send all correspondence to:
Penmore Press LLC
920 N Javelina Pl
Tucson AZ 85748

DEDICATION

To the 3rd Brigade

CHAPTER ONE:

BARRACKS

Robert Saxon paused at the open gate, his feet rooted, valise sagging from loose fingers. It was not reluctance that kept him there but reflection—reflection on the enormous change such a simple course of events had wrought in his life. Just yesterday, he had left home. Just yesterday. It had been raining, large steady drops the colour of steel. Despite the weather, his father had insisted that he wear an old evening coat and a black round hat, explaining that this was tradition, that all new gentleman cadets were to dress this way. Robert had not liked how the rain collected on the hat's shallow brim, to pour down whenever he inclined his head, but he did not complain, for he did not wish anyone's last memory of him to be one of weakness, even a trivial weakness. His family and friends had gathered in the front yard of his father's inn to say farewell, and he wore his gravest expression, shaking a few by the hand and embracing the others. Sissy had held him longest, burying her head in the folds at the front of the coat, which was much too big for him.

"Goodbye, Sissy," he murmured. Her little dog, Boxer, tried to get between them, pawing at the knees of Robert's long trousers. "I shall miss you, and Boxer, too. I shall miss you dearly."

They parted slowly, for this truly was the end of something —the long and difficult childhood they had shared. Sissy wiped away tears with crooked fingers. She and Roberts had been comrades in battle of a sort, and now their alliance was sundered.

Robert had next faced his father. The air between them chilled. They did not embrace, nor even shake hands.

"Come back when you have a commission," Thomas Saxon had said.

"Yes, sir," was Robert's reply, though he knew that if he did come back, if he ever set foot in this yard again, it would not be for long, perhaps a day or two while he was on leave. Then he would be away again, to follow his ambition, which was to go to war, to enter this new variation on an old struggle against a brutal and persistent enemy, the French, under Napoleon Bonaparte. The navy under Nelson had saved England from invasion at Trafalgar, but so far Britain's soldiers had been denied the chance to face the vaunted forces of the Corsican dictator, the man who had just crowned himself Emperor. But someday soon Robert knew that they would, and he would be with them.

Turning away from his father, Robert had said his farewells to the others who had braved the rain to see him off—some of the stable lads, and Nan, the maid with whom he had shared the occasional youthful tryst in the barn. Parting from her had not been the moment of anxiety he had feared, but more of a relief. Then, that had been that. The coachman had taken Robert's valise and thrown it up onto the coach roof, lashing it in place with the other sodden luggage. With the horses pawing and stamping, Robert had boarded the ungainly vehicle as the coachman mounted and took up his long horn, blowing out the call for the departure. There had been no other passengers, and as the whip snapped and they started forward, Robert had gazed from the window, watching as the inn receded, the place that had been his home rolling away from him. The rain had grown heavier, and its pounding on the curved sides of the coach had sounded to Robert like drums beating the long roll, the military call to arms at sunrise.

And now, here he stood, the rain having stopped and the sun boiling him in his ridiculous coat. Here he was about to enter the Royal Military Academy, and in time, after completing his course of study, he would become an officer in the Royal Regiment of Artillery.

The gate was just a gap in the grey stone wall where the lane entered. One more step would carry him inside, but he did not move. Instead, he took in the scene. The wall was about five feet high, nothing more than a fence marking the border of the Academy grounds. Beyond lay an expanse of Parade Ground, bordered on the right with a grassy field and on the left with the Academy buildings. The buildings shone in the morning light, red brick and stone facades free of the soot that covered much of London and its surrounds. In the centre was a plain square block, two stories high, with a tower in each of its four corners. The turrets on the towers reminded Robert of onions, or of pictures he had seen of Bavarian church steeples. Flanking this centre building were identical wings with flat rooftops crowned by decorative stone battlements and rows of rectangular windows. The crests of several chimneys also suggested the presence of more structures in the rear, but these were obscured.

"So, now I step into freedom," he whispered, for that was how he saw it. This was what he had wished for; this had been his dream for so many years.

He entered the Academy grounds.

"Officers of the infantry and cavalry may look upon you with some prejudice," his father had warned him. "They are fancy, aristocratic types, the lot of them, who purchase their commissions without a jot of training. They will judge you of an inferior class, for the cadets of the Royal Military Academy may be the sons of shopkeepers, butchers, bakers or innkeepers like me. Not all, mind you, but enough. Never you mind those others, for those in the Artillery and Engineering Corps are a skilled set, who require proper schooling. Funds alone would never secure you a place."

Robert had only half listened, for his father's words had come to mean less and less to him as the years passed. "I should meet some decent lads here," he said to himself, for though he would no doubt rub shoulders with members of the gentry or even nobility, it was probable that a number of the boys he would encounter would have lived a life very much like his, boys who had come to the Academy because their fathers were former gunners who insisted that their sons follow the same path.

He made his way along the edge of the Parade Ground, not across it, as his father had instructed. The Parade was for drill, not for taking a stroll. The centre building drew closer.

Beside the main door stood a sentry, stiff and solemn, in front of his wooden sentry box, musket ordered at his right side. He wore a blue coat, the collar and cuffs bright red, the buttonhole lace a startling and garish yellow. White leather belts crossed his chest, and on his head perched a tall leather shako, its brass plate gleaming. This was the uniform of the private soldier, or "gunner," as the rank was known in the Royal Artillery. As an officer, Robert would one day have a much finer suit of clothes, but he would also have a right to be described as a "gunner," for all members of the Royal Artillery, all those who served the guns, were referred to by that title, even if not by that rank.

He halted in front of the sentry. The man's eyes flickered to the right, but otherwise he remained impassive. Robert studied the soldier's uniform, but a rustle of wings drew his gaze upward. A flock of pigeons had just taken flight from one of the rooftops. Robert watched it rise, watched it twist and writhe like a cloud of smoke.

*****

Robert reported to the Orderly Room, a small closet of an office just inside the main door to the centre building. Behind an unvarnished wooden counter, the Orderly Sergeant searched for Robert's name in a ledger bearing the identities of those cadets about to be admitted.

"Saxon, aye, here you are, lad," the sergeant said. He was a gaunt veteran with sprouting grey whiskers and few remaining teeth. "Quarters in the east barracks, second floor, number eight."

A gallery connected the centre building with the east wing. At the end of the gallery, a rising stairwell brought Robert to the upper floor and a long interior corridor. He counted off the white numbers painted on the grey doors until at last he came to number eight. This was his assigned room.

The door stood slightly ajar. Voices emanated from within, light conversation, a rattle of laughter, the shuffle of papers. Other cadets were already here. For a moment Robert worried that he was late, or that perhaps the administration had no qualms about mixing new recruits with elder classmen.

Not that those worries mattered. He was here now. Giving the door a gentle push, he walked in, his shoes crunching in the sand that had been scattered on the floorboards. He halted, feet together, as he had done in the presence of his examiners when he had first applied to the Academy.

Silence met him, and four staring faces. He affected a smile, returning stare for stare. The room seemed crowded. Two boys occupied chairs at a table under the single front window, another sat on the edge of a bed, and the last stood, leaning on the mantel. All of them looked at least a year older than Robert.

"I've come to join," he said gravely, dropping his valise and doffing the round hat. He took in as much as he could of his new surroundings: the heavy green drapes on the window, the watercolours on the walls and over the fireplace, the six little folding beds in the corners, each shrouded in dull grey curtains. "The Orderly Sergeant said I was assigned to this barrack."

The boys at the table stood. One had been reading a broadsheet, and he let it flutter to the sandy floor. "Well, then," he said, "the more the merrier." He and his companion both wore the blue single-breasted coat of the R.M.A. gentleman cadet, as did the fellow on the bed. The fourth, a tall, lanky lad with a low forehead and very round, piercing blue eyes, wore a long buff coloured robe and bedroom slippers.

"Another snooker," this last said. "Let's get a look at you, then, snooker." He advanced toward Robert, looking him up and down with unconcealed contempt. "You're pretty," he added, showing his teeth. "With golden ringlets like a little girly. How old are you, my sweet girly?"

Robert met his eye. This was not a promising start, but he wondered what he had expected. Perhaps he had hoped for a friendly greeting from a group of lads in the same circumstances as he, new boys without a clue. Yet here they had put him with this bunch, elder boys who, no doubt, thought it their right to insult the younger.

"I've just turned seventeen," he said.

"Ha, just ripe for plucking! Name?"

"Robert Saxon."

"Ha. Saxon, Saxon. That rolls off the tongue with ease. I'm Wesley Rice, your cadet corporal. Which means I'm in charge, see?"

"That's right," said one of the others, a pinched fellow with features like a rat, his hair coal black. "You do what he says."

"I understand," Robert said, trying to keep the contempt from his voice. If it was his fate to be bullied, he would take it for now.   His father had explained that there would be an initiation period, that this was tradition. "I'll remember that."

"I'm Reginald Blakeley," the rat faced boy continued. "Second year cadet."

"Charles Marigold," the third said, just as a lean, striped cat suddenly crossed the room and leapt onto the table. Marigold scooped the animal into his arms and started stroking its flank. The boy had a flattened face like a bulldog's, and Robert quickly decided to think of him as Dog, a Dog with the cat in his arms, just as he had already decided that Blakeley would be Rat.

The fourth boy remained hunched on the edge of his bed. He was heavy set with a great sweep of russet hair covering part of his chubby face. He muttered something that Robert could not make out, then looked away.

"Eh, what's that Campion?" Rice said. He moved toward the chubby boy, but at that moment footsteps rang outside in the corridor. With the footsteps there rose a cheerful whistling, someone performing a rendition of "British Grenadiers."

All heads turned toward the barrack room door as it again swung open, and a fifth boy entered. Robert saw a round face, red apple cheeks covered in brown freckles, and prominent front teeth. Here was another recruit.

"Hello!" the new boy cried, loud enough to make Cadet Corporal Rice wince. Like Robert, he wore an old round hat and a long coat. "I see it's rather busy in here already, isn't it? My, my. Well, my name is George Howard, but you can call me Georgie. I've come to join the Artillery!"

"Ha!" Rice cried. "Two snookers in one day! Can you believe our luck, lads? You stay right there, Lord Georgie. We're not done with this one yet."

The newcomer blinked. "Stay here you say? And who are you, sir?"

"Stay by the door. That's your post, and I'm your corporal. Do as I say."

Georgie stiffened to a parody of attention, head tilted back. He dropped his valise with a bang. "Yes, Corporal!"

Rice grunted. "That's better. Now, let the fun begin. You, Cadet Saxon. We want to test your knowledge of basic mathematics, see what sort of roommate we have here, see? Show us a line of forty-five degrees."

Robert sighed. He wanted to wipe that smug grin off Rice's face, but it would not do to start a fight on his first day, especially with a corporal who would have the force of law behind his actions. In time these fellows would tire of their pranks, so for now he would play along.

"Do you have a ruler?" he asked.

There were snickers. "Not with a ruler, you ungracious shit, show us on the wall. Lean up against the wall at an angle of forty-five degrees."

Rice pointed to the wall beside the fireplace, twirling his finger in a circular motion. Robert tossed his hat to the table, advanced to the wall and leaned against it, tilting forward from his ankles with his arms outstretched, palms flat against the white-washed plaster. "Forty-five degrees."

"Not forward, snooker!" Rice said. "Do it backward."

That was easy enough, Robert thought, so he turned around, this time leaning back, feet braced against the sanded floor, his head hard against the wall with his hands behind as a cushion. "There you are."

"Keep your legs straight," Rat said. He produced a switch from a bucket next to the hearth, drawing it out and giving it a few test swings, letting it whistle as it cut the air. "And stay steady!"

With one sharp blow, he struck Robert across the back of the knees. Robert jerked in surprise at the sudden burning pain.

"Keep still," Rat snapped.

"And hold your position," Rice commanded, standing with one hand propped on his hip.

Robert's neck began to ache.

"Now, then, snooker," Rice said, after about half a minute had passed. "These are the rules. You take heed as well, Lord Georgie. The rules are so simple that even infants such as yourselves should have no difficulty understanding. First, no snooker—and that means you—may return a blow from one of the senior class. That includes lads that don't wear a swab on their right shoulder, a swab being a corporal's epaulette. Do you understand that, then?"

"Yes, Corporal!" Georgie exclaimed from the doorway, but Robert only said, "Understood." His legs had begun to tremble, and the flesh was cold where the switch had cut.

"Snookers are not allowed to smoke," Rice continued. "Nor are you permitted to enter a public house, save on an errand from one of us. We have our periodic sprees on the weekends, and it is the job of the snookers to fetch and carry. Do you understand?"

Robert and Georgie replied in the same manner as before.

"Lastly, snookers are not permitted to lounge or even sit in the reading room. You must fetch your book and begone. And that, my boys, is that. Simple, eh? Even irredeemable halfwits such as yourselves should have no trouble, though woe to you should you break even a single rule. Then you will be out on your ear, see? Do you understand?"

This last he spoke with a growl, as if the joking was over and he meant business. Robert rolled his eyes toward him. "I understand, Corporal."

"Good, then."

Rice kicked Robert's trembling feet from under him. Robert dropped hard on his backside, his head snapping back and striking the wall. Rice and his friends burst into laughter. "Ha ha! Welcome to the Shop!"

Robert lay on his back for a moment, massaging the sore spot on his head and staring at a lattice of cracks in the ceiling plaster. Rice, Rat and Dog had moved away and now surrounded Georgie as if they had forgotten that Robert existed. That was fine, for it meant that this treatment was nothing personal, and as torture went, it had not been particularly trying. Robert had known worse. Far worse.

If that's the best they can do, he thought, *then bugger them all*. He would study hard and have his commission as soon as the regulations allowed. His father had told him that, back in his day, some cadets had completed the entire course of study in as few as four months. Doubtless, things had changed somewhat, the material grown more complex and difficult, but Robert would not waste any time. A single year should suffice. Then none of this nonsense would matter.

He sat up. On the other side of the room, Georgie was

standing on his head. His face had turned bright scarlet and tears were starting.   When Rice bellowed, "Do you understand?" the boy sobbed, "Yes, yes! Please let me down! Please!"

Robert's teeth clenched. He knew what he could tolerate himself, which was a great deal, but the sight of another in similar circumstances was a trial. Robert's instinct was to help, a trait planted in him by his Aunt Agatha, his father's elder sister, who had seen to Robert's earliest education.

But he could not intervene here. Georgie was a cadet like him and would have to earn the respect of his peers.

Robert folded his arms and again glanced at the ceiling, as if Aunt Agatha were somehow staring down on him from heaven and scolding. He could see her now, a bland woman with a face like sour milk and lips like old prunes, though despite her appearance she had been gentle and even-tempered.

"Always look after thy sister," she told him once. "Mind her as ye would a precious flower ye found on yon hill. Ye have a duty to mind those weaker than thyself. Remember that our Lord himself said, 'Blessed are the meek.'"

That moment, and Aunt Agatha's words, seemed etched in stone, a moment of great import. Of course, Robert had never wanted any harm to come to his sister, and by extension he did not wish to see harm come to anyone like her.

Another memory surfaced, this one less pleasant but no less profound. When he was eight years old, Robert had found his Aunt Agatha sitting by the hearth, one hand tightly clamped on one knee. When Robert had touched her and called her name, he had found the hand cold and hard, like a loose bundle of old twigs.   His aunt had made no response, and did not move. Robert had crept around behind her and gazed up into her face to see eyes half closed, her mouth a strange, pinched crescent.

It was so unlike any expression he had ever seen on her face before, that he knew then that she was dead.

He had been unable to stop staring at her. It was the first human death Robert had seen. "Her body was empty," he told his mother later that day. "She was no longer there."

"No, her soul is in a better place," his mother told him. "We will pray for her."

Robert had missed her after that.

The day they buried her was fittingly solemn, the sky filled with scudding gray cloud, the rooks calling from the stark November trees. Robert had snuggled into the folds of his mother's cloak. There had still been warmth there. Sissy had blubbered, but Robert held his tears. "I will not see you weeping," his father told him, his voice like contained thunder, for the darkness was upon him that day. "A man does not weep."

And now this Georgie, this fellow recruit, was weeping without restraint. Robert watched him from his place on the floor and felt a faint contempt, but not enough to overcome his sympathy. He did not yet know the boy, did not know his strengths and weaknesses. At the moment, he was just a helpless and frustrated snooker.

Rice and his cronies let Georgie down at last, laughing and again shouting, "Welcome to the Shop!"

Georgie sat on the floor, wiping at his face with the heel of one hand. But suddenly he smiled. "That wasn't so bad, then. Thank you for the welcome, lads. I'm pleased to meet you all."

"Well, we're not pleased to meet you," Rat said. He handed Georgie a wooden pail. "Go to the well and fetch some water, snooker. We need it for tea."

Georgie struggled to his feet. "Tea! That sounds jolly nice."

The boy ran off. Rice then turned to Robert. "You, there. I

feel I did not have enough breakfast. Cooks skimping in the mess, you know. You can make the toast."

The older boys ignored Robert as he kindled a small fire. When Georgie returned with the water, they took it without thanks and thrust a broom into the new boy's hand. Rice told him to sweep.

Robert found the toaster leaning next to the hearth. There was a loaf of bread on the table, and as he cut a few slices, the smell of the room finally struck him, perhaps carried on the dust stirred by Georgie's broom. It was a scent of wool and must, of ink and leather from the books piled here and there, and it awakened more memories from Robert's childhood, of times spent in his father's study surrounded by books and papers. He remembered the tall study windows with their heavy draperies pulled aside, and the maroon carpet where he would lie, reading and dreaming. The books were the sort boys love, accounts of wars and battles, arms and armour, texts describing the different classes of artillery and fortifications. The papers were of the same ilk, sketches and diagrams of the machinery of war. With a lead pencil, Robert would either copy his favourites or create new images of cannons, limbers, wagons, gyns, men at battle struggling amidst great clouds of gunpowder smoke. He would then show the results of his work to Borgard, the wolfhound, who often lay at his side, usually snoring, or Gibraltar, the mongrel terrier. The house was always filled with lazy dogs and cats, Robert's companions, reclining in the pools of sunlight beneath the windows in summer or huddled by the hearth fender in winter. It had been a happy time, and that was how Robert had come to think of it. The happy time.

"Maybe I could be a soldier some day, father," he had said on one of these charmed afternoons. "A gunner like you were."

Thomas Saxon had turned on his stool, away from the desk where he had been figuring his business accounts. His grave face slowly changed, a light slowly kindling there until his eyes glowed.

"That would be a fine thing, my son, a fine thing," he had said. "The artillery is indeed a noble profession, truly noble, and just the sort for folk like us. A gunner knows things, and we're a family of clever, knowing people. Never forget that. A gunner knows his guns, knows the men of the crews, what they can bear. He knows how to cut a fuse, to judge speed, distance and time, and to understand Newton's principles. A gunner knows his figures. And..." His father raised his finger. "...he knows the lay of the land, where it will draw the enemy. You should do well to become a gunner some day, join His Majesty's Royal Artillery, as I did."

Robert held his pencil held in loose fingers. "A gunner in the Royal Artillery," he repeated, and there was something very fierce, very attractive about that phrase, so he said it again. "A gunner in the Royal Artillery."

After that there had never been any talk or speculation about Robert doing anything else with his life. He would join the artillery. Though his father owned a prosperous inn on the post road between Winchester and London, there was not even discussion of Robert some day assuming control of the business. Thomas Saxon had founded the inn upon his retirement from the service, as so many old soldiers and sailors hope to do, but it was just that: something for a former soldier, not a young man setting out.

The inn was called The Five Alls. Its sign depicted five figures: the King, who governed all, a bishop, who prayed for all, a lawyer, who pleaded for all, a farmer, who fed all, and last a soldier, who fought for all. Adjacent to the inn was the house where Robert had lived from the moment of his birth. It was a respectable house, sturdy and simply built. Within its walls, during the happy time, Robert had dreamed dreams and listened to stories of the king's army. His favourite tale, and perhaps his father's as well, had been that of the Great Siege of Gibraltar.

"It was that Mister Washington and his band of rebels, over in America," was how the story had most often begun. At that point a distant look would come into Thomas Saxon's eyes, and his voice would grow fainter. A strange darkness sometimes overtook him in the telling, a melancholy anger that Robert found a little frightening, but no less enthralling. War, he supposed, was a terrible thing, and its memory seemed not much less terrible.

"The American rebels had much of the British Army occupied," the story would continue, "and it seems likely that Spain thought that our attention was directed elsewhere. They sought to take advantage of our deficiency in numbers to seize our greatest stronghold, Gibraltar, beneath its great Rock, which was ever a thorn in their side. Yet they could not do it, not even after more than two years of siege. We held, and in the end, we bled them dry."

The Spanish had failed during the Great Siege, thanks to British resolve, and thanks to British artillery. "We suffered much," Thomas Saxon had so often said, adding, "A true man will endure a great deal, and still prevail against his enemies. That is something I wish for you to remember – to give in to suffering is weakness."

And at last, his voice dropping almost to a whisper, he would repeat, "It was the guns that saved us. The guns. And I was a gunner."

He had been a sergeant, he told his children. A sergeant—

someone the other men feared and obeyed. His old blue frock coat still hung in his tall wardrobe. In the evenings, he would take it out and lay it across his lap. When Robert happened upon him in such a pose, the boy would sense the darkness—as with the storytelling—filling the entire room like an invisible shadow. Robert had avoided his father at those times, even feared him, and had usually gone to fetch his mother. When he found her, he would whisper in her ear, saying, "Father is in one of his broods, Mother."

Then Mother would speak reassurances, go to Father and place her hand upon his shoulder, and soon the darkness would disappear. Only Mother had seemed to have this talent. She possessed the ability to make her husband laugh.

Robert's father had always been laughing, while Mother still lived.

Chapter Two:

Darkness

"Now, let's see your kit," Rice said next, brushing a few crumbs from his lap. Nothing remained of the toast and tea, and Georgie had been eying the empty cups and plates on the table with constrained disappointment. The snookers had not been invited to share but had been kept at the task of sweeping and dusting.

"Our kit?" Georgie said. "What is that?"

Rice threw his head back as Rat and Dog both howled with derisive laughter. "Can it be true, gentlemen?" Rice said. "Can it be that the creature doesn't know what his kit is?"

He stood from the table, clasped his hands behind his back and leaned toward Georgie. "Your kit, you great stupid lump, is your uniform and accoutrements. You may acquire these things from the Quartermaster's stores, but the former is properly your responsibility and must be procured from a tailor, fashioned on the proper regulation pattern."

"My father made no mention of my needing to procure a uniform," Robert said, realizing how stupid these words must sound.

"Not required? Did you think you would attend at table in the mess dressed like the bumpkin you, no doubt, are?" Rice looked at Rat. "Oh, we have our work cut out with these two, I fear."

"It's a heavy responsibility," Rat sneered.

"Right, then, we may as well do what we can to remedy the situation. Report to the Quartermaster's stores at once. Something moth eaten and ill-fitting is preferable to nothing at all. Lord Mumbles will escort you."

At the mention of the Quartermaster's, Georgie brightened. "Splendid!" he said. "We should look the part, shouldn't we?"

Rice snorted. "Let's hope that's not all you ever accomplish here."

"Who is Lord Mumbles, sir?" Robert asked.

Rice rounded on him. "Never ever address me as 'sir,' you damned ignoramus! I'm your cadet corporal, and you will call me 'Corporal.' Understand?"

Robert flushed, for this was an obvious mistake. "I understand."

"As for your question, if you had been paying attention you should have gathered that Mumbles is that lazy slug over there." Rice adjusted the front of his robe and pointed to the fourth older boy, the chubby fellow with the wild hair. "Come on, then, Mumbles, shift your bulk and do your duty. These two snookers are waiting."

Mumbles grumbled as he raised himself from the bed and approached the snookers. Without looking Robert in the eye, he rubbed his nose and said, "Right. Q.M. is on the south side. This way, then."

With a sigh, Robert followed. "Splendid," Georgie repeated as they returned to the corridor and made their way back toward the Centre Building. Before they reached it, they made a left turn that brought them to a heavy, iron-shod oak door. Mumbles pushed the door open and led the snookers into a wide, grassy courtyard. On the far side of the yard stood another brick building, flanked by two towers.

"East Tower and West Tower," Mumbles explained, leading the newcomers across the grass. "Q. M. is in the East Tower."

The tower loomed closer, the rooks on its battlements like tiny gargoyles etched against the blue sky. Robert folded his hands behind his back, struggling to unravel a knot of confused feelings. He suspected that his time here at the Shop was not to be comfortable, despite his hopes upon entering the gate. Even so, it could only be a step up from home. At least here, there was nowhere to go but forward.

Georgie leaned in close as they walked. "I say," he whispered, "I do hope this Corporal Rice fellow does not turn out to be a frightful bully."

Robert faced him. "Don't worry," he said. "I know how to deal with bullies."

*****

Mumbles waited outside while Robert and George entered the Quartermaster's stores, a small room with a wooden counter at the far end. Behind the counter waited a grizzled sergeant with thin wisps of grey hair clinging to his ruddy scalp.

"Names," the sergeant stated, taking a list from a peg on the wall. Behind him stretched a small cave, filled with rows and rows of wool coats, shoes, caps, hats, trousers and a variety of lesser accessories such as gloves, ribbon, lace, loose buttons, badges and buckles.

"Saxon," Robert said, gaping at the impressive array. "Robert Saxon."

The Quartermaster Sergeant found the name on his list, then narrowed his eyes. "Once served with a fellow named Saxon. Sergeant, he was."

Robert tightened his lips and made no comment. The man might have known his father, or he might have known another sergeant by that name, but Robert had no desire to discover which. He had no wish to chat about Thomas Saxon.

"I'm George Howard," Georgie chimed in. "Am I on your list?"

The sergeant glanced at him from under his iron brows. "Indeed, young sir, ye are. Now, what is it that ye require?"

Robert cleared his throat. "Uniforms."

"Ah," the sergeant said. "Well, bear in mind, ye shall be charged for all ye receive. 'Tis not free, understand. Of course, ye shall be charged for your food and housekeeping, as well." He suddenly grinned. "But never ye mind, ye shall still receive nigh on eight pence a day, more than most young gentlemen are accustomed to having in their own pockets, without father to tell them how to spend it."

Uniform issue took almost an hour. Meanwhile several other boys, snookers all, had gathered inside and outside the room, crowding each other, their excited chatter rising until the sergeant bellowed, "Quiet the lot of ye! A body can hardly hear himself think!"

The noise died at once. The sergeant brought out item after item for Robert and Georgie, and perhaps, because he was pressed for time, he was not fussy about the fit. When the issue had been completed, Robert had in his possession two caps, one a shapeless wool bonnet, the other a stovepipe shako with a brass plate and white cockade. The main article of clothing was a single-breasted blue coat with red collar and cuffs. With the coat went white knee breeches and knee-high black gaiters that were to be worn only on Sundays. For the weekdays, there was a pair of blue pantaloons and short black spat gaiters. A silk stock for the neck completed the ensemble. There was no issue of shirts or stockings or undergarments. Cadets had no option but to supply these themselves.

"Now, away to the armoury for the rest of it," the sergeant said. "I'll see the next pair of lads, there. Next pair!"

Carrying their issue clothes tied up with a leather strap, Robert and Georgie found Mumbles still waiting outside, hunched against the wall with his hands in his breeches pockets. He muttered something and led his charges to the armoury, which was located one door to the right. Beyond the door was a room smelling of wood, wax, metal, and leather. Behind the counter waited an imposing figure with arms like a bear's and a leather apron covering his massive chest.

"One stand of arms per man," the armourer said.

Robert had assumed that, as a gentleman cadet, his weapon would be a sword, but what he received was a heavy flintlock musket. "Your land pattern musket," the armourer said. With it went a wicked looking three-sided socket bayonet. The accoutrements included two buff leather shoulder belts, one for the bayonet scabbard and the other for the cartridge box.

"You must whiten your belts every day," the armourer told them, "with water and plain pipe clay. However, it is your musket that must be kept clean, else it won't spark when you need it to."

"I didn't know that I would have to march and drill like a common soldier," Robert said.

The armourer gave him a look of reproach. Robert met and held the man's gaze, for the remark had been an honest one and he saw no need for censure.

"How are you to lead common soldiers if you do not understand their duty?" the armourer inquired. "You are a cadet, boy. You must start from scratch."

"I'm game," Georgie said.

Robert nodded. The armourer's explanation seemed sound. "I understand," he said, a phrase he was finding most useful.

*****

In the time left before dinner, they returned to the barracks, where Robert and Georgie stowed their new kit in the cupboards next to their assigned beds, before Mumbles took them out again to show them the remainder of the Academy enclosure. The Royal Military Academy faced north, toward the River Thames. The central building, Mumbles explained, with its towers and turrets, had the obvious designation of "the Centre Building." Until recently it had been a workshop, hence its nickname, "the Shop." Within its walls were offices, classrooms, the fencing room, and the library.

"There are several meanings to the word 'academy,'" Mumbles explained. Robert missed most of what followed, though he got the gist. The Academy was the school, but the classrooms were also called "academies," and the various levels a cadet could achieve were also called "academies." It struck Robert as a type of built-in confusion.

In the rear of the main buildings were gardens and courts, and in addition to the Quartermaster's Stores and armourer's shop, there was a lecture hall, instructors' quarters, and the main kitchens and dining hall. The parade ground in front of the main buildings was the Front Parade, and the stretch of grass adjacent to it was the Ha Ha, though Mumbles explained, "The Ha Ha is really the hidden ditch that divides them, but everyone refers to the field by that name, (mumble), and also (mumble) for grazing animals."

He kept his hands in his pockets as he spoke, his eyes flickering here and there.

North of the Ha Ha, across the Woolwich Common Road,

stretched the wide Woolwich Common itself. Along the common's northern edge stood another complex of buildings, several rectangular structures of red brick with rows of white windows. These were the New Barracks, where the serving men and officers of the Royal Artillery were quartered. "The town of Woolwich is our home," Mumbles explained. "It is the (mumble mumble) of the regiment. The New Barracks are the depot where we may be stationed when we receive our commissions."

For now, Robert was not interested in the distant barracks. There would be time for that later. For now, he wished to know every nook and cranny of his home, here at the R.M.A.

As the three cadets crossed in front of the Centre Building, keeping to the edge of the Front Parade, a drummer emerged from the Guard Room, marched a few paces onto the Parade, and pounded out a steady rhythm.

"That means we have fifteen minutes," Mumbles said, "before dinner is served. We should go, (mumble mumble)."

"Sorry," Robert said. "What was that last bit?"

Mumbles faced him proper for the first time that day. With what seemed like an effort of breathing he said, "I said we should go to the dining hall now."

They retraced their steps, moving through the Centre Building and back across the grassy main courtyard. The dining hall took up most of the largest building on the far side, and proved to be the most impressive interior Robert had ever seen. He could not help staring upward at the vaulted ceiling with its criss-crossed lattice of dark wooden beams and the rows of Gothic windows that lined either side wall. Between the windows hung heraldic shields, suits of armour, and various antique weapons such as broadswords and polearms. The lower walls were panelled in dark wood, with rows of cabinets and shelves of books. Between them, the long tables ran crossways, each covered with a white tablecloth.

Robert's spirits began to lift. This was a room fit for a palace. The weight of history resided here, something grander than the petty scheming of boys like Wesley Rice.

"This is our table," Mumbles said, leading them to the centre of the room. The place was filling with cadets, most of them dressed in blue and red, though a few, like Robert and Georgie, still wore civilian attire. The noise of so many young men in one place was deafening, and Georgie almost shouted, "What a jolly lot of companions we are to have, eh, Robert?"

Robert made a quick survey and decided that the cadets numbered about a hundred. A hundred young men waiting to enter the king's army. Those who completed the course of study, and that would be most, would one day become officers in the Royal Regiment of Artillery. A few would become members of the Royal Engineers, the other unit in the so-called Scientific Corps. These were the young lads who would defend England and her allies from Bonaparte.

Rice entered the hall, trailed by Rat and Dog. He no longer wore his robes, but a proper uniform with a corporal's epaulette on one shoulder. He and his companions took seats at the far end of the table, grinning at Mumbles and the two snookers. Rice turned to Rat and Dog and said something that Robert could not make out, but Rat and Dog laughed.

"Never mind Corporal Rice," Mumbles said. "He likes the idea of snookers too much, but I know he took it hard when he (mumble) and now he wants (mumble) and sometimes goes too far."

"He seems a capital fellow," Georgie said, as if he had never voiced his fears of bullying to Robert. "I don't mind all that initiation type stuff. My papa explained it all. Nothing personal, he assured me."

"As long as it is only for initiation," Robert said, "and doesn't continue."

Mumbles fumbled with his fingers and made no comment.

Waiters dressed in plain white coats brought the food—roast mutton and potatoes. The waiters were older men, no doubt, enlisted gunners. The meal was simple, but Robert enjoyed the service, enjoyed having someone bring his plate, enjoyed not having to move from his chair until he was finished.

"How are the rations, generally?" he asked Mumbles.

"The same (mumble) on Monday."

"It's fine fare for a prospective soldier," Georgie said. He admired his surroundings, grinning as he chewed. "This is very fine, and just as my papa described. He is an artillery officer in the Fifth Battalion. He intends that I follow in his footsteps."

"And is that your ambition?" Robert asked. "To follow your father?"

"Certainly! I was raised on tales of the Artillery. It is the life for me, and Britain needs her sons now, doesn't she? There's really no other choice for the son of a gunner, is there?"

Robert studied Georgie's round face. For the most fleeting of moments, he had seen something pass behind the boy's eyes, then it was gone. The shadow of doubt, he supposed. Maybe, for all his outward enthusiasm, Georgie Howard was far from certain that he was in the right place.

"I was raised on tales of the Artillery too," Robert admitted. "The Great Siege of Gibraltar is engrained in my soul, I think."

"Ah, yes," Georgie said, chuckling. "Yes, the Great Siege. I wonder . . . I wonder if any of us will ever be put to such a test?"

"No doubt we will, and sooner than you think." Robert turned to Mumbles. "When do you suppose we will begin classes?"

"Tomorrow," Mumbles said. "You'll start with drill on Front Parade. 'Steady-stuff,' we call it, as the sergeant-major is always telling us to be steady. You recruit types will have your own squad and will learn the basics. Drill, drill, drill, (mumble) in the afternoon. Then we march to class. Tomorrow the lower classmen will have swot, or mathematics. Or so I (mumble)."

"I suppose this afternoon I shall have to purchase my stationary," Robert mused.

"I suggest you do," Mumbles agreed. "You should have brought it (mumble)."

Robert prodded a boiled potato with his fork, pushing it about his plate. "My father didn't mention it. In fact, I'm beginning to think there were a great many things he neglected to tell me. I don't really know what to get. I don't really know anything, yet. Will we receive any sort of schedule? How are we to know what to do, unless one of you tells us?"

Mumbles wiped his mouth with his napkin. "Orders will be posted outside the Orderly Room, explaining everything, all daily activities, order of dress and, (mumble). Rice is supposed to tell you all this, but you will find being corporal, for him, is just an opportunity to play pranks and to have fun, to wield his (mumble mumble). So always check the Orderly Room, because Rice may remember to tell us something, and he may not."

Robert sat back and folded his arms. "Well, that's a sad state of affairs."

"At times it is," Mumbles said, too quiet to hear, though from the movement of his lips the words were plain enough. "At times it is."

*****

The day swirled to a close. Robert found his stationary at a shop in town and returned just in time for a light supper of barley soup, bread, and tea in the dining hall. Then it was back

26

to barracks to sort out his new kit, and finally lights out, his first day done.

That night, after his spinning head finally ran itself down and he managed to fall asleep, he dreamed of his mother. He imagined that he remembered her face, her soft smile. He had been nine years old when he had last seen her. That was the year he had attended the Reverend Field's school for boys. His term at the school had been cut short by the news that his mother had died, attempting to give birth to what would have been another little sister.

Robert remembered the day he returned home, for it marked the end of the happy time. He had dismounted from the coach in the yard of The Five Alls. Leaving his heavy trunk in the mud, he had gone to the house to see his father, to see Sissy. The house had been silent. When Robert had opened the heavy black door, no dogs had come running, as was usual, tongues lolling and tails wagging, excited at the prospect of visitors. No one greeted him at all. There was no sign that anyone was home.

Maybe they are out for a walk, he remembered thinking. Or maybe the dogs are in the stables. Then he had stepped into the wide, gloomy hallway, his shoes making no sound on the slate tiles. On his left, the door to the parlour stood half open. He paused, squinting into the dim interior. Something shifted, made a sound like the brush of fabric on fabric.

"Hello!" he called. "I've come home!"

He was met with a gurgle, then a cough. Someone was there after all.

"So, you have come home at last," a voice said.

Robert had hesitated, for though the voice was that of his father, it had that rough, embittered resonance that Robert had always dreaded. The darkness was upon him.

"Why do you stand out there?" Thomas Saxon snapped. "Come into the parlour, boy."

There was no option but to obey, no possibility of waiting until later, until the darkness had passed. Robert pushed open the parlour door. It, too, groaned on un-oiled hinges, and as Robert took three careful steps forward, the house seemed to breathe and sigh around him in its emptiness, even though his father was there, in the room. It was then that it struck him— mother was truly gone. There was no trace of her spirit here.

Robert bowed his head, fighting tears. He wished that he had not come, that he was back at school. The school had been as grey as the stones within its walls, but he had been welcome there and adored by the faculty for his quick intelligence.

"You came by post," Thomas Saxon stated. A single stab of light through a crack in the drawn curtains illuminated his face, leaving the rest of him in near darkness, slumped in a wing chair by the cold hearth.

"Yes, sir," Robert sniffed, trying to compose himself. "Where... where is Mother?"

He meant, "where was her body?" But his father looked at him as if he had gone mad. "Your mother is dead, and already in the ground, boy."

Robert held his breath, for this news struck him like a blow. They had not waited for him? They had buried her already? He would have no chance to say his farewells....

"Where... where is Sissy?" he gasped after a moment.

"In the back garden, I should imagine, where she always is, peeling potatoes with Mrs. Greene."

"Will she be going to school with me next year?"

Thomas Saxon stood, rising on his thin legs like a shadow crawling up the wall. "No. Neither shall you be returning. From this moment, I will see to your education."

*****

Robert had, indeed, found Sissy in the garden that day, just as his father had suggested. She ran to him and almost bowled him over with her embrace, crying, "Robert! Robert is home!"

"It's good to see you, child," said Mrs. Greene, the fat and sturdy matron who kept the house. "My, you seem to have sprouted a foot in the last year!"

"You have," Sissy said. "You have indeed. You're a beanpole!"

Robert held up his arms to show the sleeves that stopped inches short of his wrists. "It's true that none of my clothes fit anymore."

Sissy took his hand. "You must tell me everything about school. Not just the things you wrote in your letters, but what really happened! I know there's more."

Robert's face clouded. "There is, and there's things you can tell me too." He looked back at the house. "I have just seen father. I... I know I've just arrived, but I want to get away from the house for a while. Until his... mood passes."

There was only one place to go. Taking their leave of Mrs. Greene, Sissy led Robert toward the high hill behind the house, almost dragging him through the back of the garden and onto the familiar path. This had been their secret place as children, their playground. The rain on the grass had dried, and they sat on the summit amongst the season's first wildflowers, gazing down at the inn and house, the stables and outbuildings, the smoke rising from the chimneys, and the brown road stretching across the green country.

"Father seemed angry," Robert said. He tugged at the grass. "Though I suppose he is just sad."

"He is angry all the time now," Sissy explained. "He yells

and shouts, and once he broke a chair. Borgard barked at him one day, because he was scared, and so he sent the dogs away. I don't know where." She sighed. "He misses mother."

"Of course he does. Yes, of course he does."

Sissy buried her face in the crook of Robert's arm. "I miss her too!"

Robert stroked her hair. "I'll get you a new dog," he told her after her muffled sobs had subsided. "One of the stable dogs will have pups."

"Thank you, Robert," she whispered.

Time stood still as they sat there on the hill, making up for the past months, their lost companionship. But they could not sit there forever, and Robert's belly was aching. The sun was low in the west when they at last came down for supper. Father was waiting in the dining room, dressed in a fine black coat and clean neck stock. There was a blackness to his manner as well. As the children entered, he slowly rose from his chair. His watch was in his hand.

"You are late, both of you."

Robert felt a prickling along his scalp. The darkness had not passed, and despite Thomas Saxon's fine appearance, there was the reek of liquor about him. He had, no doubt, been to the inn and sampled some of his own wares.

"I'm sorry, sir," Robert said, doing his best to speak with some force. But he was afraid, for the drink had always made the darkness deeper, and now there was no mother to bring the light.

"That is not acceptable. Nor is it acceptable for a young man with responsibilities to leave his trunk lying in the filth of the yard for hours on end. MacLeod found it there, and brought it in. Did they teach you to be so neglectful at that school?"

Robert stared past his father, at the wall behind his right shoulder. Sissy was hanging her head, her little hands folded in front of her. "No, sir," Robert said, and this time his voice trembled.

"Then you have neglected your lessons as well." Thomas Saxon moved away from the table and came toward his children, looming over them in judgment. "I expect obedience, and I expect discipline. A soldier knows that punctuality is of prime importance."

Robert stood still. "But I'm not a soldier, father."

One big hand lashed out, an open-handed blow across Robert's left ear. It felt like a blast of wind. He lost his footing, fell to his hands and knees. Sissy screamed, and though his ear began to throb and his cheek sting, Robert was more shocked than hurt. "No, father, no!" Sissy cried, running forward and clinging to Thomas Saxon's legs.

Robert's father grasped Sissy's shoulder and shoved her aside with a grunt. She, too, fell, dropping to a sitting position. There she remained, sobbing.

It was then that Robert found his strength, and he pushed himself to his feet. "Don't you touch her!" he shouted, though he knew that such defiance would only make matters worse. But this was injustice, and he had to stand up for himself and for Sissy. It had been Thomas Saxon himself who had always insisted that, "A man defends himself and defends what he thinks is right."

And Thomas Saxon froze, one hand in the air. He paused, fingers twitching, then his stone face seemed to melt, contorting in anguish.

"Damn you, boy!" he gasped. "Damn you!"

He turned about, sweeping out of the dining room. A moment later Robert heard him stomping up the stairs.

Robert took Sissy by the hand and led her into the parlour. There they curled up together in the biggest chair next to the hearth.

"Father is just sad," Robert kept repeating. "He didn't mean to be so awful."

"We haven't had any supper," Sissy said.

But Mrs. Greene found them there, and she took them to the inn and gave them something to eat, so they did not have to go to bed hungry that night.

*****

Robert had kept his promise and brought Sissy a mongrel pup. He had not asked his father's permission, and when Thomas Saxon saw the thing mewling and biting in play at Sissy's feet, all he said was, "Feed it."

"We will, sir," Robert promised, and at that moment he dared to hope that his father would heal, that he would come out of the dark place.

"Come with me, boy," Thomas Saxon then said, gesturing with his cane toward his study. The cane was a yard long stick of ash with a brass head, a ball not unlike a round shot. "I would discuss your schooling."

The study was warm and smelled as it always had, that scent of happy dreams. Robert's father moved toward his gun cabinet where he kept two firelocks. One was a birding piece with two barrels, the other a small-calibre Austrian rifle. Setting down his cane and opening the cabinet, Thomas Saxon took out the birding gun and passed it to his son. Robert took it, holding it in both hands, surprised at the weight.

"Feel that," his father said. "You will come to know it well. Beginning tomorrow, and continuing most days if the weather is agreeable, we will go past the hill and practice our shooting.

You will also learn the maintenance of a firelock, patience, dexterity, and of course marksmanship. These are skills a soldier must have. Indeed, it is my opinion that every man must understand the basic elements of musketry."

Robert nodded and smiled. He would look forward to that, and the chance to spend time with his father. Perhaps they would grow closer.

Thomas Saxon snatched the gun from his son and locked it away in the cabinet. Robert stared at his empty hands, but his father had already moved to one of the bookshelves and was speaking again.

"There are books here you have never seen, books that at one time would have been beyond your comprehension. I will order more, enough so that you may master the classics, gain a grounding in Greek and Latin, and also history, mathematics, artillery and engineering. I have a treatise here on the fortification principles of Vauban, and those of Coehorn, both translated from the French. Many of my military texts are from the French, which is another language you should master."

"Yes, sir," was all Robert could say. This did not sound as much fun as shooting, but he knew he was up to the task of learning new things. He supposed he had the time. He was only a boy and would not join the Royal Artillery for many years.

His father pulled a book from a shelf and placed it on the reading table. "This shall be your classroom. I have business in the inn. Before I return, you will read this. When I come back, I expect to see some progress."

Robert held the book as he had held the shotgun. This was the treatise on fortification his father had mentioned. It was very thick and seemed to weigh about five pounds.

"I'll do my best, sir," he said, though he wondered what

"progress" meant.

His father grunted and turned to go. Robert sat down and opened the book. He supposed he should at least attempt to finish the first chapter, which proved to be a biography of Marshal Sebastien de Vauban, a French military engineer who had lived in the seventeenth century. The words were thick and heavy, far beyond anything Robert had ever attempted to read at the Reverend Field's. The text was also dull and at times meandering, but he was determined to do what his father had said, and he was determined to learn.

It was growing dark by the time Thomas Saxon returned. By then Robert was dozing in his chair, the book still open in front of him. He had managed about half of the first chapter before boredom and sleep had carried him away.

He awoke as his father's cane came crashing down on the table next to his ear. He almost jumped out of his chair, heart racing. His father was another dark tower, leaning over him. Robert smelled the drink.

"Sleeping?" Thomas Saxon rumbled. "I give you a simple task, and you sleep? Have I raised a lag-about? Is that what my good money paid for at that infernal school?"

Robert could say nothing. He was still rubbing the sleep from his eyes and did not see the blow coming. It was the open palm again, across the cheek, and the force of it knocked him and his chair backwards. When he landed, only the study carpet prevented him from cracking his skull on the oak floorboards.

"You will do better," his father thundered. "You must do better."

At that moment, Robert had known that his earlier hopes would never be realized. The darkness had conquered his father, and there would never be another moment of light.

Mother had been the only one with the power to bring him back, and she was gone.

Chapter Three:

Endurance

A single stab of sunlight piercing a crack in the drapes awakened him. He winced and pushed himself toward the wall, deeper into the gloom cast by his half open bed curtains. There he lay, staring at the dust cascading in the beam from the windows. Almost at the same moment, the squeal of fifes and rumble of drums outside assaulted his senses.

"Reveille, you sloths," Rice's voice croaked. "All of you... out of bed. Out of bed."

Rice's next breath became a drawn-out sigh as he shifted onto his side and lay still. The only one to rise was Mumbles, who struggled into his uniform, then donned his accoutrements and snatched his musket from its brace against the wall.

Robert sat up and rubbed his eyes. "Where are you going with that firelock?"

"Extra drill," Mumbles said, adding something unintelligible as he moved toward the door.

"Extra drill again, hey, Lord Mumbles?" Rice said, again coming to and raising his head. "Have to be a little more diligent in your tactics, eh, Mumbles?"

Mumbles paused. He seemed on the verge of saying something, the skin on his face pulled tight as he stared into

Rice's shadowed bed.   But then he turned on his heel and stormed out, slamming the door.

Rice chuckled.

"Why does he have extra drill, Corporal?" Robert asked. It was his third day at the Shop, and the second time Mumbles had run off in the morning for extra drill.

Rice did not respond at once, but settled back within the shadows, his laughter degenerating into a series of tortured gasps, perhaps the result of too much wine the night before. "Well, my good snooker . . . Well, it is because he buggered up his drills yesterday, and the day before, I might add. Always buggering up something, is our Mumbles, if that something is drill.   The period before breakfast is reserved for those delinquents who require more practice."   He raised himself, swinging his feet out to find the floor. "The rest of us have an hour, which gives you plenty of time to fetch us some water, hey snooker?"

"Of course," Robert said. He knew that Rice meant the task to be unpleasant, but in a purely rational situation Robert thought it only just that the new boys, those who had not yet proved their worth, should have to carry out the bulk of these menial tasks. And he would not give Rice the satisfaction of seeing him rattled by these little attempts at torture.

"Oh," Rice added, "and empty the night soil pots."

Robert paused for just an instant. "Right."

Rice snickered.

Only one chamber pot was full, and Robert took it to the privy. The privy was located behind the Centre Building and consisted of several so called "black holes," each with its own enclosed cubicle. To Robert the cubicles seemed a luxury.

The pump room was next door.   Robert filled an empty bucket with cold water and returned to barracks.

The cadets washed and dressed. Robert pulled on his new uniform coat, admiring himself in the small mirror next to Mumbles's bed. The fit was not as bad as first he had thought, now that he had worn it a few times. In fact, it looked quite good.

Mumbles returned from his punishment drill, sweating, tight lipped and glowering.

"Right, we're all here," Rice said. "To the dining hall."

They moved off in single file, not exactly marching, but walking at a brisk pace. Breakfast appeared, almost the moment they sat down, and proved to be a bland milk porridge. Robert tasted one spoonful and grunted his dissatisfaction. Not all the food was proving as fine as the room in which it was served.

"Get used to it, snooker," Rice said, and laughed. "It's gruel every other day."

Robert swallowed the tasteless lump and said, "My name is Robert Saxon, Corporal."

"I think this porridge would be perfectly delightful," Georgie said, "with a little butter, perhaps."

Rice's lips were pouting. "I'll have none of your insolence! I'll call you whatever I wish."

Robert kept a straight face. "I thought perhaps you had forgotten my name, Corporal. That's all."

"I never forget a thing, Saxon." Rice tapped his chin. "Saxon, Saxon. My father tells a tale of a fellow named Saxon what went through the old Academy with him. My father's a colonel of artillery, you know. That's a rare thing, and you would do well to remember it. To be in my good books is to see yourself right, but to be in my bad books?" He shrugged. "At any rate, this Saxon fellow was a terrible bully, always lording it over the others, playing pranks and so on. A man after my own heart, save that he was stupid and vicious. Attacked my father and broke his arm, and all in front of witnesses. That was it for him, saw him chucked out on his backside."

Robert shrugged. "Nothing to do with me."

Rice swirled his porridge with his spoon. "You never had a relation who attended the Academy?"

"No. I'm the first."

"Then you need to be properly broken in, don't you?"

Robert pretended to misunderstand the remark. "I intend to do my best in all things."

"Ha! Well, we'll do our best to help you along."

*****

The period immediately after breakfast consisted of squad drill. Robert and Georgie and the other snookers, forty in all, made up one squad. This was their second day on the Parade, though yesterday all they had undergone was a detailed kit inspection. Today began in a similar fashion, with a pair of corporals pushing and prodding them into two rough ranks. When some sense of military order had been established, the recruits found themselves facing a stout sergeant, his turnip face framed by ballooning whiskers.

"My name is Sergeant Bane," he said. "And I shall be your bane, if you cross me."

Robert wondered how many times the man had used that particular witticism.

"The first thing you shall learn today," Bane went on, "is the position of a soldier. That is, how to stand at attention. You cannot do a thing else, lest you learn this position. When you have mastered it, I shall instruct this squad in the proper procedure for standing at ease. That is, for resting on Parade, though do not expect to get much in the way of rest under my tutelage."

This all sounded simple enough, and for Robert, the lesson did not prove difficult. It was no bother for him to stand perfectly still. All one had to do was control one's breathing. Robert had spent hours thus, sitting and reading in his father's study. Standing still, alone with his thoughts and the voice of the sergeant, was not much different. Though Robert wondered if ensigns in the infantry and cavalry were ever subjected to this, to having a sergeant take them out for drill. He doubted it. According to his father, infantry and cavalry officers hardly even marched in step with their men, if they could help it.

Bane strutted about in front of the two ranks of recruits, commenting on each snooker's positioning. "Good, good, young sir, you ought to show the rest how to do it. You keep your hands straight. You, there! Stop twitching! You must remain steady. A soldier on Parade, even a jumped-up, snotty-nosed little gentleman like yourself, must be steady. The foremost aspect of the British soldier's drill is his steadiness."

When Bane came to Robert, he glanced at him from head to toe and said, "Good enough."

Bane moved on to the next man. This was Georgie, standing on Robert's left. From the corner of his eye, Robert saw Bane scowling.

"Suck that lip in Mister Howard," the sergeant snapped. "And stop waggling your shoulders. You look to be the most unsteady lad out here, as if you're about to cry for your poor lost mother."

"Oh, don't worry, Sergeant," Georgie said. "I won't cry."

"Keep your mouth shut, Mister Howard!" Bane shouted. "Won't cry? I'll make you cry if you don't remember to speak only when addressed! Is that clear, Mister Howard?"

"I..."

"I asked a question, thus I demand an answer, young sir!"

"Yes, Sergeant. That's clear!"

"Good, then."

Bane moved on. His next lesson was the "stand at ease." This involved clapping and folding the hands together, dropping the right foot back six inches, and bending the left knee. Robert found it a simple movement, but Georgie had trouble again. At the end of the hour, he was the only snooker who had not succeeded in combining the hand clasp and the foot movement.

"We will take this up again tomorrow," Bane said. "All save you, Mister Howard. You're on extra drill, first thing."

"Yes, Sergeant!" Georgie bellowed.

"Right, you lot. Dismissed!"

Georgie was the only snooker to draw extra drill, but as he accompanied Robert back to barracks, all he said was, "I could use the extra drill. Didn't know it would be so hard. A bit dull, though, don't you think?"

Robert studied him, a little nonplussed at this statement. Georgie had taken the brunt of Bane's wrath for the period.

"I'm sure it won't be dull for long," Robert said. "It will be more interesting when we begin to march."

"Yes! I look forward to that day."

Robert admired Georgie's attitude. "I look forward to all of my days here," he said, gazing back across the Parade, the Ha Ha and the green Common beyond. The sky was the piercing blue of September, and for a moment he had a sense of complete freedom, a lightness of soul. Here, the worst thing that could befall a gentleman cadet was extra drill, which, as Georgie seemed to understand, did not really amount to punishment at all, but a drive to ensure every cadet managed to reach the desired standard of proficiency in his chosen profession. Robert would not have minded extra drill either. What was having a corporal or a sergeant bellow at you, compared to what he had endured as a child? It was nothing, nothing at all.

No one here, Robert decided, would raise a hand to him. Not Sergeant Bane and not Cadet Corporal Rice. Here he would learn to be a man, and men did not accept abuse from others. Men defended themselves.

His father had taught him that as well.

*****

In the years following his mother's death, Robert had lived under the constant threat of a good thrashing. Somehow, he endured it, and somehow, he forgave his father. Father missed mother still, Robert told himself, and it was the drink that drove him to despair. And at no time did Robert ever cry out or weep. He refused to show weakness, and perhaps that was his father's intention as well, to build strength. Thus, for Robert to cry would have been to fail utterly. He would deny the pain, deny the hurt to both his flesh and his spirit. It was his only sense of victory in a helpless position.

Sometimes the beatings were minor, a momentary rage. After a single blow, Thomas Saxon would throw down his cane, the passion seeming to drain out of him, and he would begin speaking in a far away manner, usually telling the story of the great siege of Gibraltar, of the Spanish fire ships that failed, of the special gun platforms the British built to allow their cannon to fire down from the top of the great Rock. "I was a sergeant," he would repeat. "I was a sergeant." But on other nights the opposite happened, and the rage was greater. Then Robert could see that the darkness had taken complete control, and there was nothing he could do, no proper answer he could give, that would not elicit savage punishment. Mercifully, on those nights, his father was also so weak from the drink that his blows would not land true, and he would tire soon, slumping into a chair and sinking into unconsciousness.

Robert had borne it. Some would have become cowed, broken, withdrawn, their lives fragmenting. Robert remained defiant, a defiance that had already been instilled in him by the very person who now offered him such brutality. And though Robert could not fight his father, could not return blow for blow and believed that no child ever could, he vowed that no one else would ever treat him so. He would brook no malice nor abuse from anyone. Nor would he ever be cruel to anyone else, or accept such evil in others. He would protect those weaker, as his late aunt had instructed, and he would begin with his sister.

Robert had been determined never to allow his father to hurt Sissy in any way.

Sissy divided her days between helping Mrs. Greene at the inn and receiving her schooling from father. There was no more talk of her attending a proper school, and this, Robert knew, had broken her little heart. Robert did all he could to make her laugh, and to assure her that one day things would be better, and he would remind her that both Mother and Aunt Agatha were watching over them from heaven.

"I know that no one can hurt me," she told him, "as long as I know you're here, Robert."

And so they passed the remaining years of their childhood, the seasons rolling by, the guests coming to the inn and leaving again. Robert worked in the stables, where he grew to know horses and their ways. The work was hard, but it kept his body strong and healthy. For his mind, he had books, new books that father ordered from London every month. They arrived in large wooden crates, and soon the study and parlour were full of them; great unstable towers of them on the shelves, on the side tables, the mantle.

And all the while Robert missed his mother and Aunt Agatha, by now a dim memory. He missed his days at school, but he was learning, despite the harsh methods, and he promised himself that he would distil something good from the bitter fruit of his days. He would not waste this time.

He did not learn for his father's sake; he did so for his own.

*****

On a night in spring when the hour had grown late, Robert had tired of his book and decided it was safe to set it aside. Sissy had curled up on the settle across from him with her dog Boxer, her constant companion, curled at her feet. Their father was not yet home from the inn.

"Its time for bed," Robert had said. "Let's go up."

The candle cast its misshapen shadows on the walls of the stairwell as they ascended. In their shared room, Robert placed the candle on the table between their beds. Boxer took his customary place on the rug.

"It's chilly tonight," Sissy said, pulling open her bed curtains.

Below they heard the front door swing open, the still un-oiled hinges seeming to groan in agony. Robert froze. He had dared to hope that his father had drunk himself into a stupor and would not be coming home at all tonight.

There was a bang as the door slammed shut, like the crack of a three-pounder cannon. The house shook. A moment later there was the tramp of heavy feet on the flags.

"Where are you, boy!" Thomas Saxon's voice thundered. "Don't hide from me, for I'll find you!"

Sissy jumped like a startled mouse. "He is angry tonight," she said. She pressed both fists under her chin and let out a whimper.

"Get into the wardrobe," Robert told her.

The tramp of feet continued, growing as it made its way up the stairs. Sissy was just climbing into the wardrobe when father entered the room. He staggered, one hand fumbling for the door handle. The candle on the table cast his figure upon the wall, and it resembled some twisted giant from a fairy story.

"There you are, you damned rascal," he shouted.

Robert turned and faced him, determined to stand his ground. He was almost sixteen now, almost a man. Boxer, no help at all, scrambled under Sissy's bed. Sissy squeaked in fright from within the wardrobe, but Thomas Saxon did not appear to have heard. He crossed the room to bury his fingers in the front of Robert's nightshirt, and with one heave, lifted the boy from the floor. His breath was foul and his crimson eyes blazed.

But it was not anger that Robert saw there. It was triumph.

"I have my letter!" Thomas Saxon said. "It came by today's post, from the Master General of the Ordnance himself. My request has been approved, and you shall go to Woolwich and take the examination!"

Robert stared, conflicted, afraid yet buoyed by this news. "Woolwich?" he cried.

Thomas Saxon laughed. "A place has been secured! My son shall go to the Royal Military Academy, learn to be an officer and a gentleman. No private soldier like me. Yes, my son shall be an officer!"

He let go of Robert's shirt. Robert dropped hard, the impact shivering from his heels to his hips. His father repeated, "An officer," belching as he staggered backwards, toward the door.

His foot caught on something, a slight rise in the floorboards, and he stumbled, collapsing in the doorway. He made one feeble attempt to rise, but when that failed, he lay there in a heap. Within a moment, the air filled with the stench of his urine.

Robert stared in disgust, but he could not prevent the slow smile that began to spread across his face. At last, his way out, his escape, was here. He was to attend the Royal Military Academy, the school for officers of the Royal Artillery and Royal Engineers. He was to be a soldier, just as he had always wished. And he would leave this house.

"I'll be a better soldier than you ever were," he swore to Thomas Saxon's unconscious form. "I'll be more than just a sergeant. Much more."

The door to the wardrobe creaked open. Sissy padded across the floor and wrapped her arms around him.

"That means," she said, "that you will be leaving me."

*****

Not long after that, Robert and his father had taken the post to London, thence south of the Thames, though Greenwich to Woolwich. The exam was not held at the Academy, but close to the river, in a building that was part of the old Woolwich Arsenal. The school had once been housed there but had recently moved to a new location. Now the Arsenal buildings contained offices, storerooms for cannon, foundries and workshops for making guns.

Robert remembered how his stomach had danced, how he had only paid the grim and sooty structures passing attention. On any other day he would have been pleased to see the blue coated sentries, to watch them march their beats, or to examine the many cannon that lay scattered about in the courtyard. But not that day. On that day all he had noticed was the smell of brick and stone and metal.

"You possess a sound grounding in mathematics," Thomas Saxon had told him before setting out, "and comprehend your English and Latin grammar better than most. You should have little trouble."

Robert shrugged. He had all that, and more. He knew he need not fear, but fear was no rational thing. If he should fail here, he would have to endure his father's wrath for many months, until another attempt could be made.

He had entered the examination room alone. The place was an empty cavern, its walls a dingy gray and unadorned, the ceiling a distant shadow. The single table at the opposite end of the room seemed very far away.

Four examiners waited behind the table. Two wore gold-encrusted artillery uniforms, the other two, sombre black civilian dress. This was the Board of Admittance, a body that included the Lieutenant Governor of the Academy, the inspector, and two of the masters. For a moment Robert hesitated, for these men had the power to change the course of his life, for better or worse. But he reminded himself that he was cleverer than most, and there was no doubt that he would be successful. No doubt at all. He could not fail, unless he allowed fear to cloud his judgement.

He advanced, walking as he expected a soldier should, with his chin up, his chest out, and his hands by his side. His shoes echoed on the polished wooden floor, and this helped him keep an even cadence. They would be impressed with his quick march, he thought.

When he halted before the board, a mouse emerged from some hole and scampered across his path. He watched it enter another hole on the other side of the room.

"Robert Saxon," said the man in the center of the table. He was the oldest—one of the civilians. Two of his companions were almost as old, aged and very serious men, who must have glowered as a point of habit. The fourth, another civilian, was young, and in contrast, wore the perpetual hint of a smile. "Yes, Saxon. I remember this petition. Stop looking at the mouse, boy. We are not here for such frivolities."

Robert met his eye. "Sir."

"Yes," the man grumbled, then launched at once into the exam, asking a simple question about grammar. "Describe to me the parts of a sentence, in English."

Robert answered with no difficulty. "Subject, verb, object, Sir." He expected the exam would grow more difficult as it progressed. It did not. The questions came in rapid order, but Robert answered every one without hesitation, save for a few arithmetic problems that he was permitted to figure on a small slate that the examiners provided.

When the exam had finished, Robert knew that he had answered every question correctly.

He marched back the length of the room. When he reached the door, the beginnings of elation started to rise deep within his breast. By the time he had descended the stairs and was making his into the entry hall where his father waited, he had begun to chuckle. Soon the chuckle became a laugh, and at that, he had to stop, leaning against the wall until the fit passed. That was when the laughter changed to sobs.

He would be leaving home. He would escape into the world, and though he would become a soldier and so face the horrors of war, his future seemed nothing more than a sun-washed green field, over which rode an ever-expanding sky of deepest blue.

Chapter Four

Attack

Rice had shown Robert and Georgie where the notices and schedules were posted outside the Orderly Room. "You are both in the third academy," he told them. He placed his hands on his hips. "The third academy, you ought to know, is at the bottom, and therefore utterly useless. Being a member of that lofty corps means that you're not fit to lick our boots." He gave Georgie a cuff on the ear. "Now I'm only going to show you and tell you this once. Here is your schedule of study: maths, Latin, and Classics. Stuff I mastered when I was still wetting myself."

Robert sighed, unable to express the various witticisms and insults that sprang to mind. "You were still wetting yourself last year?" he especially wanted to ask, but the rules would not allow it. No doubt this inability to respond was some method by which the Academy taught recruits some restraint, some discipline. Perhaps this was all part of the training. Corporals were to taunt the snookers, bait them, try to provoke a reaction. A good snooker, Robert supposed, would not rise to that bait.

"Thank you, Corporal Rice," Robert said.

"Don't thank me, you bloody snooker! Looking after your lot is thankless and will forever remain so."

Robert had soon learned that study periods and lectures

were held three times a day, at eight o'clock, two o'clock, and six o'clock. Each period lasted two hours, and whether the period would be used for a lecture or study varied. The lectures were formal, but much of the study was left to the discretion of the cadet. The professors presented their subjects, taught their lessons, and the cadets decided how best to reinforce those lessons with their readings.

The eight o'clock period was almost always filled with a lecture. This took place in one of the spacious Academy rooms on the first floor of the Centre Building. Every day a separate subject was scheduled, and in this way, Robert was introduced to his academic instructors, one day at a time. The professors were not soldiers, but civilian masters of their respective fields. The first to appear was Professor Marconi, the Latin Master, an excitable Italian who seemed always in a rush, always in a sweat, and always slightly late. He smelled of garlic, though he was good tempered and the passion he felt for his subject was unquestionable. The cadets warmed to him, for he made the lessons simple to comprehend, unlike the mathematics instructor, Professor Wendt, who spoke in an accented monotone and approached his lessons as if he was always beginning in the middle. A small man with a very round head and tiny spectacles, Wendt had a habit of turning his back to the cadets and speaking to the slate board as he figured some obscure equation. Meanwhile, the cadets would hurl bits of paper and slate pencils at each other. Wendt never seemed to notice. When introducing a topic, the German would simply take a position at the head of the room, fold his hands behind his back, and say something such as, "We will now add these fractions."

The English Master was Professor Blackwood, a stern, dark pillar in an old-fashioned frock coat, with dust on his shoulders and fine, pale skin like old wax. He scowled at the snookers and taught the tales of the ancient Greeks as if for punishment, and grammar as if it were the backbone of all learning, which he often stated as fact.

Robert was not intimidated by any of these men, nor their subjects. The curriculum for the lower classmen was rudimentary, a repeat of lessons he had undertaken with his father. Robert planned to work through it and begin preparing for entry to the middle academy. The academic rules at the Shop made this possible. Every academy, lower, middle, and upper, required its students to complete several projects, but there was no strict deadline for any of these, nor was a lower classman prohibited from plunging ahead and beginning work on his middle academy requirements. Under this system, Robert could understand how some clever cadets had managed to gain their commissions in a single year or less by simply completing every project for all three academies.

"As soon as the opportunity arises," he told Georgie, "I'm going to take the exam to enter the middle academy. I feel like I'm wasting my time here with these subjects that I've already mastered. I don't see the need to go over the same ground."

Ground hard won, he did not add, with his father, night after night, enduring his potential wrath, his shameful drunkenness.

Georgie's perpetual smile wavered. "Do you think I could try to pass as well? I mean, we're chums after all, aren't we Robert?"

"Of course," Robert said. "Of course we're chums." He had come to think of Georgie as an agreeable and gentle soul, and one who would stand by his companions if they would stand with him. The world needed more fellows like him to help counter the overpowering number of disagreeable fellows like

Rice.

"Look, if you want," Robert added, "I'll tutor you. I don't really need to spend my time learning this for myself."

Georgie sat up quickly, almost losing his balance and pitching forward from his chair. Righting himself, he ran his hands over his rounded skull. "That would be most welcome, and most appreciated. You're a capital fellow, Robbie Saxon! I'll have to write father and tell him, for he worries about my grasp of mathematics. He will be relieved to know that I have some help."

*****

Squad drill under Sergeant Bane progressed. Bane instructed Robert and his fellow snookers in the basics of forming a line at close order, of advancing and retiring, facing to the right and left, and to the right and left about. Bane taught them how to dress their line, shouting, "Eyes – right! Dress! Move up, Mister Howard! Move up two whole inches, you horrid little fellow. Want to be an officer, do you? Steady there. Eyes – front!"

Bane also introduced his gentleman cadets to the British Army firelock, or musket, the artillery's version of old Brown Bess.

"This is shorter than the infantry pattern by two inches," Bane said. "That, my fine young gentlemen, makes it less cumbersome when working around our guns."

Bane's lessons included how to place the musket at the "order," the "shoulder," "port," "advance," and "support." He taught the cadets how to fix and unfix their bayonets, and promised that, when he judged them ready, he would teach them how to load and fire, as if he was doing the cadets a favour, and not simply his duty. Such was squad drill.

On most days there was also a Second Drill Parade, this one on a company scale. For this session every cadet from every academy assembled as a single body. The commander of the cadet company Parade was Lieutenant Flushing, a tall, lanky officer with delicate, almost womanly features, his nose pencil thin, his mouth a pinched bauble. He sat his horse with arrogant ease, one hand poised on his hip, his uniform spotless, the gorget at his neck gleaming, his cocked hat worn at a jaunty angle. He would begin every Parade thus mounted, perhaps for the sake of appearances, dismounting within a few minutes, handing the horse to a groom, and proceeding on foot, though looking no less fine or pleased with himself.

"We call him Flashdash," Rat told Robert after his first company drill. "No doubt, you will discover why soon enough."

Robert had already guessed the reason and knew he would never warm to Lieutenant Flushing. Robert liked his professors well enough, for they knew their subjects, and he respected Sergeant Bane, for his instruction was clear, fair, and efficient. Yet Flushing, or "Flashdash," cared for one thing, and that was turnout. He wanted his cadets to show the same dash he, no doubt, believed he personified. He loved nothing more than a shiny button, a whitened belt, a blackened shoe. Other officers loved these things as well, but the problem with Flashdash was that he displayed no interest in any other aspect of a soldier's training. His inspection was interminable, taking up the bulk of the Parade. Worse, it seemed designed to find fault.

"There is dust on the bottom of your gaiters," he once said to Robert. "You must not have dust on your gaiters, cadet."

"Uh....Yes, sir," Robert had replied, confused, for his gaiters had been clean when he had put them on. The only time dust could have collected was in the last few minutes as the cadets had formed their lines, shuffling their feet as they jostled for position.

As the days passed, Flashdash would mention that dust again, and soon Robert understood why. The lieutenant had a store of faults he reached into whenever he could find no other deficiency with a cadet's appearance. Flashdash lectured even those whose kit was pristine, and was brutal to those whose kit was not. He delighted in assigning extra drill and extra fatigues.

At the end of every inspection, which most often lasted about three quarters of the hour allotted for drill, Flashdash would make the same statement. "You are gentlemen, and you must maintain the appearance of gentlemen." This single sentence signalled the second part of the drill. For the remaining fifteen minutes, the lieutenant would attempt to march the company to and fro across the square. His patience for this was thin, and he would invariably end up shouting, "Keep that line straight! Stop wobbling about on the left! Move up – oh, you pack of ruffians!"

If the company's performance was worse than usual, Flashdash would call a halt. Here the men would have a break, for the lieutenant would stand them easy as he stewed in his own frustration. But the breaks were short, and always followed by an outburst against whoever Flashdash had decided was to blame for the wobbly line or the improper turn.

"Sergeant Bane, that man there has no sense of timing," he declared one day, pointing to Georgie with his cane. "He cannot keep the step and is confusing the men to either side. Be so good as to examine his shoes to see if he has two left feet."

Sergeant Bane made a show of checking, and said, "Two different feet, sir."

Flashdash looked as if he had sucked a lemon. "Well, he should learn to use them. Take his name. Extra drill in the morning!"

From his place two files away on Robert's left, Georgie made a strangled gurgle. Robert glanced at him, saw him tilt his head back, eyes closed. This was the third time that week that Flashdash had placed him on extra drill. It meant another early morning for Georgie, another day of struggling into his full marching kit before his comrades rose from their beds.

Flashdash moved to the edge of the Parade, muttering under his breath. Robert watched him, wondered how it was possible that the officer still did not know Georgie's name. The lieutenant halted on the green border of the Ha Ha, where a small group of spectators had gathered to watch the cadets. The lieutenant suddenly swept off his hat and began chatting with a young woman, glancing now and then toward the cadets and shaking his head. She smiled and giggled at something he said, one hand to her mouth.

Robert turned to Mumbles, who was on his right, and whispered, "Who is that Flashdash is talking to? Do you know?"

Mumbles grunted something that Robert thought may have been, "His wife."

"His wife? That's Flashdash's wife?"

Mumbles darted a glance at Sergeant Bane, who had positioned himself on the right flank of the cadet company as covering sergeant. Though the cadets were standing easy and could relax, talking was not permitted. But Bane was staring to his front and did not appear to have heard their whispered conversation.

"She's the most beautiful woman in Woolwich," Mumbles ventured, shielding his mouth with his hand. "Everyone says so."

"And small wonder," Robert remarked. He could not see

her eyes at this distance, but he imagined they were a deep brown to match the chestnut curls that spilled from the edges of her bonnet. Her fashionable dress was a light off-white, her little velvet jacket burgundy. Robert fancied he met her eye, though only for a fraction of an instant, and then her gaze swept on. She laughed again, and Flashdash shied to one side, blocking her from Robert's view.

"Our Flashdash is a fortunate soul, to have a wife like that," he murmured. Fortunate like all those of his class, the sort of man who had never needed to struggle to acquire his present status. A puffed-up buffoon, the kind that Robert held in contempt.

*****

Supper followed Company Parade. After that, the cadets had another period of independent study. On the day that Robert had spied Flashdash's wife, he returned to barracks determined to do some reading. With the library off limits, the barrack room was one of his only certain havens. That and the corridor.

Georgie and Mumbles joined him. Mumbles took a seat at the table under the window while Georgie crashed onto his bed. "Extra drill again," he cried, though his smile was broad, showing his teeth. A forced smile. "I'll be a master before long!"

"You had better be," Robert said. "Learn something from your mistakes."

Georgie sighed. "Yes...."

Robert hefted a volume of Latin and sat on the edge of his folded bedstead. The door to the room stood ajar, and Dog's little cat suddenly slid in through the gap and pranced toward Mumbles. The cat sat back on its haunches and dropped something at Mumbles's feet.

"Oh, look, he has caught a bird," Georgie said. "Well done, little man!"

Mumbles reached down and retrieved the little corpse. "He's forever bringing in birds." He held the bird to the light, stretching out the tiny wings to reveal the interlocking feathers, silky and brown. "A common song sparrow, I think. But (mumble mumble) specimen."

Robert had admired the pair of miniature watercolours pasted to the wall near Mumbles's bed, one depicting an English robin and the other a kestrel about to dive. "Birds are an enthusiasm of yours?"

Mumbles had already begun to sketch the sparrow with a charcoal pencil. "Yes."

"Well, your depictions are very fine. Very detailed and lifelike."

Mumbles kept his eyes on his work, his shoulders hunching forward. "I think... I think my best subject, (mumble mumble) drawing and design."

The door burst open. Rice strode in, laughing and trailed by Dog and Rat. The cat leapt to the windowsill, back arched.

"Ah, Mumbles and the snookers!" Rice cried. "I had hoped you would all be here. I'll need one of you to fetch me a bottle of something later. I'm planning a spree for the weekend."

Robert raised his book, pretending to read, but he knew this was an end to his peace. He would have to read in the corridor after all, though there was always a chance that Rice and his cronies would grow bored and not stay long, that they would run off somewhere to plan their party, just as they did every weekend. Rice was a whirlwind of cadet society, always arranging some outing or another. The corporal was a popular cadet, though, in Robert's view, for all the wrong reasons.

"On Saturday I intend to celebrate," Rice continued. He snatched a slender stick of kindling from the firebox and began an idle tapping against the hearth frame. "I received a letter from my father yesterday. He tells me that I'll likely have a company to command, soon after I leave the Academy, as soon as the vacancy comes up. He'll see to that."

Robert put down his book. Rice never missed a chance to mention his father, to remind his barrack mates that his was an old and distinguished family, fully superior to theirs. It was irritating. Robert knew he should not say anything, but his evening had already been spoiled, and his self control was starting to erode. "Why didn't you join the infantry or cavalry," he said, "purchase your commission and have done with it?"

"Shut your mouth, you bloody snooker!" Rice cried, throwing down the stick with a clatter. "You have no right to question me. Though for your information, the men in my family have always been gunners. This is my birthright, my duty to command, unlike some in this room who have never had a relation attend this lofty institution. Artillery is in my blood."

"Some here don't know their place," Rat sneered, glaring venom in Robert's direction.

But Rice's attention had already moved on. "Now, what are you up to, Lord Mumbles?" he said, crossing the room and leaning over the table.

Mumbles had frozen in the act of drawing. Robert saw his hand begin to tremble.

"Ugh! Is that a dead bird?" Rice suddenly shouted. "Get that thing out of here!"

Rice slapped Mumbles on the left ear. Mumbles cowered in his chair, his left hand springing open to let the sparrow fall to the table. Rice then swept the tiny, feathered corpse onto the floor, where the cat, bounding down from the window, snatched it up in its jaws.

Rice pointed at the cat and turned to Georgie. "You, Snooker Howard. Throw away that bit of rubbish."

Georgie almost fell off his bed in his haste to obey, licking his lips as he approached the cat. Robert closed his book and sat up to watch. Something in the air had changed, some malevolent energy having been ignited. Rice was in a mood to provoke; that was clear.

The cat eyed Georgie with curiosity. "There's a good kitty," Georgie said, reaching out to take hold of the cat's collar with one hand and the bird with the other. The attempt was met with a hiss and a darted slash from a forepaw. Georgie yelped and backed away, favouring a great gouge on the back of one hand.

"Oh, for heaven's sake," Rice lamented. "Saxon, you do it."

Robert had not expected to get away without some form of humiliation. There was no option to refuse. It would be best if he simply threw away the bird and had done with it. Then maybe Rice would lose interest and leave. Then Robert could get some work done.

Crouching before the cat, Robert called, "Puss, puss," kissing the air and letting his hand crawl forward on its fingers. The cat sat back, dropped the bird, and started licking its paws. Robert grabbed the bird and stood.

Rice did not hide his disappointment. "So, Mister Marigold's pet has a fancy for you, I suppose. Get rid of the bird, then."

Without a word, Robert moved toward the door, but Rice stopped him, saying, "No, not like that, snooker. Eat it. Eat the bird to get rid of it."

Robert stopped. It felt as if a bolt of lightning had just

struck him between the shoulder blades. "What?"

Rice folded his arms. "I believe you heard me."

Robert stared at him. The air seemed to thicken, and his breathing rushed in his ears. He supposed Rice was joking, that he did not really mean it.

"Right," Robert said, turning back for the door.

"Stand where you are!" Rice shouted. "I gave you an order, Saxon!"

Robert froze. His heart began to pound. "Corporal?"

Rice's lips pulled back. "I should not be surprised at your defiance. I don't care for you, snooker. Did you know that? I like you even less than that lump," he jabbed his chin at Georgie, "over there. You put on airs. I think you need a lesson in manners. Eat the sparrow."

Robert tossed the bird to the floor. He was trapped. He had been given an impossible order, and now he would be punished for refusing. But he was certainly not going to degrade himself for the pleasure of this lot, so there was only one choice open to him.

Rice bristled. "Are you disobeying a direct order?"

"It's not an order," Robert said, but he had heard the relish in Rice's voice. His fate was sealed, and thus, with nothing to lose, he added, "It's just a damned fool trick."

There was a moment of heavy silence. Then Rice said, "Get him."

Robert did not try to run. Rat and Dog leapt in on either side, seizing his arms and pulling them behind him. He struggled for a moment, but stopped, knowing that the custom forbade him to fight back. There was no sense in making this worse, no sense in giving Rice a legitimate crime that would bring further punishment. Robert would break no rules, even one so convenient, cowardly, and easily abused.

They laughed as they half lifted and half dragged him from the room, his shoes slipping in the scattered sand until Rice grabbed his feet. They carried him down the stairs, out the back entrance and into the grassy courtyard. It was late and there were no other cadets about, but even if there had been, it was unlikely anyone would have intervened.

To one side of the yard was a door which led to a racket court. The court was an empty enclosure of high whitewashed walls, open to the air, its floor of polished flags. Once inside the court, Robert's attackers threw him face first against the wall. He grunted, the wind blasting from his lungs. Rat and Dog were upon him at once, pinning his arms and legs, and Rice suddenly grabbed the back of Robert's breeches, jerking them down so hard his braces buttons flew. The breeches fell in a tangle around his ankles. Something struck Robert hard across the buttocks, and he convulsed in pain and surprise, gasping.

"That's for insubordination," Rice cried with far too much glee. Leather snapped the air, and Robert realized that Rice had brought a cartridge box belt.

So, this is to be beating, Robert thought, and a surge of hot rage filled him. He had resolved to endure whatever prank they had in mind, but not this. How dare they strike him? Rice was not his father. He had no right. They had no right to do this....

"And this is for insolence," Rice said, lashing out with the belt again. Rat was cackling, clucking like an old hen, Dog snickering close to Robert's ear. Robert could smell Dog's breath, and almost gagged at the stench, for the boy had bad teeth.

"This is for being a no-good snooker," Rice said. Another blow, harder than the first two. Robert knew his skin would tear on the next, his blood oozing, flesh ruptured.

But then they let him go. Rat and Dog released their grip,

and without their support, Robert dropped back and collapsed onto the floor. He landed in a sitting position, and at last he groaned. His assailants were already running, peeling with laugher. Robert sat still, the pain now searing down his legs. He heard Rice pause in the doorway.

"Don't be late for evening Roll Call, you damned snooker!"

Then Robert was alone, sitting and struggling to retrieve his fallen breeches.

*****

Roll Call was at ten o'clock. It took place on the Front Parade by torchlight, the torches set in iron brackets thrust into the turf along the edge of the Ha Ha. Every evening the cadets formed their ranks while Orderly Sergeant Webber, a squat gunner with a face pocked like an old cheese, called each name in his incongruous, high-pitched voice. He then marked every cadet as either present or absent on his list.

Robert was not late. He had returned to barracks and, without a word, had replaced his missing buttons. Rice and his friends had snickered amongst themselves but had said nothing more to him. Now he stood in his place, Mumbles on his right, and answered, "Present," when his name was called. He spoke without a hint of rage or agony.

When the Parade was dismissed, it was "Out Lights," the end of the day. Robert returned to barracks, where he lay down quietly amongst the boys who had attacked him. His anger and indignation were strong, so strong he knew he would pass a sleepless night.

He reminded himself that he was not permitted to strike back. Those were the rules. But he would not always be a snooker, would cease to rate as such, as soon as he passed his first exam. And he would not forget this day.

He rolled over and listened to the growl of Mumbles snoring.

Chapter Five:

Bayonet

Robert's first examination took place on a Monday, at eight o'clock in the morning, in one of the Centre Building "academies." Sunlight spilling through the eastern windows illuminated the members of the examining panel. The panel included the Academy Inspector, who was there to ensure the test was fair, and Professors Wendt and Blackwood. Marconi also appeared, though he was late and dishevelled, muttering under his breath as he hurried into the room and took a seat with his colleagues, facing Robert. Robert stood with hands folded behind his back.

"I trust you are not here to waste our time, Mister Saxon?" Professor Blackwood said, squinting from the sun as he leaned forward on his elbows. "You have been with the Academy only a few weeks."

"I feel I am ready, sir," Robert said.

Blackwood made a sound in his throat. The Inspector sat as still and impassive as a sentry. Blackwood's eyes flicked toward him, then back to Robert.

"Very well, then," Blackwood said.

The questions began. Marconi asked his with a smile and a flourish of his hands, though the others seemed to do their best to intimidate, each maintaining a stern gaze and pronouncing his words with just an edge of hostility. But there were no threats here for Robert, no canes or open palms if he answered incorrectly. They could not hurt him, could not even frighten him. And these simple questions of English usage, of French grammar and of addition and subtraction, were nothing.

After an hour, after watching Blackwood's scepticism turn first to mild surprise, then soften to pleased wonderment, he knew that he had passed.

"Thank you, Mister Saxon," Blackwood said at length. Robert detected the ghost of a rare smile on the man's thin lips. "That will be all."

Robert left, buoyant with triumph as he made for the stairwell. Coming up the stairs was Georgie, and when Robert saw him, he said, "Nothing to fear! Just answer the questions."

Georgie's face was pallid and glistened with sweat. He paused at the top of the stairs, hands twitching where they hung limp at his sides.

"Second thoughts?" Robert asked, hopeful, for he did not think Georgie was ready for this. Georgie had declared that if Robert could take the exam now, so could he. It would be something to put in a letter to his father.

"You don't have to go through with this if you're not ready," Robert added. "Just let them know."

Georgie swallowed. "What, and admit that I'm a coward? Never that, Robert."

"There's nothing cowardly about admitting your weaknesses, Georgie, but I won't argue with you anymore. Just try not to panic. The questions are simple schoolboy stuff."

Georgie found his smile. "Oh, I'm fine, Robert! Just a little jittery. Once I'm in the room, I'll be first rate, never fear."

This sudden confidence appeared genuine enough, and

Robert nodded. "Good. I'll see you at drawing. That's your favourite class, isn't it? Something to look forward to."

Georgie smoothed the front of his coatee and took a few slow steps toward the academy door. "Of course! I will see you there, Robbie."

Robert continued toward the stairs, but before he descended, he paused to add, "Maybe by then we'll no longer be snookers."

*****

The Chief Drawing Master was a young man whose hair was already thinning to cobwebs and greying at the temples. His name was Henry Crawford, and to him, the ability to draw, to reproduce an image gleaned from the physical world, was as important as the ability to write. Today he took the thirty members of the third academy to Woolwich Common for a "field trip," as he called it. There just beyond the border of the Ha Ha, he formed his students in a half circle, facing across the spreading field of grass and goldenrod gone to seed.

Robert usually enjoyed the class, but this time, he found he had little interest. The results of his exam, and of Georgie's, would be posted in the Orderly Room later than day. He knew he had passed, that he no longer belonged here with these other boys, these other snookers. This would be his last drawing class with Professor Crawford, and to him, it was more of an outing, a pleasant interlude. It was a fine day for painting—the first of October, a day of steaming breath and a sky running with high batches of clouds like men of war under full sail. The trees bordering the grounds of the Shop were beginning to blossom with colour—gold and rust. The air was still, and if the sun remained warm and it did not rain, Robert guessed that, by the middle afternoon, it would be a perfect day for sitting out under a tree and simply letting his mind wander.

"Perspective is key to understanding distance," Crawford was saying. "And to reproduce that perspective on the two dimensions available to the drawing pad. Tell me, how far is it from this point to that stand of beech trees?"

He swept his gaze across the front line of cadets, finally lighting on Georgie. "How far are those trees?" he repeated. "Can you determine the distance, Cadet Howard?"

Georgie grinned like an idiot and shifted from foot to foot. "Well, it looks rather far, doesn't it? I should think... er... I should think... three hundred yards?"

The Drawing Master's face betrayed his disgust. "You should not think," he said, "for that is a gross exaggeration. What is your estimation, Cadet Saxon?"

Robert had only half noticed that Georgie had answered wrong, but at the mention of his name he shaded his eyes, looked at the far trees, and said, "About sixty or seventy yards."

Crawford held up a finger, and he smiled. "Exactly! That copse is sixty-five yards from this position."

There were nods amongst the gathered boys. Georgie chuckled. "Oh, well, that's a lesson, isn't it? It certainly seemed farther."

"Indeed," Crawford said, the smile vanishing. "Distance can be deceptive. A difficult thing to learn, but you must master it if you are to ever sight artillery. And to that end, you must master the art of the landscape. To see it in your mind first, then to reproduce it on your canvas, or, in this case, on your sketch pad. Now if you will all take up your black lead pencils...."

The cadets sat on the grass to draw the scene before them, a simple one of an open field, a few trees, a flock of grazing sheep, and overhead, the riding clouds. Robert's hand flickered across the paper. For him this was a lark. He had been drawing such scenes for years, with a master far more demanding than Crawford hovering at his elbow.

*****

Robert attacked Monday's mutton quickly and with relish, his spirits high.   Next to him Georgie picked at his food. Mumbles tapped Georgie on the arm and said something, to which Georgie replied, "What?"

Mumbles cleared his throat and said, "Your results will be ready soon?"

"Yes, yes," Georgie cried. "As soon as dinner is over." He leaned on one elbow with a wan smile. "I'm afraid I didn't fare half so well as Robbie here."

"Get your elbows off the table, snooker!" Rice snapped from three seats down.

When dinner was over, Robert marched to the Orderly Room with Georgie trailing behind him. There was the notice already pinned to the wooden bulletin board, a dozen names, each with a single word beside it. Pass or fail. Robert leaned in, hands behind his back. He had passed, as expected. And Georgie had not.

Orderly Sergeant Webber appeared at the door, polishing his spectacles. "So, you've run your guns straight up to the wall, eh young Mister Saxon?   Not content to sit back and take ranging shots?" The sergeant chuckled at his own wit.

"Yes, sir," Robert said. "I don't like to fight over the same ground twice."

"It's congratulations are in order then.   A pity for you though, Mister Howard. You'll try again soon, I presume?"

Georgie was trembling.   "Yes, yes, sir.   I think I know... where I went wrong."

"Then a fail is not a failure, is it, when you learn from it?"

They wandered back to barracks. Robert's triumph was tempered by his disappointment for Georgie, though he realized that despite his encouraging words, he had not expected Georgie to pass. And as they walked, he felt the sweetness of his own success begin to truly sour, for his tutorship had not done Georgie much good. In that respect, he had failed, as well.

I tried, he told himself. I tried, and knew he was not ready. He needs more time, more practice.

That was it. More time, more practice, and that would be up to Georgie. Robert wondered if he would still have the luxury of helping him much from here on, for now he had to concentrate on the next rung, to pass the exam for the upper class. To become a corporal, like Rice, one had to be a member of the upper class. And to graduate with a commission, one had to be a corporal.

In barracks, Georgie scooped up Dog's little cat and sat on the edge of his bed. He stroked the cat's smooth flank, and it began a gentle rolling purr. "It was mathematics," Georgie said. "Always mathematics. But I wouldn't have gained anything if I hadn't tried. And I'll try again in two months."

"That's the spirit," Robert said. He admired Georgie's efforts to always put up a brave front, to keep some shred of good cheer, even when it did not always work, as now. For Robert often saw that briefest flash of despair, like a flicker of distant lightning, before Georgie mastered it and the smile returned.

Georgie let the cat go.

"We're still chums, aren't we, Robert?" he asked. "I mean, now that you will be moving up a notch, you won't begin shunning me as a snooker, will you?"

Robert was astonished at this suggestion, that he would fall into the game he hated so much. They were all here to train as officers, all here to fight the same enemy. "Of course we're still chums! We still share barracks, and I'm not here to lord it over anyone. I'm just here to get my commission, then get my stroke at Bonaparte."

"I knew that. I knew it, of course. You're a right fellow, Robbie Saxon."

Robert looked away, feeling himself flush. His throat closed over, and for a moment he could not speak. He sought to do the right thing, sought to uphold all that his mother and aunt had taught him, and to counter all that his father had stood for. Yet he never knew whether he was a success of not, and to have someone praise him as Georgie had done....

He cleared his throat. "We're still chums, Georgie," he repeated. "Never you worry."

*****

Things changed at once. Robert entered the second, or middle academy, where the course curriculum included decimal fractions and French as well as Latin. Again, he discovered that he was familiar with these subjects and was confident that soon, within a month perhaps, he could pass into the first and final academy. Then, after Christmas, he would have that level mastered, receive his cadet corporalship, take the exam for graduation and so win his commission, finishing within the year as he so desired.

And he would return home one day, walking tall, striding into the hallway, an officer of artillery. An officer who no one could touch, and no one could hurt.

Meanwhile his life became easier, something he had not expected, his suspicion of greater and more difficult challenges proving unjustified. He even found time for some recreation, for getting to know his new comrades, older lads who were less innocent and ignorant than many of the snookers in the lower academy. There were sprees in the local pubs, from which Robert was no longer barred, and there were bets and games of racquets. There were practical lessons now as well as academic. He enjoyed dance instruction and fencing, which became a particular favourite, though like most cadets, he became merely competent with the foil and no master swordsman.

Best of all, he was now permitted to lounge in the reading room, with its heady scent of leather, and to read under the glorious light of the front windows.

I am no longer a snooker, he told himself one day as he returned from the library, carrying a volume of *Caesar's Commentaries*—part of the Classics study. *I am not a snooker, and anyone who dares treat me like one, who dares to play a single prank or utter a single insult, will soon regret it.*

He reached his barrack room, stepping through the door to find the others busy readying themselves for the Midday Parade. Georgie was brushing one of his shoes, whistling a cheery tune, and when he saw Robert he declared, "What a fine day for drill it is! Clear and crisp, but with a warming sunshine."

Robert had worn his plain blue undress coat in the reading room, having packed away his clean dress coat to keep it fresh for the Parade. He only needed to give himself a last once-over before facing Lieutenant Flashdash. "Better sun than rain," he said, kneeling and taking the carefully folded garment from the trunk at the foot of his bed. He then raised the coat to let the folds fall open.

As the coat unfurled, its buttons, every one of them, fell off, spilling to the floor like the links in a broken necklace, ringing and dancing in little brass sparkles.

Robert stared, mouth hanging open. Rice was laughing. Rice, Rat and Dog. A few random buttons were still spinning on the floor.

Robert's anger was swift and hot. "What are you playing at, Rice?" he shouted, crumpling the coat in one fist. It was obvious that Rice had tampered with his kit, taken his coat and cut off his buttons. "You had no right to do this!"

Rice continued to chuckle. "Now, that's no way to speak to your corporal, Saxon! Especially when you have no more than ten minutes until Parade. Make sure you spruce up. I hear Flashdash is in a temper today."

Rice slapped his shako onto his head and gave a jaunty wave, exiting the room with Rat and Dog at his heels. Mumbles shrugged in sympathy, uttered a few grunts of gibberish, then also departed.

"Damn him, damn him," Robert repeated. Rice had not done a thing, had not played a single prank, since Robert had entered the middle academy. He had barely spoken an unfriendly or hostile word, and Robert had dared to think that he had been respecting the rules, but now he knew Rice had just been biding his time.

He let loose a wordless growl of frustration. By showing his anger, his outrage, he had simply made Rice's victory all the greater.

There was no time for further worry. He had a sewing kit, a gift from Mrs. Greene, from home. But he could not sew and shank nine buttons so quickly. He would have to resort to pins.

"Can I help?" Georgie asked. He was the only barrack mate to have lingered, risking lateness himself.

Robert shook his head. "Just get down to the Parade before you're in it as well."

Georgie turned to go, but he paused in the doorway. "I'd help if I could," he said. "You know I would."

"Yes, yes. Now get going!"

Robert worked quickly. He managed to stitch two of the nine buttons, the top and bottom. The rest he rigged with straight pins, thrust through the loop on the back of the button, then bent back so that the sharp end was hidden in the fabric. The entire procedure took him less than four minutes, and when he was done, he threw on his coat and his belts, snatched his musket and thundered down the stairs.

On Parade, he fell into his usual place in the front rank, dressed onto Mumbles's left elbow. He was not late.

The sergeant-major formed the company at open order and dressed the ranks. On the sergeant-major's last cry of, "Eyes front," Robert felt one of the pins pop open.

The sergeant major stood the company at ease and turned about, ready to pass command of the Parade to Flashdash. Robert winced as the sprung pin stabbed into his chest.

Flashdash was lingering on the edge of the Ha Ha, making the men wait as he chatted with his wife for a moment more. Then he blew her a kiss with one gloved hand and advanced on foot toward the cadet company, holding his sword against his left leg as he walked.

Sweat had begun to bead Robert's forehead, despite the crisp and cool air that Georgie had praised. Flashdash started his inspection and was moving down the line. It took the lieutenant about fifteen minutes to reach Robert's file. When he did, he stopped at once, staring down his long nose with a look of shock, shock that quickly changed to disgust and disappointment.

"Mister Saxon," he said, "that is the most absurd thing I have ever had the displeasure to see on my Parade. Did you think to fool me? You have lost a button, and I can see the pin plain." He let loose an elongated sigh of exasperation. "You have until now been a fair hand at drill. Fair, mind you, fair. Yet this shows poor management of time if not simple sloth. You are on extra drill for the morrow."

Then he moved on. Robert stared to his front across the Parade Square toward the Ha Ha. He saw Flashdash's wife, watching, noticed that she was eying him, doubtless wondering what had made his husband pause.

Now she will think I'm a bad soldier, Robert thought, and the burning shame that brought surprised him. Why should he care what she thought? He did not know her, and he thought her husband a fool. Yet, he cared, nonetheless, against his will.

The inspection continued, as usual dragging on for almost an hour. When the marching commenced, the sprung pin stabbed deep into Robert's flesh, just above his heart.

*****

During his period of extra drill the next morning, Robert could think of nothing else but how to retaliate. He was no longer a snooker, and he had no time for childish games, in particular those that might damage his standing.

That afternoon, he waited outside, his sketch pad under his arm. Every cadet was required to produce a book of plates before the conclusion of their first year, and as a pretext for what he was about to do, Robert had intended to make a drawing of the Academy buildings. Then he had noticed a battery of field guns parked along the west end of the Front Parade and thought they would make a much better subject. Six-pounders, complete with carriages and limbers, the most common field piece in use by the Royal Artillery. The six-pounder was a small gun with the power to inflict only slight damage on the enemy, and there was talk amongst the elder cadets that the army was considering replacing it with the nine-pounder as the new standard. The Academy used its six-pounders for training, and as Robert ran a finger along one smooth brass gun barrel, he wondered how long it would be before he did more than simply sketch guns like these. Soon, he hoped. Maybe even before Christmas.

He held the sketch pad open before him, bracing one edge against his chest, his left hand clamping the pages in place, his right darting here and there as the image slowly formed. He took particular pains to capture the appearance of the new British carriage, with its single, tapered oak trail. The trail was light and well balanced, designed to allow the gun commander to easily shift it from left to right when laying a gun on target. It was considered a far superior design to the old, heavy, double bracket carriage, with its two iron-bound oak sides, the carriage still used by most continental armies.

Robert paused in his work and blew on his frigid hands. A flock of geese passed overhead, like a squadron of cavalry, despite all their honking and rustling, cutting across an autumn sky that was the colour of steel. A stray gust of wind twisted Robert's page, and he cursed. This was no good. It was too cold to draw. He closed the sketch pad with a snap, shivering as another gust managed to penetrate the flap of his heavy greatcoat.

With the pad again tucked under his arm, he moved away from the guns, following the west perimeter wall and veering toward the barracks. He might find a little shelter in one of the doorways. Anyone who saw him would no doubt wonder what he was doing, why he would loiter outside on such a day as this, but he still had his sketch pad, and he hoped that would allay any suspicions.

But even as he gave himself this reassurance, a figure suddenly entered the grounds through the west gate. Robert took one stuttering step, managing at the last second not to trip. He had not expected to feel such acute anxiety, such a fear of discovery. Or worse, of having his plan interrupted. But the figure was that of Flashdash's wife, and she was not likely to stop and question him. She would probably not even notice him, even though she was making for the junior officer's quarters in the west barracks and her path would cross his. She was not looking up as she walked, but fussing with the bit of pink ribbon that secured her bonnet. The long skirts of her Roman style dress, all the rage these days, billowed about her legs, revealing, for a moment, her black shoes.

The freshening breeze suddenly snatched her bonnet from her head, the ribbon coming loose. She cried out, a faint squeak caught in the wind. The bonnet spiralled away, then began rolling in a straight line like a lost carriage wheel.

Robert was upon it in three quick hops. Stooping, he caught it in his free hand.

Flashdash's wife scurried toward him. She was laughing.

"Thank you, thank you!" she cried. "My gallant cadet!"

He straightened, the bonnet clutched in tight fingers. He had dropped his sketch pad and it lay on the ground behind him, pages fluttering. He paid it no mind.

"My, you're a tall one," she added when she reached him. "I had not observed how tall from back there!"

"Your bonnet, Mrs. Flash . . . er, Mrs. Flushing," he said, offering the rescued headdress.

"You are a true gentleman cadet," she said, taking the bonnet and holding it. Free tendrils of dark hair writhed about her head. "I have seen you before. Yes, I have." Her brow furrowed. "Please tell me your name, so I can thank you properly."

Yes, you have seen me, he thought. *Seen me made a fool for your idiot husband.*

"Robert Saxon, madam."

"Robert Saxon. An earnest name for such an earnest young gentleman, with such a serious face." She showed her teeth, two perfect rows. There was nothing flippant about her words, only humour and honest gratitude for this small thing he had done. For a moment, his heart fluttered, and he found himself staring, with nothing to say. It was true that she was the most beautiful woman in Woolwich, and more lovely up close than seen from the edge of the Ha Ha. And he could smell her scent, some sort if perfume, he supposed, like rose water.

Flashdash did not deserve her.

"I will remember your name, Mister Saxon," she added, inclining her head and dropping a small curtsey. "And your height, as well."

He bowed at the waist and was grateful when an appropriate response came to mind. "You compliment me, madam. I'm happy to be of service, however small. Though I think the barracks wall would have stopped your bonnet if I'd missed."

"Perhaps." She began to move away, but turned back once. "Goodbye, then. I will mention you to my husband."

He watched her as she entered the central door in the west wing.

Somewhere in the town, the bells of a clock tower struck three. It was time.

*****

Robert had not studied Rice's daily routine, but it was hard to share a room with someone and not come to know their habits. Every day at about three, Rice paid a visit to the privy in the annex between the Centre Building and the west barracks. And he always chose the same seat of ease in the same little stall.

Today Rice was late, but that was just as well, for Robert might have missed him as he chatted with Flashdash's wife. But no sooner had she disappeared than Robert spotted Rice coming along the open arcade. A moment later he entered the annex. If he had spotted or recognized Robert, still standing on the Parade, he gave no indication.

Robert started after him. When he reached the annex, he hesitated before deciding to prop his sketch pad in a corner. He needed his hands free, and the pad would not be missed, nor the rude charcoal drawing he had begun.

The privies were in a small room, just to the left of the annex doorway. Robert stepped inside, pausing to listen. He heard shuffling in the last stall in the row, but nothing from the other four. The privies were usually empty at this time of day, which was why, he presumed, Rice preferred this hour to do his business. It seemed that the cadet corporal liked his privacy, at least in some things.

Robert unbuttoned his greatcoat. Underneath, concealed in the coat's folds, he wore his bayonet. Reaching into his coat pocket, he first drew out a small wedge of wood, which he then jammed under the door. Then he slid the fifteen-inch bayonet blade from its scabbard and held it close against his right arm, fingers tight around the socket.

Step by step, on his toes, he crept toward Rice's stall. Robert could see the tips of Rice's shoes sticking out from the edge of the dividing wall.

"Who's that?" said Rice's voice, raised more in irritation than alarm. "I can hear you out there."

Robert moved quickly. The stalls had no doors; were just set apart by thin wooden dividers. Rice was perched on the edge of the wooden seat, his breeches about his ankles, and his look of indignation at once turned to one of shock as he clapped his naked knees together and squirmed backward, just as Robert fell on him, shoving him against the wall with his left forearm and bringing the point of the bayonet to his throat. Robert's left knee pinned Rice's legs, his right bracing against the edge of the seat of ease. A stench rose from the black hole, mingling with the stink of Rice's sweat.

"Don't say a thing," Robert hissed, "or I'll run this through your throat!"

"Saxon," Rice said. "What—?"

"Shut up," Robert snapped. Rice's arms were free, and he might have put up a fight, but Robert had decided to trust in fear. If Rice believed his throat would be cut, that Robert would make good his threat, he would remain still. "I have a message for you, Corporal Rice. I'm no snooker anymore, and I won't have any more of your tricks. I was willing to play along for the sake of the rules, for the sake of tradition, but not anymore. Another bit of fun out of you at my expense, and I'll kill you. Do you understand me?"

"You're stark raving mad!" Rice gasped. "I never meant any harm! It's just in good fun! All in good fun! I had the same happen to me! All snookers do."

There was some sincerity in Rice's desperation, a true incomprehension at Robert's inability to see things his way, and for a moment, Robert hesitated. Maybe Rice did think it was all harmless fun. Maybe he did not understand the consequences of his own actions.

But that, Robert decided, made it all the worse. A flash of memory from the racquet court, of the beating, brought a new flush of rage, and he pressed the bayonet into Rice's neck. Rice let out a whimper, a pathetic animal whine.

"You're a damn fool," Robert said. "So much as look at me the wrong way from now on, and I'll find you."

"You don't really mean it," Rice said, his breath coming in short gasps. "You're just bluffing."

Robert twisted the bayonet. It would be so easy, so simple a thing....

His hand started to shake. "You know I'm not bluffing, but if you squeal a word of this, I'll deny it all, and you'll look an even bigger fool. Then I'll gut you when you least expect it. Remember that there are no witnesses here, just you and me, but just imagine the shame you would have to endure, with you, the high and mighty corporal, and me a recent snooker, catching you out in the black holes?"

"You wouldn't do it," Rice said, though now his eyes were closed and Robert fancied he saw tears in the gloom. "You wouldn't."

"I would. Or should you care to test that?"

He backed away, keeping the bayonet point against Rice's neck with one outstretched arm. He withdrew the bayonet at the last second, just as he slipped out of the stall, dashed to the door and quickly pulled out the wedge. He sheathed the bayonet as he emerged into the annex, buttoning his coat as he stepped through the portal to the main court.

Moving at a brisk march, he doubled along the back wall of the Centre Building, turning into the east arcade, emerging again onto the Front Parade. There he stopped, drawing in a deep breath.

The air, devoid of the stink of shit and fear, smelled sweet, but cold sweat stood out on his forehead, and he fought to control his sudden trembling. He was afraid now, though not of being caught. He was afraid because he knew that he had not been bluffing. For a moment, he had truly wanted to drive the bayonet home, to take his revenge for the beating in the racquet court. It had taken an effort, an incredible effort of will, not to do it then and there, in the stall, to just let the bayonet tip slide into the soft, defenceless flesh.

What had he just done? He had threatened the life of a fellow cadet. He had planned it, thinking to just frighten him, to show him that he was not to be crossed. But he had not really thought it through; he had simply acted. And he had almost killed his intended target.

He leaned against the wall to steady himself. His limbs still shook. He had something of his father's darkness, after all. He had just done a wicked thing, a savage thing. He feared he was capable of much worse. Much, much worse, if pushed.

I must master this thing, he told himself. *Master it before it masters me. I am not a murderer. And I am not my father.*

He pushed himself to his feet and straightened his coat. In a moment he was back in front of the west arcade. He stooped, retrieving his sketch pad. The thing was done, and the day would go on like any other. Perhaps he would finish the sketch? But no, his hands were still unsteady, and the air was, if anything, colder. He needed warmth and comfort.

Thrusting the pad under his arm, he entered the Centre Building and made for the library.

*****

He saw Rice again later, in the barracks. Their eyes met for an instant, but Rice looked away, his skin pallid, sheened with sweat. Robert had wondered if he would feel shame, remorse and sympathy when he next saw Rice, and was grateful that he did not. He felt no emotion at all, his heart cold.

"You are not yourself this afternoon, old fellow," Dog commented, as Rice pulled a chair away from the table, the legs making streaks in the sand.

"I feel a touch... a touch ill," Rice said. "Perhaps it was the mutton."

Dog chuckled. "I should think you'd grown accustomed to that by now."

"I think it's not what you ate," Mumbles said, "but that, (mumble) eating you."

"Shut up, Lord Mumbles," Rice said, but without his usual force.

Robert rolled over on his bed, letting a slow smile spread across his features. The smile came unbidden, and for a moment he thought he might laugh. No one knew about what he had done. He had told no one, and it was obvious that Rice had told no one, either. Like so many bullies Rice was all bravado and bluster, only daring to attack what was too weak to strike back. He was a spoiled weakling who had no doubt led a soft life with a family who doted on him and catered to his every whim.

"Did you do this today?" Georgie said. Robert had left his sketchbook lying open on his bed, the drawing of the guns displayed. "You certainly have an eye for perspective and detail."

"Thank you," Robert said. "Just something I... something I did quickly, while I was waiting for someone."

"Oh, I suppose it's a bit rough," Georgie added, "but the start of something anyway."

Now Robert could not stifle a chuckle. "Yes. Yes, I think I did some good work today!"

Rice threw off his boots and pitched into his bed, closing the curtains after him with a snap. Robert stared after him for a moment, doing his best to stifle more laughter. A little nervous hysteria, he realized. A little relief, as well. For, despite his initial misgivings, it was clear that his actions had paid off. He had won. He sensed that he would have no more trouble from Rice.

He would not have to fight that inner darkness again, for Rice would never again give him a reason

Chapter Six:

Secret

Rice avoided Robert as much as possible, even in the barracks. Robert did not find the situation awkward, oppressive, or disagreeable in any way. To him it meant peace. Peace at last, and time to delve into his studies. And he had much to occupy his mind as he simultaneously strove to master algebra, read Horace and Cicero, and translate Marmontel's *Travels of Cyrus and Belisarius* into French. But his progress pleased him, and by late November, with the trees surrounding Woolwich Common stripped bare and black, he was ready for his next examination, this one for admission to the first academy.

The exam proved no match for him. He left knowing that he had answered every question correctly. He was in a buoyant mood. He was halfway through his first year at Woolwich, and already he was an upper classman. He was on schedule.

One thing marred the day for him. As before, Georgie chose this time to make his second attempt to pass for the second academy. Robert knew that this was premature, but he had been unable to get Georgie to see reason. "I can do it," Georgie had insisted. "I don't need another month."

Robert half feared and half anticipated hearing the results.

"Well?" he asked Georgie at supper. "How did you fare?"

His question was met with silence. Georgie continued eating as if he had not heard.

"You didn't pass," Robert stated.

The radiant smile that suddenly spread across Georgie's face made Robert doubt that analysis for a moment, but just for a moment.

"I was closer this time," Georgie said. "Closer! There were only two questions that gave me great difficulty, and I know I can master them next time. I believe I have a sound understanding of Euclid, but the accuracy of my arithmetic needs work. That is the whole of it, Robert. There's no need for me to be downcast."

"And I see that you're not."

"No. Of course not, when I know what I must do."

Robert looked away, his feelings mixed. There was logic to what Georgie said, and maybe this second failure was just another step on the road to success. Maybe.

"I had a letter from my father," Georgie continued, holding up a folded sheet of paper, the criss-crossed lines of tight handwriting plain. "He agrees that perhaps I am rushing myself. After all, we can't all be like you, off to the races. I should stop competing with you."

"I had no idea you were competing with me."

"Well, perhaps not competing. Perhaps I take... inspiration from your drive."

"I had a sound grounding in the subject matter before arriving, that's all," Robert stated. He drained the dregs of his tea and reclined in his chair, wishing that Georgie would not try to follow him, that he would wait until the end of his first year before taking the exam again. Another mishap would mean utter ruin, and that would be a shame, for Robert thought

Georgie would make a decent officer. Unexceptional, but decent. Robert's father had always said that the sergeants ran things. Officers issued orders, sergeants saw those orders carried out, and a good sergeant would look to the details. Meanwhile it was the officer's duty to inspire the men through his confidence and enthusiasm, and in that, Georgie was second to none. Robert thought that it would be better if more officers took an active role in training and instruction, something his father had told him, with some contempt, that they did not do. Robert believed that the truly exceptional ones must, but if so many did not, then Georgie would never stand out for incompetence, even if he knew next to nothing of algebra and trigonometry. He would, no doubt, treat his men with respect, and would never lose hope, even when all seemed lost. He would at least be as good as Rice, or Mumbles. None of them knew a thing about soldiering yet, and Georgie had as much a chance as any to distinguish himself in the campaigns to come.

"My father is... concerned, you see," Georgie went on. "If I should take and fail the exam a third time, I would be out on my ear." He chuckled. "Funny expression that, 'out on your ear.'"

"You won't be out on your ear, Georgie," Robert said. "But I urge you to take your time. Just take your time and wait until you're ready. Most of the cadets give it at least two years."

Georgie nodded, bobbing his head in quick jerks. "I will, Robert. I will. Never you worry."

*****

After supper they retired to barracks. Mumbles was already there, sitting at the little table and sketching by candlelight. Robert lit another brand, and by its light began polishing the buttons of his dress coat, every one of them newly stitched and shanked.   Georgie unfolded his bed with a thump, then collapsed onto the straw palliasse and stared at the canopy. It was a quiet evening, one like many others.

Then the barrack door opened and Rice burst in.

"Ah, look who we have here," he said, as if there was something unusual about the presence of his barrack mates. Dropping into the chair opposite Mumbles, he began humming an overloud version of the "Grenadier's Slow March." Robert paused in his task, fixing Rice with his best stare of disapproval, but Rice was ignoring him, all his attention on Mumbles, who did not falter in his work until Rice stretched out one long leg and gave him a little kick on the ankle.

"What's that you're up to, Lord Mumbles?" Rice said. "More of your birdies, again? My, you certainly have a thing for them.   Better at making feathered friends than real ones, I should imagine."

Mumbles muttered something. "What's that you say?" Rice cried, cupping one ear. He leaned across the table, suddenly snatching the sketch book out from under Mumbles's pencil. Mumbles simply froze.

Rice was on his feet, holding the sketch book under the light of the candle, pretending to accidentally get it too close to the flames.   "Well, I can't tell what it is," Rice declared after a minute.   "Then again, drawing was never your strongest subject."

"I am very good at drawing," Mumbles said, every word clear.

Rice chuckled and tossed the sketch to the table. "Don't take offence, now, my dear Mumbles. I'm only keeping you sharp, you see. What's the good of being a corporal, if I can't push you lesser mortals around now and then?"

"That's your problem, Rice," Robert interjected. "You think that's all being a corporal is for. Pushing the lads around."

Rice shot him a look of pure malice. "I'll have you on charges if I hear any more remarks like that."

"I doubt it," Robert said. He turned back to his buttons.

His face a dark mask, Rice moved to his bed, sat and pulled off one buckled shoe. He then rubbed his arms, affecting a shiver, though a fire was smouldering in the grate. Waving one hand toward Georgie, he said, "It's damned freezing in here. Snooker, go and fetch some coal."

"But the bin is full," Georgie said.

Rice lobbed his shoe at Georgie. Georgie covered his face, crying out in pain when the shoe heel bit into his forearm. "Then we will have extra! Now get on with it!"

Georgie rolled out of bed and scurried off. Robert watched him go, then turned his gaze on Rice. Rice at last met his eye, if only for the briefest moment, his lip twitching.

So, it's the same old game, Robert thought. *If you can't make my life hell, you will focus your attention on Mumbles and Georgie.*

And it was true that now Georgie did all the little tasks in barracks, "fagging" for the older boys, for Rice, Dog and Rat. He did their laundry, made their snacks, fetched them bottles of the best wine and often paid for it, as they conveniently forgot their pocketbooks. And now this pointless errand for coal, when Rice must have known that Georgie had failed his exam again. And the time that Georgie consumed on these pointless tasks was time that he should have used for his studies.

I will have to teach Rice another lesson, Robert vowed, if this keeps up.

*****

That month the French invaded Portugal. For several days

after the news reached England it was all the cadets could talk about. "Britain can't sit idle on this one," Robert said to Mumbles. "Portugal is our oldest ally."

"What can we do?" Mumbles said. "The army is (mumble mumble)."

Robert paused on one of the broad steps and faced Mumbles. They had been descending the grand east stairwell in the Centre Building, passing the hanging portraits of former Master Generals of the Ordnance. "The army is what?"

"Too small," Mumbles asserted. "Ours is the smallest army in Europe. If the Portuguese won't stand, what could we do by ourselves to help them?"

"We can fight! We have to make our own stand at some point."

Mumbles shrugged and swiped at a lock of hair that drooped over his forehead. Cadets streamed past them, hurrying down the stairs as they always did after study period. Always in a rush to get to where they were going. Professor Blackwood was hovering on the broad upper landing, keeping a watchful eye and glowering in his usual apparent disapproval.

"Since Trafalgar we've sat on out backsides," Robert continued, "letting Bonaparte overrun all of Europe. It's almost as if we can't be bothered. All our attempts to fight the French on land have been puny, little pinpricks to help an ally who is already beaten, like the Duke of York and his bloody mess in the Low Countries. It's time we committed to something larger, grander. Helping Portugal could be our opportunity. And shouldn't it be our duty to stand with such an old friend?"

Mumbles stared at his fidgeting hands. "You're thinking of your future in the army. Of a chance to (mumble)."

"Of course. I joined to fight, not to sit here in England! I would like to believe that every one of the gentlemen cadets here at the Academy did the same, and surely, when we graduate, the army can find us all useful employment." He started down the stairs again. "Really, I'm surprised that a prospective British officer would suggest anything else."

The stairs were quiet now, the rush of cadets having passed. "We must not rush headlong into something," Mumbles added, "without considering it carefully."

"Our army doesn't lack for planning so much as commitment, direction."

They resumed their descent to the next landing, but before they reached it, they paused again, this time in surprise. Georgie and Rice were both there. Georgie had his back against the wall, standing as if at attention, balanced on one leg. Rice faced him, hands on his hips.

"Don't drop that foot, you damned useless snooker," Rice was saying. "Keep it up! Drop it and then I'll really teach you to be in such a damned hurry."

Sweat stood out on Georgie's forehead, his rotund body quivering as he struggled to maintain his balance. Only inches to his right, the next flight of stairs fell away to the ground floor.

"Rice, what are you doing?" Robert demanded.

Rice started, his head snapping around. "None of your business!"

Robert descended the last few stairs toward the landing. Mumbles remained behind. "It is my business," Robert said.

"It's your business that this damned snooker shoved in front of his betters on the stairs?" Rice cried. "I'm teaching him some respect, something you could also do well to learn."

"Leave him alone."

Rice screwed up his face. "Oh, why do you care so much for this nothing?"

"He's my comrade. It's my duty to see that he comes to no

harm."

"Your duty? What sort of rot is that?"

Robert kept his temper in check. Rice would obey him. "Do as I say."

But Rice only smiled. "Very well."

He gave Georgie a push. It was just a small tap on the arm, but enough so that Georgie lost his balance. With a shout, he fell sideways and tumbled down the stairs. Robert reacted at once, leaping past Rice. Georgie came to rest at the bottom, a shapeless heap of arms and legs. He just managed to raise himself on his hands, a look of stunned disbelief on his face, when Robert reached his side.

"Are you hurt?" Robert asked, kneeling. "Are you all right, Georgie? Are you all right?"

"Yes, yes," Georgie winced, for the fall had not been as bad as it looked. He forced himself to a sitting position and rubbed his right arm. "I'll be all right, Robert. Just a few scratches.... It will take worse than a drop of that length to get me down." He laughed.

"Oh, I can give you worse!" Rice shouted from the landing.

Robert slowly rose to his feet, but Rice was running, skipping past Mumbles and bounding back up the stairs, leaving a trail of laughter.

"Coward," Mumbles said.

"You have a lot to answer for, Corporal Rice!" Robert cried, but there was no answer. Rice had already gone.

*****

Georgie was fine, but Robert had seen enough and did not wait. He knew where to find Rice, and find him he did, twenty minutes after Company Parade.

Rice had gone to the recreation room where dancing and

fencing were taught. He wore only shirt and breeches and was practicing his guard and thrust against one of the padded fencing targets. When he saw Robert enter the room, he staggered back as if struck.

There were two other boys present, members of the Second Academy that Robert knew only by name. Robert said, "I would appreciate it if you gentlemen could leave us alone for a few minutes."

The boys exchanged a glance, and one said, "Certainly. We understand."

Then Robert was alone with Rice and advancing, the memory of that awful day in the racquet court coming back to him, feeding his anger. He reached for Rice's foil, but Rice danced out of the way, crying, "What do you think you're doing?"

With one sweeping blow, Robert struck Rice on the wrist. Rice groaned and the foil went clattering and skidding across the hardwood floor. Robert then seized Rice by the front of his shirt and pushed him back, back, slamming him against the far wall. Rice shouted and gasped at the same time, and Robert hissed in his ear, "You could have killed him, you puffed up bastard."

"Let me go," Rice said, struggling, though he could not break Robert's grip.

"You're going to stop tormenting him, do you hear me? Stop from this moment. Do you understand?"

But this time Rice did not cower, and a look of defiance overcame him. "Or you'll what, Saxon? You'll gut me like a fish? Go ahead, then! Do it!"

"I will," Robert insisted.

Rice shook his head. "I don't believe you! You wouldn't do it!"

Robert slammed Rice against the wall twice. Rice grimaced in pain. "Do you want to put that to the test?"

Rice regained his composure, and his chin jutted. "Yes, I do."

Robert released him, letting him slide to the floor. He stood back. The walls were closing in on him. There was only Rice, there in front of him, his enemy, vulnerable. He could snap Rice's neck here and now, have done with it.... "I'll break your arm," he growled, and that decision brought satisfaction. Yes, a compromise, a deal with the darkness. He could not kill this piece of filth, but he could hurt him, see him howl and writhe in agony.

"Don't touch me! Don't touch me or I'll expose your dirty secret!"

Robert had the arm in his grip. "What secret?"

"I'll tell them who your father was!"

Robert froze. "What do you mean?"

Rice's pale skin was slick with sweat. "I didn't believe you when you said no one in your family attended the Academy before, so I wrote to my father. It was your father all right, who made his life hell, and who was booted out. Booted out, and then he went and joined the ranks, of all things!"

Robert felt as if Rice had just punched him in the gut. He tightened his grip on the arm, fighting the sudden sickness, the odd rushing in his ears. "My father was a sergeant."

"Well, perhaps he managed to get that far. I don't bloody care. He was a failed cadet who was forced to join the ranks, and you lied to me. You hid the truth, and if you harm me, I'll let everyone know. I'll expose your shameful little secret!"

Robert at last let him go, stepping back. His head was whirling. "What the hell are you talking about? I never lied to you. My father never told me...."

He stopped.

Rice was rubbing his arm, gaping at him. Then his eyes widened, and he barked a sharp, spiteful laugh. "Is it possible that you don't know? That he was a cadet here, and that he was kicked into the street for being the undesirable that he was?"

Robert could think of nothing to say, no defence. Rice seemed to sense his triumph, the course of battle turning. He drew himself up and laughed out loud. "He never told you, then, did he? He always told you he was a sergeant. Well, I suppose his shame was as great as it should have been."

Robert's fists clenched. "Tell me what you know, or I'll beat you senseless."

Rice folded his arms. "Saxon thought he ruled the roost, exercised a reign of terror. Not just on the snookers, which is permitted, but on everybody. A bloody madman, just like you will no doubt turn out to be. A madman who went too far. Attacked my father in a crowded barrack, nearly strangled him, and they were both upper classmen. There were witnesses, and your father had tangled with the wrong man. Foolish enough to let himself be caught; you see. Had the inspector throw him out in front of all the other cadets. A rare Dismissal Parade! Ruined his career." Rice laughed again. "And you never knew!"

The blood was drumming in Robert's ears. All his anger seemed to have drained away, leaving nothing but a vast weariness, a heaviness as if someone had dropped a sodden greatcoat over his shoulders. He wanted to shout out that this was all lies, but somehow, he could no longer summon the rage.

"So, what, you will blackmail me now?" he said. "Tell everyone that my father was a bully? And got himself kicked out?"

"Yes."

"Don't you see that even if that is so, he never did anything that you haven't done?"

Rice's face flushed scarlet. "I have a host of friends amongst the members of the upper academy. It's tradition to make you snookers answer to discipline! Tradition! Can't you get that through your thick, stupid skull? What's the matter with you? I am no villain!"

Robert started to back away. None of this seemed to matter. Nothing mattered.

"My father is a drunk and a bastard," he said. "You can't hurt me by slandering him. I don't care. I don't care one bit."

Then he turned and left the room, walking with calm, deliberate steps.

*****

The library brought a torrent of memories, of days spent on his father's study floor, pouring through the books and drawings and imagining himself a soldier, a gunner. It was the smell, the wood and paper and must. He supposed all libraries, no matter their size, must smell the same, but to him that scent would always mean the happy time. There was magic and discovery in his father's bookshelves, in both the leather books and the unpublished bundles of drawings and paintings, landscapes, diagrams of fortifications, gun carriages. Why would a sergeant have those things? Robert had never questioned it before, but now it struck him as unusual. Sergeants were not required to produce such detailed designs.

One section of the library at Woolwich contained the selected works of past gentleman cadets. Books of plates mostly, sketches and drawings. Almost every cadet who had ever attended the Royal Military Academy was represented. Almost every cadet. Robert knew that if he did not find anything, that would not disprove what Rice had said.

But there under "S," he saw it. Thomas Saxon, 1775. A bundle of lead sketches. With trembling hands, Robert took it to a reading table in the corner, almost tearing at the ribbon that bound it, causing an explosion of dust motes that danced in the veil of light from the window, the gold of late autumn, the glory of a dying year.

He recognized the style of the drawings. One was a rough sketch of a watercolour landscape he recognized. Recognized from home.

He gripped the arms of his chair and stared out the window. He stared out the window for a long time.

After a while his stomach snarled, while outside fifes and drums announced that it was fifteen minutes until supper hour. Tying the bundle, Robert returned it to its place on the shelf. He would have no one else find it on the table.

Somehow his coat had become rumpled. Smoothing it with his hands, he left the library, descending the spiral staircase that curled through the middle of the Centre Building. At the landing he turned and made his way along the central corridor, toward the west exit. From there his feet seemed to propel him onward without any conscious command from his brain, taking him through the arcade, then into the main courtyard and so to the dining hall. He walked with his head down, his only thought a vague understanding that he needed to have his supper. With food in his belly, he could make sense of what he had just learned.

He nearly stumbled into a group of cadets gathered outside the dining hall doors, just stopping himself in time and staggering to a halt. He knew these fellows, boys from the second academy. They were talking in excited tones, some apparently delighted, others seeming in distress.

"What's this about, lads?" Robert said. "Has Bonaparte

captured Lisbon?"

A grinning face full or freckles turned to him. It was Bernard Henry, the son of a clergyman from Sussex. "Robert! Have you not heard the news?"

Robert shook his head. "No, what news? I've been studying in the library."

"Of course you would be. But it concerns one of your barrack mates, Wesley Rice."

Robert perked up, suddenly interested. "What is it? What happened?"

Henry seemed eager to tell the tale. "It seems he pushed a snooker down the stairs. Old Blackwood saw the whole thing. Or heard it, I think."

"Blackwood?" Robert echoed. Blackwood had seen Rice push Georgie? "What did he do? There must be more to it than that! What's to happen to Corporal Rice?"

"That's just it. They've broken him, stripped him of his corporalship! Can you believe it? He was almost ready to take his final exam for a commission. Now he will have to wait, win his rank back. And all for giving it to a snooker!"

"It's a damned shame," someone said. "A damned shame."

"Daft, as I see it. Some of these fellows go too far, taunting the snookers, make a sport of it."

Robert was no longer listening. An involuntary smile was spreading across his face. "Foolish enough to let yourself be caught, Mister Rice," he murmured, and then he laughed. Laughed as he pushed through the crowd and entered the dining hall.

CHAPTER SEVEN:

CORPORAL

The fourth of December was Saint Barbara's Day, and on that day a feast was held in the dining hall. The commandant, inspector and all the masters were present, and as part of the Grace, Professor Blackwood made a brief speech, explaining the reason for the celebration. "For refusing to recant her faith in our Lord, Jesus Christ, our blessed patron's pagan father ordered her beheaded, and so was struck down, in turn, by a bolt of lighting from heaven. Thus, Saint Barbara watches over all those who work with fire."

The feast was the last occasion before the Christmas holiday. Just days later the first cadets began to leave, departing for home, returning to their families on furlough until after the New Year.

"Goodbye then, Georgie," Robert said when Saint Barbara's Day was a week gone. He shook his friend's hand. "Happy Christmas."

"A shame you will have to stay here," Georgie said, "but then, there are others in the same boat. You won't lack for company."

"I don't mind," Robert said. He alone of his barrack mates would remain at the Shop during the holiday. He missed Sissy, but he had no intention of returning to the Five Alls. He would not see his father, would not confront him with what he had learned. Not yet. Not until he had studied it, turned it about in his mind, found a way that he could see it, comprehend it, make it fit.

"Hopefully they will have a decent dinner for you here," Georgie added, hefting his valise. "Something like the feast last week. That was a fine evening!"

"Yes. I hope so too."

Mumbles was the next to say goodbye, and Robert shook his hand as well, repeating, "Happy Christmas." Robert even wished Rat and Dog a pleasant holiday, and though Rice had, no doubt, poisoned them against him completely, they were both decent enough to nod. Dog, with his cat draped across his shoulders like a fur collar, even managed a, "Thank you, and to you as well."

Rice was the last to depart. Two servants carried his uniforms, packed in a trunk, out to a carriage waiting in the lane. Rice followed, and Robert thought that he had seen the last of him until the New Year, but a moment later he returned. He hovered in the doorway, staring. Robert put down the book he had just opened. "Forgot something, did you?" Robert said.

"I'll have my corporal's swab back by the middle of the winter," Rice said. "And I promise you that I'll have my commission by the spring."

Robert smiled. "Probably true. But so will I."

With a final look of scorn, Rice left.

*****

The days grew colder. Robert read in his silent barrack room, wrapped in his greatcoat, a single candle burning. He studied R. W. Adye's *Bombardier and Pocket Gunner*, a volume of useful advice on every subject for artillerymen, and poured over the notebooks left by former cadets, determined to master the lore of artillery, of guns, carriages, ammunition, gun manufacture, ranges, powder charges, transport, drill, and British tactics. He read most of the books on the course curriculum, some more than once. And every afternoon, he took a walk alone, crossing the ditch of the Ha Ha, then wandering across the stretch of field to the edge of Woolwich Common, hands behind his back, reciting range tables or some other series of facts or figures, muttering to himself like a lost vagrant.

On Christmas Eve a light snow fall accompanied him on his walk. The snow was fat and wet, and it settled on his shako and piled up on the wide collar of his coat, making tiny mountains on his shoulders. Once across the Ha Ha, he paused to brush himself off, looking back toward the Academy buildings as he did so. They seemed removed and distant, as seen through a fog, their brick walls faded to a dull brown like old blood.

He resumed his walk. Ahead a figure loomed, details shrouded by the snow. But as the figure drew closer, he saw that it was a woman, hands in a muff, a fur-trimmed hood concealing her features.

He touched his shako as she passed. "Good afternoon," he said.

She stopped. He went on two more paces before coming to a halt, aware that he she was looking at him. Two rich brown eyes spied out from the dark confines of the hood.

"Mrs. Flushing," he said.

"Good afternoon to you, too," she said.

He quickly took off his shako, holding it upside down as if to catch the snow. "Mrs. Flushing, you shouldn't be out in this sort of weather."

Her saw the flash of her teeth. "It is Mister Saxon, is it not? I was certain that I recognized you by your height. My, but you are a bold one, aren't you?"

There was something strange about the way she paid him compliments. "Bold, ma'am?"

"To lecture an officer's wife on what she should do or not do?"

Her flippant tone told him that he had not really given offence. "It seemed appropriate, ma'am. It's my duty... to have concern for the well being of an officer's family."

She laughed. "Of course; I remember now. You are my hero, the rescuer of my bonnet. Well, then, if you are so concerned, you must do me another favour. Escort me through this blizzard to my husband's quarters. We are to dine with friends tonight, and tomorrow we go to his family house in the town."

It meant retracing his steps, but he did not hesitate to offer his arm. As they made their way back, her tight gloved fingers gripping his coat, he wondered if she was this friendly with the other cadets. She had recognized him, remembered him, and he dared to think that he must be unique. The notion filled him with a warm glow, even though, in the end, it did not really matter. It was a pleasure to share her company, even if she shared it the same with others.

A sudden gust of wind swirled around him, and she gave a little cry, pulling him closer. Through his coat and hers, he could feel the softness and warmth of her body, bringing flashes of memory, of smell and touch, of other girls he had known at the inn, of Nan the maid, who he had sometimes met in the stables. A boyhood tryst that had gone nowhere, had nowhere to go, though he recalled it with nothing but fondness and pleasure. It had been an escape, a glimpse of what life had to offer, away from the iron hand of his father.

The gust had passed, but she did not release her hold on him. He glanced at her, saw the curve of her nose in profile. *If you were not already married to Flashdash*, he thought, *I would give him a fight.*

He took her all the way to the west barracks, the same location as their last brief exchange. She faced him and said, "So, you have rescued me a second time."

He forced himself to step back and saluted. "I am just doing my duty, Mrs. Flushing."

She gave him a sidelong smile, arching one eyebrow as she said, "I think not."

He stared at her as she turned away. "What," he began, but then she was facing the orderly, who was opening the door for her. She waved, saying, "Happy Christmas, young Mister Saxon."

He was left standing on the steps, with the snow piling again on his shoulders.

*****

They had a proper dinner on Christmas Day, with goose, veal, greens, potatoes, apple pies and a decent plum pudding. Georgie would have been pleased, Robert decided, for he was not wanting for Christmas cheer. The dining hall was near empty but far from quiet, the remaining cadets filling a single table and making the most of it. Outside the day was gray and still, as it should have been.

Another week of study came and went, the year 1807 passing away, and so began 1808. And Robert's barrack mates returned.

Georgie greeted him with, "Hello, hello, Robbie! I trust

things weren't too bleak?" Robert assured him they were not. Mumbles was next, saying something that ended with, "A fine holiday?" To which Robert replied, "Finer than I could have hoped. I accomplished a great deal."

Rat and Dog greeted him as well, politely if not warmly, but Rice said nothing at all.

Later that evening they all gathered again before Out Lights, and Robert readied his kit for the resumption of drills on the morrow. As he buffed his cartridge box, Rice regaled Rat and Dog with the tale of his holidays, and how he regretted the unavailability of Portuguese wine, concluding with, "Damn that Bonaparte."

"Why is it not available?" Georgie asked.

Rice threw him a look of disgust. "What do you mean, why isn't it available? You're bloody stupider than you look."

Rat and Dog laughed, though Georgie just looked baffled. "Well?" Georgie said.   "Am I ... am I forgetting something? Does anyone know? Robert?"

"Boney invaded Portugal in November," Mumbles reminded him.

"Oh." Georgie dropped heavily onto his bed. "Then I did forget something. I suppose the French have cut off the export of wine."

"Those who thought that this would bring a time of enlightenment," Mumbles continued, "of *liberté, égalité, et fraternatié*, have come up for a rude awakening.   This is (mumble mumble) and outright oppression."

"What sort of oppression?" Georgie asked.

"My, you're full of questions," Dog said. His cat perched on his shoulder, nibbling the fingertips of one upraised hand.

"Looting," Mumbles said with a shrug. "Robbing the royal family (mumble mumble) sending it all back to France."

Georgie wrung his hands. "Oh dear, oh dear. War can be a terrible thing. I wonder if we shall be sending ships, perhaps an expeditionary force?"

"We should all be so lucky," Rice quipped.

"I don't know. I don't know."

Robert finished polishing his kit and hung his cartridge box on its peg in his designated cupboard. He was tired and wished for nothing more than the call for Out Lights and the feel of his bed, but Georgie was hovering at his elbow.

"It's rather frightening, isn't it?" Georgie whispered. "This talk of more war on the continent."

"There's been war on the continent since I was a little boy," Robert said.

Georgie tried to smile, but for once he failed. "Well, it frightens me. You see... you see... I had rather an uncomfortable holiday, Robert. Father is not happy with me. He thinks that I lose my nerve, and that's why I failed two examinations. He says that I know my arithmetic, but the stress of the moment gets the better of me. The unfortunate thing is, that I think he is right. I can't imagine myself in a war."

Robert scrubbed his hands through his hair, cropped short in the new style of the cadet corps. "Georgie, you're to be an officer in the army. The army fights wars. Some day, every cadet in Woolwich will make his mark against the French. That's why we're here."

"Oh, I know, I know. I'll have to learn, won't I? Father expects it, if nothing else."

"We all have a lot to learn," Robert offered as consolation. "Keep to your studies, Georgie. Fight one enemy at a time."

But Georgie again failed to smile.

*****

And now with the new term Robert at last began to learn the rudiments of soldiering. Some subjects he already had become familiar with over the holiday, including the principles of fortification, of the attack and defence, and though these were interesting enough he found that military drafting, the use of the square, compass and protractor, gave him greater pleasure. But best of all was what he could never have learned from a book, and that was the basics of artillery drill. With the new term, Robert at last got a crack at the guns.

Artillery exercises took place on a section of Woolwich Common, an expanse of dead grass and mud criss-crossed by the ruts of many carriage and limber wheels, pocked with the footprints of both men and beasts, and spattered with great lumps of horse manure. From the vantage of this wide-open field, Robert enjoyed the view of Woolwich in winter, the distant houses and buildings of the New Barracks dark red against the landscape of brown and white, the trees black, the Thames beyond a leaden grey. In the west, a pall of coal smoke marked distant London.

Sergeant Bane was the principal gunnery instructor. The cadets exercised a battery of six field guns, the same brass six-pounders that Robert had seen on the edge of the Front Parade. Their carriages had been given a fresh coat of grey paint for the winter, for as Robert was to learn, the guns were Lieutenant Flushing's pride and joy.

"Keeping your line is foremost in battle," Flashdash said during one early lesson. This was a maxim that Robert met with scepticism, for he already knew that the lieutenant had never been in battle, and the meticulous alignment of artillery had not figured prominently in Adye's book. "A battery of guns must keep its muzzles properly aligned, and on this I insist. At the beginning and conclusion of every exercise, every muzzle is to be aligned. I shall check myself. See that this is so, Sergeant Bane."

"Very good, sir!" Bane snapped.

Flashdash leaned forward in his saddle, placing one hand on his hip, a pose he often affected. "You are all gentleman cadets, and I cannot stress the need to remain gentlemen, in all things. You will care for these guns as you would your mothers, sisters and sweethearts, and treat them well. I expect their barrels and all brass furnishings to be burnished, and all grease and dirt to be removed, just as you do with your personal kit. You will expect nothing less from your men once you are commissioned. These guns are our ladies," and he smiled, "and I wish to see them shine always."

Again, Robert was not impressed, for a great shiny, glittering gun, exposed here in this field, without cover of any kind, would make a very nice target for the enemy. Though, of course, this was practice and it would not be the same when they faced Bonaparte in the field. Surely not.

The cadets took turns learning every position in a gun detachment. The gun positions were numbered, and according to Adye, the system varied. As Flashdash taught it, Number Seven wormed, rammed and sponged, Number Eight placed the cartridge and shot into the muzzle, Number Nine served the vent and primed the cartridge, and Number Ten fired the gun. Number Eleven was the gun commander. The rest of the men, up to Number Fifteen, brought up ammunition and supplies from the ammunition chests on the limber, and also cared for the horses.

After two weeks Robert knew the operation of the six-pounder on the field carriage as well as any second-year cadet.

The first part of the drill dealt with bringing the guns to bear on the enemy. While in transport, the gun reclined in an awkward, unusable position, with its carriage trail attached to the limber and its barrel facing the rear. In order to swing the gun into action, the horses and limber had to be removed and pulled to safety, then the gun itself turned to face the enemy, which might be in front, to left, right, or even rear. After that the gun had to be wormed, sponged, loaded, primed, aimed, and fired. This procedure involved a complex series of movements, a kind of martial dance in which a misstep could lead to failure, but the better Robert came to know this dance, the simpler it seemed, the more logical.

Throughout the training, he observed the older cadets in his division, saw how they did things, especially those who took the Number Eleven or command position. Some gun commanders pushed the crew, gave them advice and encouragement. Some were quick with their commands, while others were slow, as if they had to constantly think about what came next. Some ignored the other numbers and simply saw to their own task. Robert decided which methods he preferred, which allowed the gun crew to operate to the fullest, and when Bane at last let him take control of a gun, he put those methods into effect. Speed and energy, he decided, were key. Keep the men moving and keep them excited.

After three weeks, Bane introduced an exercise in which each gun commander was required to drive his piece forward, unlimber it, fire five blank saluting rounds, then limber up and move back to the starting point on the south side of the shooting range. Every member of every gun crew would get a chance at this exercise. Flashdash would serve as the battery commander while Bane observed and took notes.

"I want to see precision, gentlemen," Bane said. "No

mistakes, you hear?"

Rice was the first commander on Robert's gun. Robert was a limber man, and when the commands began to ring out, he helped pull the limber to the rear, then halted and released the pin to unhitch the horse team. It was his job to then pass ammunition forward, and from this position he had a clear view of the main gun crew. They were certainly precise in their movements, almost too stiff, like infantry on Parade. Rice was one of those methodical types, with a need to control minutiae. There were few mistakes, as Bane had so ordered, but when the exercise was finished, it had taken the crew a full ten minutes to fire their five rounds and make it back to the starting point.

"Good, Mister Rice," Bane said, "though a trifle slow. I near fell asleep waiting for you. Change round!"

Robert was the next commander. The horses were hitched, and he climbed aboard the limber, palms sweating, waiting for the command to start, for the drivers to crack their whips and start them forward. His mouth was fixed in a firm line. This would not take him ten minutes.

"Walk-march," Flashdash called. The six guns started off, rattling across the hill. They had gone about forty paces when Flashdash shouted, "Action front!"

"Action front!" Robert and every other gun commander repeated. The limber men leapt to their task, while the drivers turned their teams one hundred and eighty degrees, pulling them to the rear and leaving the range open. As the limber wheels passed the gun carriage, Robert cried, "Spin!" The four carriage men, two on the trail and one on each wheel, spun the gun, its long brass barrel revolving to face the front. Dropping the trail to the ground, the cadets unhitched the sidearms – the rammer and sponge, the worm, the linstock with its wrap of slowmatch – while Robert fitted the trail handspike in place.

Another cadet placed the sponge bucket, its water already black from use, next to the righthand wheel.

"Five rounds saluting cartridge," Flashdash called, "Load!"

"With five rounds, load!" Robert cried, and his crew sprang into action, sponging the barrel and ramming home the cartridge and wad. They were slow, but Robert quickly identified who were the problem men and admonished them, crying, "Number twelve, be quicker with the ammunition! Number nine, prime with a single thrust. Don't waste time! Move, lads!"

The gun cracked as it fired, flame jetting from the muzzle and from the quill Number Ten had inserted into the vent. The smoke blew backward, engulfing the men. The lads were often stunned after a gun fired, a momentary awe, but Robert had anticipated this phenomenon, barking the command to load again, knowing that the human voice could be just as powerful, the aggressive use of words enough to propel the men to action.

The second round was slow as well, but by the third they had the pattern. The fourth and fifth came in rapid succession, and Robert was shouting, "Front limber up!" The horses came back, and again the cry of, "Spin!" This time the members of his crew, now grinning and inspired by their own efficiency, nearly bowled each other over in their eagerness, and as they brought the trail forward to reattach it to the limber, one man tripped. The heavy oak timber of the trail dropped, landing with full force across his knee. He howled as he fell.

Robert reached out and pulled the boy to his feet with one heave, but it was clear that the boy was in too much pain to continue. Robert spotted Numbers Twelve, Thirteen and Fourteen, shouted, "You, here, now! Thirteen and fourteen, get this man to the rear!"

The replacement dashed in, the injured man pulled clear,

and the drill carried on with hardly a minute lost. With the carriage now hitched to the limber, the horses started forward.

Robert pulled out his watch and snapped open the lid. His gun was the first in the battery to complete the exercise, the first to make it back to the south end of the range. And the entire drill had lasted only about four minutes.

I could do better, he thought.

When the exercise was over, Flashdash and Bane approached Robert's crew. Bane was grinning. Robert knew he deserved congratulations for having the speediest time, though he suspected the one mistake would cost him a penalty, perhaps a few added seconds.

Flashdash leaned down from his saddle. "Mister Saxon, a speedy performance. Yes, the most speedy of the lot, and I have no doubt, some here are impressed. However," he sniffed, "I am not one of them. That was a display of pure recklessness. Pure recklessness."

"Yes, sir," Robert said, speaking quickly to help mask his immediate indignation.   He could not disagree with his superior, could not argue his case, for that was not permitted. But he had not been reckless. "Reckless" implied that he had shown a disregard for the requirements of the gun and its crew in the pursuit of a personal goal, though to Robert killing the enemy before the enemy killed you was not reckless. Recklessness was exposing your guns by polishing them.

"You must look to the safety of your crew," the officer added. "You must not push them beyond their limits. They are only men, after all. Do you understand me?"

Robert nodded, a jab of his chin. "Yes, sir."

"Well then, have you anything else to say?"

Robert would have been content to keep his mouth shut, but Flashdash had given him permission to voice his displeasure.

Maybe, if he did so with tact, he could speak his mind after all.

"Will not the crew be safe when the enemy is dead, sir? And is not the best way to ensure their death to fire as many rounds as quickly as possible?"

Flashdash looked down his nose, affecting a mild, yet patronising smile. "If you incapacitate your own men and fire all of your ammunition too quickly, the French will kill you as surely as if you were standing still."

Robert digested this advice, deciding almost at once that it was irrelevant. The point of the exercise had not been to worry about the many factors they might encounter on campaign. A crew needed to be trained in speed in case it was necessary. They would conserve ammunition when they needed to, fire it all when they needed to.

He could have explained this view but decided that he had only really been allowed one comment, and Flashdash had corrected him. That was the final word. So, he simply added another, "Yes, sir, I understand, sir."

"Indeed. Sergeant Bane, change round."

"Next relief!" Bane shouted.

The crew rotated. The cadet who had dropped the trail insisted on falling in, though he walked with a limp. Robert became Number Seven. Rice, as Number Eight, faced him across the gleaming brass barrel.

"Lucky you didn't kill that fellow," Rice said. "It's just as I always suspected. You're a menace, Saxon."

Robert held his tongue. It was not seemly to bicker in public. Rice only made himself look petty.

When the exercise was over, the guns went back to the Academy, the drivers parking them in their customary place on the edge of the Front Parade. The drivers then took the horses back to the stables as the cadets formed ranks to march the fifty or so paces back to barracks. When they broke off, the cadets did not disperse at once, but splintered into smaller groups to chatter in rising excitement, something that always seemed to happen after gun drill. This time, the main topic under review was Robert's crew, their speed and the accident.

Robert was not happy with himself, and now that the exercise was over, his pride and certainty in his position began to give way under the memory of Flashdash's admonishment. The injury had been his fault, a fact that he could not dispute. He had pushed for speed that had been beyond the capabilities of his comrades in the gun crew, and now he overheard several opinions that agreed with that assessment. He tried to close his ears to it, tried to ignore comments such as, "They ought to give him extra drill for a week."

"Mister Saxon!" a gruff voice snapped. "Mister Saxon!"

Robert started, rounding. He found himself facing Sergeant Bane.

"You are to report to the Orderly Room at once," Bane told him.

Robert sighed. "Yes, Sergeant."

So, it seemed that the incident was not to end here. Flashdash had no doubt devised some dreary punishment.

Robert lost no time in obeying his instructions. The less time he spent on this, the better. He pushed open the Orderly Room door and halted before the counter, standing at attention.

"Ah, Mister Saxon," Sergeant Webber greeted him. "It is a fine day, young sir, a fine day."

Robert did not relax at the sergeant's friendly tone. "Reporting as ordered, Sergeant."

"That I see." Webber pulled a folded piece of paper from a pigeonhole and passed it over the counter. "Your orders, Mister

Saxon."

Robert took the paper. "What is it?"

Webber grinned. "You will have to see for yourself."

Robert began to doubt his assumption of punishment. He stared at the paper, mystified, only half aware of his own feet as they propelled him outside. The winter air sighed around him, a fiercer bite than that on the Common. The paper was sealed with the crest of the Royal Regiment of Artillery. He broke it with a snap, unfolded the paper, and read.

He had been promoted to corporal.

The paper fluttered in his hand, crackling like new ice. He read the order over again. It consisted of just three lines. "You are hereby granted the rank of corporal within the corps of gentlemen cadets, to repair at once to the Quartermaster's...."

He would have his swab before Rice.

A laugh bubbled up, uncontainable. He had expected sanction, and here was promotion! To hell with Flashdash, then, and to all those who had condemned him today.

And to hell with Rice, for now, at least for a little while, he was Robert's subordinate.

Chapter Eight:

Commission

The corporal's swab made an awkward lump under Robert's greatcoat, but even after two weeks it still gave him satisfaction, if not outright pleasure. His step was lighter than it had been in years, his feet gliding over the thin covering of snow, his breath steaming in bitter cold that he no longer noticed. His studies were nothing more than rungs in a ladder now, necessary but no hindrance, no obstacle. One more exam, perhaps at the beginning of spring, and he would be an officer in the Royal Regiment of Artillery.

He crossed the main courtyard, shoes creaking, making for the model room. He enjoyed modeling, constructing miniature gun emplacements, miniature trenches and field fortifications— all good practice if he ever needed to build the real thing, which he was certain he would. The air was the colour of steel, the few huddled figures he passed, black and cramped. All save one, a cadet who sat on one of the benches on the side of the path, hands in pockets and shako pushed far back to reveal a rounded forehead. Robert frowned, for it was no day to be sitting outside for any length of time.

"Georgie!" he cried, at last recognizing the figure by its slouch. He ran the last few steps to Georgie's side. Georgie said nothing, did not even look up, his eyes vacant as they stared across the courtyard.

The snow and frozen ground groaned as Robert took one last step. "Georgie," he repeated. "What are you doing here, sitting out alone? It's far too cold!"

Georgie's eyelids fluttered and he kicked at the turf, but though his lips moved and his head shook slightly, he said nothing.

"Frozen already?" Robert said, an attempt at flippancy, though, in fact, he was alarmed. Georgie continued to profess his happiness at every turn, but he had begun to brood more and more often, lapsing into long periods of still silence, as now.

"I say, wake up!" Robert added, giving Georgie a shove.

"What?" Georgie suddenly cried. "What, is that you?" A broad smile split his ruddy features. "Oh, no, I like the cold! It's refreshing, bracing...."

"No, no," Robert said, dropping onto the bench. "Don't play your games, George. Did you receive another letter from your father?"

"Oh, no, no! I was just pondering mathematics." Georgie cleared his throat. "Sitting and pondering."

"Pondering? What's left to ponder? You know basic arithmetic inside and out. How many rehearsal exams have we run? You have passed every one. There's nothing left to ponder."

Georgie did not answer for a moment. "I'll tell you, then. I'm concerned. Yes, I may pass a rehearsal exam, time and again. That's a proven fact. Yet, I remain concerned that I have only one more chance to pass the proper exam. If I should fail... if I should fail, I will be out...."

His face crumpled, and for a moment he could not speak.

His lips quivered. Robert waited, his alarm increasing, but he did not speak; he just waited for the moment to pass. Georgie squeezed his eyes shut and took several long draughts of air, and after a moment collected himself enough to state, "My father expects this of me, you see. He expects it. We have been gunners in my family for three generations."

Robert leaned back against the bench. The wooden slats were cold, even through his heavy woollen coat. "You'll be gunners for four generations."

"Yes. I fear—"

"You fear *fear*, and that's bloody foolish. Listen to me. You're ready. You won't fail the examination a third time."

Georgie swiped at his eyes with the back of his bare hand, the flesh already blue from cold. "I cannot fail it. I cannot....My father, you see, he doesn't like the way the other cadets annoy me. Rice and the others. I spoke of it with him, raised it as a concern of mine, and he told me to accept it and be quiet—or to act. Still, I have not acted. I'm afraid... I'm afraid he thinks I'm a...."

The words caught in his throat, stuck, his breath coming in little gasps. But Robert knew what he was unable to say. His father thought him a coward.

Well, we're only boys, after all, Robert thought. *Not men yet*. Georgie needed – no, he deserved – more time to learn. It would not be so difficult once he made the move into the middle academy, proved to himself that he could succeed.

Robert stood and slapped his arms against the cold. He could work on his models later. He did not think Georgie should be left alone at this hour. "This is pointless. You should find something to do rather than sitting here, freezing to death."

"Maybe it would be better if I froze to death."

Something about that statement sent a stab of ice through Robert's heart. Georgie had never said anything so defeatist. Of course, they were just words, no doubt hyperbole, but Robert found himself strangely unnerved.

"Oh, bollocks!" he said. "Don't say such things. Look, I have just the thing to cheer you up. They're turning some new ordnance down at the Arsenal, in the Royal Gun Factory. We could go and watch."

Georgie shrugged, a tepid hunch of one shoulder. "I... yes, so?"

"They're brass field pieces, the new nine-pounders. I believe that today the bores are to be drilled."

It took Georgie a moment to make up his mind, but at last he agreed. "All right. Yes, that would be interesting. Let's go, then."

Robert took him away from the Shop, down toward the river. This would keep Georgie's mind occupied, prevent him from forming any more ridiculous paranoid notions. And in no time, he would be fine.

But there was a persistent glumness about their visit to the gun factory, one that even the ear-splitting grind of the drills, the flash and shower of sparks, and rumbling of the lathes could not dispel. And the heat of the place made the outside air feel all the more biting later, when they emerged, smelling of soot and hot metal, to slowly make their way back to barracks. With their faces pulled down within the collars of their coats, they spoke very little.

They unbuttoned their coats in the barracks corridor. The door to their room was ajar, and when Robert heard the laughter emanating from within, he knew that Rice was having one of his little parties. He saw Georgie hesitate, saw the fear in his eyes, the sudden spring of sweat on his forehead.

"They can't hurt you, Georgie," Robert said. "I'm corporal now."

"Yes, of course." Georgie's shoulders relaxed. "I'm all right."

The laughter abruptly ceased as Robert strode into the room. Rice was sprawled in a chair by the windows, with Dog opposite, cradling his cat. Rat was at the hearth, stoking the fire. The room smelled of spirits, and there were two bottles on the table, one of green glass, containing red wine. The other bottle was squat and black.

Robert pointed at the black bottle. "What on earth is that?" he demanded.

"Rum, from the West Indies," Rat said, as if it should have been the most obvious thing in the world. "We have been wondering what the other ranks see in it."

Georgie struggled out of his greatcoat and his blue coat. His shirt was stained under the arms, despite the cold. The sweat of fear.

"You're celebrating something?" Robert asked Rat. "It's rather early for a spree, isn't it?"

Rice sat forward, aglow with triumph. "Yes, we're bloody celebrating something! I have regained my corporalship. I plan to have some fun, unless you object?"

Robert had not expected Rice to win his rank back so soon, and he felt a stab of alarm. Then he reminded himself that it did not really matter. Rice was nothing to him now.

"This will be my last day in this barrack room," Rice went on. "I'm moving. I'll have a whole new batch of snookers under my wing, and to that end, in addition to the rum, I have procured a bottle of Portuguese wine, smuggled through the lines. Would you care for a glass?"

Robert turned away. He had no intention of raising a glass

with Rice. "No, thank you."

"I thought not." Rice filled his glass from the green bottle. Dog and Rat each held cups that Robert presumed were filled with rum. They would, no doubt, be drunk for Evening Parade, which would do them no good.

"You will have a whole parcel of little innocents to look after, Wesley," Rat said. He faced Georgie, stared him up and down. "Little sweaty fellows like Georgie, here."

"We should call him Piggy, not Georgie," Dog remarked. "He's always reminded me of a little piggy. Oink oink!"

"That's enough of that," Robert snapped. He had taken off his coat and was busy folding it, taking great care as always.

Rat wrinkled his nose. "Poouh! You stink, Georgie. Stinks like a pig, all right."

"He does!" Dog added. "I cam smell it from here. We should do something about it." He stood, cup in hand, and advanced to where Georgie sat on his bed. "Here's your perfume, piggy!"

He upended his cup of rum over Georgie's head. Georgie held up his hands to shield himself, saying, "Don't!"

"Damn it, what are you doing!" Robert cried, throwing down his coat. Dog leapt backward, suddenly wary, but behind him Rat had pulled a brand from the fire, saying, "There is only once surefire cure for such a stench."

Rice had not moved, and he was laughing. "Yes, yes! Do it!"

Robert saw what Rat intended, but too late. He stepped forward, but he was too far away, too far to stop Rat from thrusting the burning brand outward.

The fumes from the rum burst into small, hot blue flames.

Georgie screamed and beat at his face and hair. Robert shoved Dog aside, grabbed Georgie's coat and threw it over Georgie's head. Rice was still laughing, crying, "Oh, well done!"

Robert held the coat in place until he was sure the flames had gone out. Georgie was on his knees, gasping and moaning.

Robert cast the coat aside and could see that the boy's eyebrows had been singed off, his hair burned, and there were raw, red burns on his scalp and forehead. Georgie reached for the wounds with trembling hands. "Well, I'm sure it's an improvement," he said, but his voice broke on the last word.

Robert rounded on Rat. "I mean to have you removed from the Academy for this," he said. He did not raise his voice.

Rat folded his arms. "Oh, you do, do you?"

"Yes. In fact, I'll call on the provosts on my way back from the hospital. You should begin packing your things."

Rat made to step forward, but his face had turned white, and his hands balled into fists. Behind him, Rice had at last gone silent.

"You wouldn't dare!"

For a fleeting instant, Robert wanted to strike him, smash his face, but he would not give in. Not today. "Why wouldn't I? I'm your corporal, and you're no friend of mine. I warned you, warned all of you to stop this outrageous behaviour. And now this assault? Spare me your excuses. You're a damned disgrace, and to hell with you." He pulled Georgie to his feet. "Come on, I'll take you."

Georgie just nodded. Robert gathered up his coat, throwing it over his shoulders. The others just watched as he escorted Georgie out of the room, but as he moved into the corridor, Rat followed, crying, "I'll remember your name, Robert Saxon!"

Robert called over his shoulder, "You will have no choice but to remember it!"

The hospital was outside the main compound, across the road that ran along the east wall. The sky was already growing dark. Robert chewed his lip as they walked, the frozen ground creaking as if in protest. How had he allowed this to happen? He had failed as a corporal, failed to stop this abuse.

It was Rice, he decided. It was Rice who had egged them on.

"I can't take much more of this, Robert," Georgie murmured as they passed through the east gate.

"You'll be all right," Robert assured him. "Just a little further. The hospital will be warm."

"No, I'm not all right.   I told you earlier... my father considers me a disappointment, a weakling."   There was something dead about his tone of voice, quiet and ominous. "My mother always taught me to laugh at the world. But father...."

"Father what?" Robert demanded after a few minutes. The dim orange lights from the square two-story hospital building glimmered ahead.

"It's nothing," Georgie said. "Nothing...."

The hospital was tiny, consisting of an anteroom, a surgery, and a single dark, chilly barrack. It was not a warm place as Robert had promised, but cold and uninviting. In the anteroom the orderly corporal on duty admitted them.   Robert told Georgie, "I'm for the provosts now. I mean to have Rat arrested tonight."

Georgie did not seem interested.   He just stared at the ceiling.

"I won't allow any more bullying, Georgie."

"Oh, I trust you'll do your best. You've been a good friend to me, Robert."

Robert touched his comrade's shoulder. "Chin up, Georgie."

Then he left him, moving back outside, seeking the provosts.

*****

Rat remained in his own bed that night, for gentlemen cadets were not thrown into lockup like common soldiers. At roll call, both he and Georgie were absent, though for different reasons. Georgie was on the sick list. At breakfast, Robert sat apart with Mumbles, who had come into barracks only after Robert and Georgie had left. Robert explained the details of the incident.

"Not fit for the service," Mumbles said. "Some of these people...."

Robert nodded. This, he realized with a sick churning in his stomach, was how it must have been when his father had been dismissed from the Academy. This same awful, uncomfortable sequence of events. There would have been the injury, the witnesses, the report, the resentment of his father's friends. And there would have been those who had said that he was not fit to hold a king's commission.

And they would have been right.

After breakfast, Robert returned to the hospital. It was a study period, but he could afford to spend the time otherwise.

There was a different orderly on duty, a squat corporal with a pocked face. "I'm here to see Gentleman Cadet Georgie Howard," Robert said.

"Not here," the orderly replied.

Robert assumed a mistake. "Yes, he is. I brought him here last night, with injuries from burns."

The corporal was nodding. "That's right, but there ain't no one by that name nor with burns in that barrack room now."

Robert leaned on the counter. "Do you mean he left? Did someone take him?"

"Don't know. He just weren't here no more, this morning."

"But where did he go?" Robert said, and just then, the same surgeon he had seen yesterday emerged from the barrack room.

"Sir, sir! I've come to see Georgie Howard. I brought him in yesterday, but the corporal says that he left."

The surgeon eyed him. He had a puffy face, his eyes red, and he smelled of drink. "Mister Saxon, is it not? Yes, I remember. The corporal is correct. He left just before Out Lights."

Robert felt the first hint of real concern. This made no sense, for Georgie had not returned to barracks last night. "And you let him leave? Just like that?"

The surgeon frowned. "Mind who you are speaking to, Mister Saxon! I dressed Mister Howard's burns, which were superficial. He rested for a while, and then he left by his own decision. There was no reason to keep him here against his will."

Robert was already turning away. "He didn't go back to barracks. Why didn't he go back?"

Outside, he stared across the Ha Ha toward the Common. There was a sprinkle of fresh snow on the ground. It had been cold last night, unusually cold. He understood why Georgie would not have wanted to go back to their room, but if not, why not just stay in the hospital? Where else was there for him?

He had not been at roll call.

Robert started to run, back along the road, in through the gate, fearing the worst.

*****

It was a company of the 5th Battalion, Royal Artillery, that found him. The company had marched out to the Common to exercise their guns, for they used the same field as the cadets. Georgie was lying on the edge of the common, half covered in new snow. The regular gunners recognized his cadet uniform, and one of their officers rode, at once, to the Academy to report.

Meanwhile, the artillerymen carried on with their drill.

Robert learned these details later. He searched for Georgie throughout the morning, asking everyone he met if they had seen him. No one knew a thing. Then at the end of Morning Drill Parade, Sergeant Bane told him to report to the Orderly Room. "There are special orders there for you," Bane explained.

Robert's curiosity was piqued, but he did not for a moment think this was anything to do with Georgie. When he entered the room, Sergeant Webber was there with Lieutenant Flushing. Flashdash's face was long and grey, and at the look of him, at his mere presence, Robert froze in his tracks, his heart leaping. These were not special orders.

"Ah, Mister Saxon," Flashdash began. "I have unfortunate news. A tragic event has occurred which involves one of the gentleman cadets from your barracks room. We have summoned you here to avoid rumour, in the hopes that you will inform the others, and do so properly and truthfully."

"What has happened, sir?" Robert said.

Flashdash told him what the gunners had found. "It appeared as if he had been sitting on the ground for some time, and that he fell asleep. A clear trail from the hospital was easily discerned within the new snow." Flashdash shook his head. "A bad business, and unfortunate. Most unfortunate! It was the cold that did it."

Robert listened, stunned. "Georgie is dead?" he cried. "Are you sure, sir? I only spoke to him last night."

Flashdash seemed uncomfortable with this outburst, but he said, "I am only too sure, Mister Saxon. A tragedy that we now must keep from becoming an unnecessary scandal. This appears to have been an accident. We must think of the family."

Robert staggered back, his hands seeking the wooden back of a chair. "He let himself freeze to death," he said. He thought of the previous afternoon, when he had come upon Georgie on the bench.

"That is precisely the sort of talk I wish to avoid!" Flashdash snapped. "I have explicit instructions that we do not speak of this in terms of Mister Howard having taken his own life. There is no reason to believe that this was anything other than, as I have said, an unfortunate accident."

Robert gave him a blank stare. So be it, then, if they wanted to avoid scandal. It hardly seemed to matter anyway. Georgie had been trapped, trapped by his own fear, by his immense need to avoid disappointing his father. And now he had escaped, and there was nothing else to it.

I failed him, Robert thought, as he left the Orderly Room, his feet shuffling, dragging. *I took him on, promised to help him through, and I failed. And I failed to protect him from Rice and his cronies.*

He returned to barracks. It was quiet; only Mumbles and Dog were present. Getting ready to go to dinner, Robert presumed. Mumbles was brushing his shoes. Dog buried his face in a book when Robert entered.

"Where's Rice?" Robert demanded.

"Already been reassigned," Mumbles said. "Received word after Parade (mumble mumble). Rat will be leaving, too, it seems." A smile flashed across Mumbles's normally gloomy features. "That leaves two vacancies. I wonder if we're to get any snookers?"

Robert sank onto his bed with a sigh. "Three vacancies, my dear Lord Mumbles," he said. "There are three vacancies."

And at last, his voice cracked, and he covered his face to stifle a sob. Death was easy, and common enough, but he would never grow used to it.

*****

Rat was dismissed from the Academy. A guard detachment came to the barracks to remove his belongings, and also those of George Howard. As the detachment was about to leave, the sergeant in charge remarked, "A shame to lose two of our young gentlemen."

Flashdash made a short speech during the general Parade that day, expressing his sympathy to those cadets who had known Georgie, and reiterating that, "We should not speculate about the cause, but remember him with honour, as we recall all those of this company. We shall miss him."

In the weeks that followed, Robert carried on with his studies, but his actions were mechanical, and he seemed to move in a daze. Now he wished more than ever to be done with the Academy, to move north to the Artillery Barracks, to start anew, and to forget.

"Perhaps he did not mean to die," Mumbles suggested one day. "Perhaps (mumble mumble) wished to run, to flee, and in his injured state, he simply did not understand what he was doing."

"It makes no difference," Robert said. "He was pushed to the brink, and so he fell. That's all." Pushed by Rice. Pushed by his father.

March brought the first warm winds, and rain, and the first flowers. But none of these things held any joy for Robert. He studied.

The first day of spring was grey but mild. The entire cadet company formed on the Front Parade for a general inspection by the Lieutenant Governor of the Academy, Lieutenant Colonel Twiss of the Royal Engineers, and the Inspector,

Captain Hall, who also served as Assistant Commandant. A Royal Artillery band was present for the event, and for a time Robert enjoyed himself. Enjoyed the music, the pageantry, and the smell of new grass emanating from the Ha Ha.

When Twiss had finished his inspection, the company stood at ease. The commandant faced the men, sitting tall on the back of his black gelding, and declared that he had never seen a finer body of gentlemen cadets. Those cadets were required now more than ever. The army, the colonel said, was undergoing a period of rapid expansion. With the tyrant Bonaparte's rampage through Europe, and the recent invasion and subjugation of Portugal, more men and officers were needed and needed at once. Therefore, he has been directed by the War Office to grant commissions to a number of senior gentlemen cadets, those who, in the eyes of their instructors, had met the requirements. There would be no final examinations. They were not necessary.

The names had already been chosen. They would be posted, and the commissions granted that very day.

When the Parade dismissed, the company broke into subdivisions by academy. The sergeants then read the names of those who were to report to the Orderly Room. The names were read in alphabetical order. "Wesley Rice," was followed immediately by, "Robert Saxon."

The cadets broke off.

A March breeze began to freshen, but it was warm and hinted of the coming summer. Robert told himself to forget about Georgie. Georgie had been his own man. There was nothing Robert could do about what had happened, and there was no sense in dwelling on the heartbreak and tragedy that was life. He had never done so and would not do so now.

He had what he had come here for.

He waited in the queue outside the Orderly Room. The lads were excited, laughing, boasting about what they would do to Bonaparte, wondering where the army would take them. Robert wished to join in but could not. His ears felt stuffed with cotton.

When he, at last, received his orders from Sergeant Webber, he turned without a word and made his way along the edge of the Front Parade. It was then that he saw her approaching.

At once, his heavy heart grew a fraction lighter. She smiled when she saw him, as she always did. And as was usual, he stopped and saluted. She did not always pause to speak to him when he did this, but today he hoped she would. Today of all days, he hoped she would.

"Good afternoon, Mister Saxon," she said.

"Good afternoon, ma'am," he replied, and with a sudden burst of gratitude and pride, he held up the sealed orders for her to see. "I have received a commission in the Royal Artillery. I will be leaving the Academy."

"Oh, how wonderful for you!" she chimed, clapping her hands. "You must be thrilled!"

At last, he was able to smile. "I am, Mrs. Flushing!"

"My husband has also received a new posting," she said. "He will be leaving as well. So, you see, we will all be moving."

"Then, congratulations to you."

"A shame to leave, but the world turns. Perhaps we shall see each other again?"

"I look forward to the day."

"As do I, Mister Saxon. It may be sooner than you think. Good day!"

She carried on, but he caught her eye when she looked back.

There was an attraction, then. It was obvious, though of course it was not something that could ever have grown into anything beyond a word and a look here and there. But he had enjoyed it, enjoyed putting one over on bloody Flashdash, who obviously was not man enough to keep his wife's eye from wandering. He enjoyed having her brighten his days—days like this one. And it was a shame that he would probably not see her again, despite her words.

In his barracks, he sat at the little table and tore open his orders. He was to be commissioned second-lieutenant in the new 11th Battalion, Royal Regiment of Artillery. He read the statement through several times, savouring its simplicity, its bold message. He was a gunner now, really and truly. He was commanded to repair to the officer's quarters in the New Barracks, Woolwich Common. The barracks he had stared at all year. For now, he had six days leave, to get his affairs in order.

He folded the order, placing it in his pocket. Then, for the first time since arriving at the Shop, he began writing a letter to his father.

"I know that you were a gentleman cadet here, and that you were dismissed and so joined the ranks. I would like you to know that I have passed all my examinations and am to be commissioned in the new 11th Battalion."

He stared at the page, at the pale brownish wash of the cheap ink that he and Mumbles had purchased. The words had a nasty knife edge to them, and that was not what he truly wanted.

He tore up the letter. He had six days, and that was plenty of time. Plenty of time to go home, to see Sissy and so face his father.

Chapter Nine:

Home

The road was a rutted mire, the potholes filled with the churned remains of a spring rain. Robert stepped with care as he dismounted the post coach. He wore his cadet's dress coatee, and with the corporal's swab on his right shoulder, he knew he must have looked like someone of consequence, someone who commanded respect, for this time, the coach driver did not cast his trunk into the filth of the yard. This time the driver carried the trunk to the door of the inn and said, "There you be, young sir."

The coach remained in the yard as the horses were changed. Robert looked at the inn. The sign with its five figures was faded and starting to peel, and some of the thatch above the door was ragged and in need of mending. The place had not been maintained, though it could not have been for lack of business. The churned yard, with its hoof prints, ruts and piles of manure suggested high traffic, and the noise coming from inside suggested a full common room.

Father has not bothered to hire anyone to do the work, he thought. *Not since I left.*

He decided not to go into the inn. At least not into the common room. Not yet. That would mean facing the welcoming cries of Mrs. Greene, and perhaps seeing Sissy, or even Nan, and having himself congratulated and slapped on the back by his old mates from the stables. He could not endure those things right now, for he had to settle business with his father first. If father was at the inn, he would be behind the bar or in the kitchen. Robert thought he might enter through the back way, but then the kitchen staff would see him. And his father might not be at the inn. He could be at the house.

Robert left the trunk beside the door, deciding that its great weight would deter any would be thieves, and made his way to the house. His stomach was dancing and his mouth was dry. He had no wish to do this, but he had no choice. He hoped his father was not in the inn, that he was here instead, that this business could be concluded in private.

The front door was unlocked. Robert pushed it open, and it swung on creaking hinges. The hinges had never creaked before. No barking greeted him. There were no dogs about. Maybe they were all kennelled in the stables.

The hall was unlit, the floorboards protesting with every step. Robert entered his father's study, and there he stopped. He let the scent of the books and papers fill him, and if he closed his eyes for a moment, he could imagine that he was a little boy again, a little boy full of dreams, and that mother still lived. But then, other memories intruded, of the later years, when he had studied here under the constant threat of the belt or the open palm. His dancing stomach clenched. He backed out of the room.

"Hello?" he called when he was again in the dark hall. "Father, are you here? It's me, Robert. I'm home."

There was no answer, just the remnants of a dull echo. Then silence, save for the dull, metallic ticking of a clock. No sounds of life, not even the scuttle of a mouse. The house seemed old, tired, only half aware.

"There's no one here," he said, turning, but as he passed the doorway to the parlour, he paused. Something had stirred within, some flicker of movement. He heard a man clearing his throat, and a dark hump shifted on the settee against the far wall.

"Father?" Robert whispered, entering the room. The curtains were drawn, and as his eyes adjusted, he saw that the place had not changed. Its unexpected tidiness, so in contrast to everything else he had seen today, were a testament to the continuing efforts of Mrs. Greene. The figure of his father sat with his back to the wall, eyes closed and mouth half open. The room stank of him, stank of liquor. *He must be drunk all the time now*, Robert thought.

He knelt to the carpet, repeating, "Father? It's Robert."

Thomas Saxon stirred again, one eye cracking open. Though it had been less than a year since their last meeting, his hair had paled to grey wire, his cheeks had sunken, his chin covered in iron stubble.

"Is that you?" he said, and he coughed. When the coughing ceased, he said, "Is that you, boy?"

"I'm home on leave," Robert stated. "I've learned... a few things."

His father stared at him with dull eyes that slowly grew more alert. "Learned things at the Academy?"

Robert hesitated, but that was never a good tactic. His best course was to attack at once. "I learned that you were a cadet, and that you were dismissed. You were sent packing from the Academy. And you never told me."

"I was never sent packing," his father croaked, struggling to rise, to escape the settee. "I was... who is that? Is that Robert? Robert?"

"Yes, yes, it's me. I'm not some drunken vision, if that's what you're afraid of, father."

"Damn you, boy, I demand you show respect!"

Thomas Saxon lurched to his feet, fists raised. Robert rose and caught his father's hand just as the blow was about to land. "No, sir, never again!" He forced the hand down, and his father lost his balance. As he fell forward onto the carpet, Robert felt a sickness in his gut, that he had needed to defend himself against his father, and that now he had humiliated the man who had raised him.

Robert went to the windows and took hold of the curtains, tearing them open. As light filled the room, Thomas Saxon managed to stand, though he swayed like an ancient oak in a thunderstorm.

Robert folded his arms. "You didn't complete your time at the Academy, and you never told me."

"I will not be questioned." With unsteady steps, Robert's father moved to the mantel and leaned there, face to the wall. "Though I suppose... I suppose you were bound to find out. There are still those in the regiment who know me."

"I have a commission now," Robert said. "I am a second-lieutenant of the Royal Artillery, the Eleventh Battalion."

His father stiffened, and one hand went to his mouth.

"You should be proud, father. It's what you wanted for me."

"Yes... what I wanted. Damn you, you were quick about it."

"I have no more need of you now," Robert added, for that was why he had come home. That was what he had wanted to say.

His father looked at him at last. The eyes were alive now, but there was nothing but hurt there. *This will kill him*, Robert thought. But he told himself he did not care.

"You will serve... as I should have served," his father said at length.

"Why did you lie?"

"I was a sergeant. That was no lie." He turned again to face the wall. "Now get out of this house, if you have no more need of me. I have no more need of you."

Robert felt his face flush, and a strange tingling flowed through his arms. For a moment he could not move, and he drew in several long breaths, struggling to maintain his anger, not to allow it to change into something else. He would not let himself weep. A man does not weep.

"I'm going to the inn," he said, grateful that his voice remained steady. "I'm going to see Sissy and Mrs. Greene."

Thomas Saxon said nothing. Robert lingered for another moment, then turned on his heel, his shoes loud on the boards as he stomped out of the house.

*****

But he did not go to the inn as he had said, but up the hill, climbing to the summit where he could look down on the greening landscape. The trees were just beginning to bud, and the hill was awash with the first primroses.

He sat on the grass, legs stretched out before him. His stomach was settling, his jaw beginning to unclench. This was his contented place. It was the one place about the inn and its surroundings that seemed unsullied. He gazed down upon the softening land of green fields and darker hedgerows, the rusty houses and other buildings, like incongruous outcroppings of even-cut stone, and another memory came to him—a memory of a day long ago when he had sat here with Sissy.

"Look, if I had a cannon," he had said to his sister, "like one of father's cannon, I wager I could knock down the church bell tower from here."

Sissy had screwed up her face. "Why would you do that, Robert?"

He had shrugged, wary of displeasing his sister. "I don't know. That would not be a kind thing to do, I suppose." But it would be a joy nonetheless, to wield all that force and power, to cause such devastation at your word, all with this instrument, the gun. Or so it always seemed in father's stories.

He was still wondering why his mind had conjured that moment when he saw her coming up the hill from the inn yard, like a vision of herself. She held the skirt of her dress in one hand and her sun bonnet in the other. He stood when she reached him.

"Oh, Robert!" she cried. "They said you had come back! I didn't believe it, but I had to see!"

She threw herself into his arms, and he laughed, crying, "There's my little sister!"

Then she pulled away and slapped his arm hard enough to sting, and balling her fists, she demanded, "Why didn't you tell anyone you had come? Old MacLeod saw you from the inn windows, getting out of the coach!"

For a moment he could not face her, could not face that he had hurt her, even a little. "I'm not ready to go down to the inn yet. I needed some time. You see, I saw father."

Her face darkened. "Did he speak to you?"

"He was drunk." Robert fought to keep his voice even. "He didn't recognize me at first, I think. Then he was... he was...."

"It's all right," she told him, taking his arm. "He is always like that now. No one can speak to him."

"Then, who is running the inn?"

Suddenly, she smiled. "I am."

"You are?" His little sister, barely seventeen, was an innkeeper? "You have taken over from him?"

"I keep the books. I pay the workers. I see that we are supplied."

"Father is completely useless, then? Is that why the place needs repair? You can't be expected to...."

"Old MacLeod helps some." She sighed. "I would hire a man to do the work, but Father would not allow me to. There have been rare days when he has been himself, and he claims that he will affect the repairs himself. He retains control in name. He is still the owner of the property. I think it would not be wise to defy him too much."

"To hell with him. Do what you think best. The inn should be yours now. Yours forever, if you want it."

She looked at her feet. "I would do, if I could. Perhaps in time." Suddenly she threw her arms around him again. "We need you here, we need you back! I have missed you, Robert!"

He held her, but he needed her to understand that they had but the briefest of moments together. "I miss you too, but I'll be here only for a few days. I'm to return to Woolwich. You may visit me there, as often as you're able, but the odds are, I'll be sent on campaign soon. There's talk of Portugal, and even a ridiculous rumour of South America."

She gasped. "South America!"

He shrugged. "It's possible. Our only true success against Bonaparte has been on the seas and in the colonies, though as I see it, the only sensible course of action now is for us to give help to Portugal."

She looked around at the hill. "I feared this when you left, feared that this was the end of everything we've known. And now it's come to pass, and it's all changed, changed forever."

He did not like this sort of talk. His career in the army seemed nothing but promise now, one of the only truly good things he knew. That, and ensuring Sissy's happiness. "We have to make something of ourselves, Sissy. I told you before that I'm to be a soldier. That's the only thing I can ever imagine myself doing, especially with a tyrant loose in Europe. I don't care much for tyrants."

And I will gain fame and riches in my campaigns, a voice inside promised, *enough to secure the inn, which is certain to fall into ruin. And I'll rise up the ladder of promotion, as much as possible in the Royal Artillery, and we will all prosper.*

They lingered on the hill for some time, not saying much, but as supper approached, they made their way down, hand in hand. "Mrs. Greene will wonder where I have gone," Sissy said, then giggled. "Though she has no right to be cross. Now, I give her orders!"

"You should have told me of your enterprise in your letters! Though I suppose I didn't write to tell of my commission, so you have a right to your surprise. I am a mere lieutenant, but here you are, lieutenant-colonel in charge of the inn!"

She squeezed his hand. "I want to be the colonel."

*****

Robert remained at The Five Alls for three more days. In that time, he made himself useful. He repaired the thatch, replaced a rotted hitching post in the yard, and painted a new inn sign. He was most proud of the sign, for he had learned much about drawing, and he had no doubt that the new image was far superior to the old. And now, the five figures had the faces of real people, namely his barrack mates, including Mumbles, Rat, Dog, and Rice. He could not bring himself to paint Georgie, so the fifth figure, that of the soldier, he painted as himself.

He saw his father only once more, as the old man entered the common room. Their eyes met, and for a moment they held each other's gaze. It was Thomas Saxon who looked away, with a grimace and a hunch of his shoulders.

When he prepared to leave, Robert once again said his farewells, just as he had done all those months before. This time, old MacLeod shook his hand, saying, "The young master is a proper gentleman now."

Robert returned the firm grip of the old Scots sergeant. MacLeod, he realized, must have known his father's secret, but he had never uttered a peep. There was something both infuriating and admirable about that.

As before, Robert embraced Sissy last. "Thank you for everything you have done," she said, drying her tears on the shoulder of his coat. "I'll miss you, Robert. I'll miss you more this time."

"Look after the inn," he said. "I won't be gone forever."

And as he stood back from her, he saw his father standing over her left shoulder. Robert's muscles stiffened, but he did not look or turn away. His father held a bundle about two feet in length, wrapped in an old scrap of blanket.

"Sir," Robert said. "I'm returning to Woolwich."

"You shan't return without this," his father grunted, letting the blanket fall from the object in his hands. It was an officer's small sword, long and slim. Sunlight glinted from the straight blade. It was in pristine condition, a sword from an earlier era, an older British Army, one that had fought in an earlier revolution. Its guard was plated with gold, the grip of carved bone. The maker's mark read Bland of London. Robert had never seen the sword before, had not known of its existence, and as he took its offered hilt in his hand, it was with a strange sort of awe. He felt the perfect balance, the whip strength in the light steel. He sought appropriate words, but his feelings were a jumble, and he only managed to croak, "Thank you. I'm in need of a sword."

"It was mine, when I was at the Academy. My last gift to you. You shall never receive another thing from me."

Words to sour the gesture, but Robert suspected his father was no longer capable of pleasantness. No doubt, whatever had compelled him to make this gift embarrassed him now, but it did not matter. The gesture had been made.

"Goodbye, then," Robert said. The post was waiting, and the driver blew a great blast on his horn. Robert's trunk was again on the roof of the coach, and soon he, too, was aboard, propped on the patched leather bench.

After several short delays, the coach at last pulled away, bound for London. Robert stared from the side window at the little gathering in the yard. Sissy, Mrs. Greene, MacLeod. There was no longer any sign of his father.

*****

The inn had no longer felt like home. Home, Robert hoped, would be with his new regiment. He was now Second-Lieutenant Saxon (although he would be addressed as "Lieutenant" as a courtesy), No. 1 Company, 11th Battalion, Royal Regiment of Artillery, with headquarters at the New Barracks, Woolwich. The barracks had been constructed in 1777, during Robert's father's time, and thus, they were no longer new, despite their name. Some gunners had begun referring to the buildings simply as the Royal Artillery Barracks, for that was what they were. That was their sole function, and no other regiment would ever reside there.

Robert did not go to the barracks at once but made a stop at the shop of Joseph Rackham and Son, military tailors, to inquire of the progress on his new uniforms. He had ordered them immediately upon the receipt of his commission.

"There is the one set ready," said Rackham, a wizened little fellow who resembled a gnome. "The additional dress coat and your undress must wait, Lieutenant Saxon. You understand that I have many orders to fill these days, and it would not do to rush."

Robert stood before the tall mirror, admiring the finished dress coat and white summer breeches. They were a far superior fit to his second-hand cadet uniforms. "This will do well for now," he said. He grinned at his reflection, for he seemed a man made new, no longer a boy. The coat was blue, faced with red, with the addition of gold lace edging the collar, cuffs and buttonholes. The flat, gilt buttons bore the Ordnance arms, a shield showing three round shot, all in a row, above a stack of three guns. He had purchased his single bullion epaulette separately, and it was not yet fastened to the coat's right shoulder; but nevertheless, he thought he looked very fine.

"The fit is perfect," he declared.

The tailor wrapped the coat and the summer breeches in paper, tied with string. "The winter breeches must wait," he said, repeating, "I have so many orders. It would not do to rush."

"It's a miracle you were able to do this much at all, sir. Thank you."

Next, it was a trip to the hatters, where he purchased a plain, black wool cocked hat and a new leather shako, both of regulation pattern. With these and his paper package under his arm, he set off up Plumstead Road, intending to walk the rest of the way. But as he rounded a corner, he pulled up short, almost colliding with a young woman coming from the other direction. They both managed to halt themselves at the last second, the woman crying out, "Oh!"

Robert dropped his packages. "Pardon me, pardon me," he

cried. "I shouldn't have been walking so close to the edge of the road!"

Then he realized that he was looking into a face he knew, one as astonished as his must have seemed. It was Flashdash's wife. For a few heartbeats, his words caught in his throat, for she should not have been here. She was a creature of the Academy, who had no existence beyond its walls and influence. But here she was.

"Mrs. Flushing," he at last managed. "I do apologize for startling you."

Her hands flew to her cheeks. "Oh, Mister Saxon, I have made you drop your packages."

"It's nothing," he said, stooping and gathering up the bundles. "They won't be ruined."

"Let me help you."

"No, see, I already have them." He rose to his full height, the packages again under his arms.

"Another chance meeting, Mrs. Flushing," he said. "Again, I apologize for not looking where I was going."

Her lips curved into a slow smile. "Well, we seem to meet so often, you must at least begin to call me Marion."

He nodded. "Marion." It was a strange thrill to speak her name.

She brushed at the water stain soaking into the brown paper of his uniform package. "Oh, you are trying to save my feelings by saying your things have not been ruined. It is I who should apologize. You must let me make it up to you."

"It's nothing, ma'am. Just a little water. It will dry—"

"Oh, at least allow me to buy you coffee, or perhaps chocolate. There is a lovely shop nearby that I have only just discovered."

He hesitated. The offer was welcome, but it did not seem

entirely proper to take coffee with the wife of a superior officer. It was not the same as a chance encounter, for there was design behind it. Yet the design was on her part, and coffee houses were all the rage these days. Robert had never been to one. Taverns in abundance, yes, but not coffee shops. Places where the gentry gathered, he supposed, or naval officers, who were fond of their coffee. He would be out of his element, but he was also curious. He had to begin living the life of a gentleman some time.

And there was that smile of hers, that perfect smile.

He said, "I do have some time. I would be delighted. Thank you."

The shop was just around the corner, a warm place with an unusual large glass window in front. They sat on high stools inside, overlooking the street. Robert ordered a cup of bitter chocolate, and when it came and he took his first sips, he discovered that it was refreshing and invigorating.

For a moment they sat in an awkward silence. He had never been in such an intimate situation with her, one so sustained. A proper conversation was expected, and now he found he had no words.

"Where do you come from, Mister Saxon?" she asked at length.

He told her, told her about the inn, though he did not mention that his father had been a sergeant. Instead, he said, "I hail from an artillery family."

She rested her chin in one hand. "So many of them do, it seems."

"Your husband as well? Lieutenant Flushing?"

"He is a third-generation gunner. It is his life, the artillery. All he cares about."

There was another silence. Robert sipped his chocolate.

"And what of yourself, Mrs. Flushing? I mean, Marion."

She stirred her coffee with a spoon, an idle movement for which there was no need. "My family is from Hertfordshire. We have some distant relationship to the Flushings, who are, as I said, an artillery family. My father was in the cavalry. He served in the Flanders campaign, when all this war nonsense started. He lies there still, in some unrecorded place. I was very young when he died, just a girl."

"Unfortunate," Robert said, a little gruffly. "What regiment was your father with?"

For a moment something clouded her perfect features. She mastered it quickly, but Robert was certain he had seen it. "The Fifteenth Light Dragoons. He was... riding near their head. One of the few to fall, in some mad charge at a place called Villers en Cauchies."

"You don't care much for the Army then, do you?" he said, for it suddenly struck him that this was so. She looked at him sharply, and again the shadow marred her soft beauty.

"No, Lieutenant Saxon. I do not. Is it so obvious?"

He cleared his throat. "Maybe not. I fancy I have a keen eye... but it's just how you speak, how you say it. You hate that it took away your father, and how it is...taking away your husband."

He knew he had gone too far. She sat upright, her fingers twisted together.

"You are impertinent, Lieutenant Saxon."

"I apologize." Cold sweat started on his forehead. Why had he said those things? He would always say what he thought, even when it was not appropriate in every situation. "It's none of my business, of course. I've spent too much time at my studies, trying to get to the heart of things. It's a bad habit, I suppose."

After a pause, her smile returned. "Well, you are very good at your bad habit, Mister Saxon."

He wanted to change the subject, and said, "If I'm to call you Marion, you must call me Robert."

"Very well, Robert. Very well."

They drained their cups.

When they had returned to the street, Robert thanked her. "I must be off to the barracks, but I enjoyed our talk."

"As did I. And it does not have to end, for I am headed in the same direction. You may escort me."

He was tempted to take her arm, but better judgement prevailed, so they simply walked. They did not say very much. The mild air smelled of rain.

"You are living in the barracks now?" he asked.

She laughed. "Yes. Our new posting was not very distant, was it?"

Robert nodded. "You are still in Woolwich, then."

"Yes. I had not realized either!"

They walked along, moving slowly, neither in a hurry. And from somewhere deep inside, Robert felt something he had not known for a very long time, rising up from some unknown reservoir. It was happiness. Pure, unexpected happiness.

Chapter Ten:

Company

The Parade Square at the New Barracks was identical to that of the Royal Military Academy, a strip of beaten earth in front of the main buildings, bordering the Common. Robert paused to watch a full company of troops at exercise. The troops marched in line, then changed to column, looking for all the world like infantry, although they were Royal Artillery, in blue coats with red facings and glaring yellow lace. They wore the leather stovepipe shako, and every man's hair was pulled into a tight queue, powdered white and tied with black ribbon. All very neat.

That could be my company, Robert thought.

He made his way along the edge of the Parade, pausing once to avoid a group of small boys who mimicked the soldiers, stomping by in step with each other, one of them belting out, "Left, right, left!" Robert smiled to himself, then carried on, moving along the front of the long, long face of the barracks, which stretched for what seemed a mile. He paused before the center of the vast building, staring upward at the black face of a clock with bright gold hands that pointed at Roman numerals. Ten o'clock in the morning.

The door was on the Parade level. Robert stepped inside

and found himself in a narrow corridor. The Orderly Room was the first room on his right.

"Hello," he said as he entered, sweeping off his new cocked hat. The room was bright, its walls whitewashed and hung with portraits of gunners from earlier ages, fellows in three-sided hats and powdered wigs. "I'm here to join the Eleventh Battalion. Could you please show me the location of the adjutant's office?"

"You're in the right place, sir," said the Orderly Sergeant, a grey-haired veteran with commodious side whiskers. "The adjutant is Lieutenant Buckley, and he, like the rest of your people, is located in the west wing, sir."

It took Robert some time to find the office, owing to the enormous size of the barracks complex, and even then, a corporal serving as clerk made him wait half an hour. At last, he went in, and there sat a pinched-looking fellow with a receding hairline, small round spectacles, and a mouth that seemed to have just swallowed a lemon.

"You are to be placed in Number One Company," Buckley stated, after Robert had reported, though this was not news. "They're still setting up. You should report to Captain Flushing, who I believe to be in his office. It's at the end of the corridor, last door."

"Yes, sir. Did you say Captain Flushing?"

"I did."

Robert hesitated. "The same who was recently an instructor at the Academy?"

"Indeed."

Robert rocked back on his heels. This was a surprise, a genuine surprise, and not welcome at all. His heart sank. So, this was Flashdash's promotion, his new assignment. It had been a joy to know that his wife, that Marion, would be close, but this was more than a foil for that bit of good fortune. And of course, it was not in the least bit appropriate to be pleased at the thought of spending time with a brother officer's wife, and his commanding officer, to boot.

Commanding officer. Bloody Flashdash was his commanding officer....

Buckley was glaring at him over the lenses of his spectacles. "Was there something else, Lieutenant? Or do you enjoy casting a shadow?"

"No, sir," Robert almost growled. He resented the man's tone and considered sarcasm unbecoming in a superior officer. He almost spoke his mind, but military discipline, drilled into him over so many months on the Parade under Sergeant Bane, took over. He nodded. "I'll be on my way."

On his way to see Flashdash.

The captain's office door stood ajar. Robert knocked, and a familiar voice said, "Come."

Robert halted before the mahogany desk, standing at attention, hat propped under his left arm. "Second-Lieutenant Saxon reporting for duty, sir."

Flashdash's half-moon frown rivalled Buckley's. "Saxon, yes. I remember you. Good student, a bit on the untamed side, if I recall."

Robert could think of no reply that his new captain would not find offensive, so as with the adjutant, he held his tongue.

Flashdash leaned back in his stuffed chair. "The lapels of your coat are not folded back properly, Lieutenant."

Robert's right hand went to the front of his coat, but he could detect nothing awry. "Sir?"

"Four fastened buttons must be visible above your waist sash, and the top three buttons should be left unfastened, the lapels turned back to reveal the lace inside. You are showing four unfastened buttons.”

Robert took a breath. “I was not aware that there was such a regulation, sir.”

“In this subunit, there is.   I intend to run an orderly company, one with tight discipline and standards the rest of the battalion will envy. And we won’t have any of that gallivanting about, like we saw on the Common. You will instruct your men to be methodical and precise in their drills. Speed will come later.”

“Yes, sir.”

“I am aware of your father’s reputation, you see, Mister Saxon. I would not have a repeat of the same behaviour.”

If Flashdash had leapt across the desk and tried to throttle him, Robert would not have been more astonished. Flashdash knew of his father?

“What... behaviour is that, sir?”

The captain sighed and folded his hands. “I shouldn’t like to speculate. Perhaps I should not have mentioned it. You’re new at this, and I can’t expect perfect compliance at once. I intend for you to continue learning, as you did at the Academy. I wish for us all to get on, and in that respect, I think we are lucky. We have chosen officers to serve together who learned together, former brother gentlemen cadets.   You are well acquainted with the other lieutenants, Mister Rice and Mister Campion. Lieutenant Rice, as the formally senior gentleman cadet, will serve as my acting Second Captain.”

Robert felt the remaining blood drain from his face. He did not recall a Campion, but Rice—not bloody Rice!

He swallowed. “Did you say Rice, sir?”

“Yes. Second-Lieutenant Wesley Rice. Now acting in the capacity as Second Captain, due to our shortages. I understand you were barrack mates.”

"Yes, sir. That we were."

"Then, as I say, you should get on splendidly."

Robert emerged from the interview with a blazing anger. He needed air and hurried outside. There he leaned his back against the brick wall. This was not a good start, not the promising beginning he had hoped for. It troubled him to think that Flashdash had known about his father's career at the Academy before he had himself, and also that the captain was so obtuse as to think that he and Rice were friends. Everyone at the Academy had known they were enemies.

"This is not the Academy," he murmured. There could be no bullying or foolish pranks here, amongst commissioned officers. Maybe in time, he and Rice would learn to get along.

On the Parade, the gunners continued to drill, marching in line, to and fro, along the great width of the barracks front.

*****

Robert found his quarters in the west wing. They consisted of a single room divided by a wooden partition into a parlour and sleeping chamber. A single fireplace, a coal grate, served to heat the entire room. Fortunately, the quarters were furnished, though sparsely. In the parlour was a settee, two wing chairs with threadbare arms, a few side tables, and a mirror over the mantel. In the bed chamber stood a plain four poster with no curtains, a side table and a chair, a washstand with a cracked porcelain basin and a chamber pot.

Robert decided that it would do. He would spruce it up on his own, and it was a damn sight better than the barracks, where the men lived.

The hour was drawing late. Turning to the mirror, he adjusted his neck stock, then buttoned his lapels so that four fastened buttons showed above his silk waist sash.

The officers' mess was a single large room divided by its furnishings. A long mahogany dining table dominated the far end, while nearer the entrance was a cluster of stuffed chairs, side tables and foot stools. The walls were panelled in dark hardwood, perhaps oak, and there was something comforting in their warm silence, something that made Robert stop and take a steadying breath. Within a few minutes he was feeling better, for this place reminded him that he had entered a world much larger than what he had seen at the Academy. This was the meeting place of all those who had come before him, all those officers who had made the Royal Artillery what it was, what it would become. And this was where Robert would come to know the other officers in his battalion, and the other battalions stationed in the depot.

Another of those officers was already present, propped in one of the arm-chairs, a glass of Madeira on a table at his elbow. He was reading a newspaper, and though it obscured his face, with a start, Robert realized who it was. He knew him by the way he lounged, feet up, left leg over his right, one toe idly twitching. It was Rice.

Robert folded his hands behind his back. For a moment some invisible force kept him in check, but then he stepped forward, toward one of the other chairs. Its springs protested when he sat, and at that Rice dropped his paper. His eyes locked with Robert's.

Rice made a sound low in his throat and pushed himself back in his chair.

"Hello, Wesley," Robert said. "It seems we're to serve together again."

Rice's face took on a look of pure disgust. "So I hear," he said slowly. "And here you are, just like before. Seems I can't get rid of you."

Robert crossed his legs. "So, you've tried, have you?"

Rice threw down his newspaper with a snap. "No, I have not, though if I knew a way I wouldn't hesitate to use it."

Robert locked his hands together. He could feel himself teetering on the edge of an intolerable situation, an unworkable situation. He had defeated Rice twice, both times using the same tactic, a bold and unrelenting assault, but Rice was still here, and he had not changed. Their little war had come to nothing. It was time that it ended, and though the very thought made his stomach writhe, and though the ghost of Georgie still cried out for revenge, Robert knew that only he could end it. Rice would not, for he was too stubborn, too stupid to see the full effects of his actions and his attitude.

For the good of this new company, Robert told himself, for the good of this company that he had striven so hard to become a part of, he would find a way for them to settle their differences.

"I suppose you're just being honest," he said, "so I'll return the favour. We detest each other, but now we have to serve together. We have no choice, for we must follow orders."

Rice was shaking his head. "Oh, I know this, I know what you're about to say, that we have to get on. But that's all rot. Captain Flushing has made a grave mistake by choosing you. A grave mistake."

"He made a mistake by placing us together, but we can't do anything about it."

Rice rolled his eyes. "No, no, my dear Saxon. The mistake was choosing you. You – you're the detriment here. How is it possible that I could ever trust you, after what you did? Pushing and bullying your way through, throwing around your threats, all for your absurd obsession with obtaining a commission in under a year, no doubt to prove that you aren't the failure your father was. That's how you do things, by pushing everyone around, forcing them to do things your way."

For a moment Robert was at a loss for how to respond. Was Rice so unaware of his own behaviour? "Rice, you're the one who lorded it over the snookers, especially Georgie, and even poor Mumbles, and encouraged your friends to do the same." He leaned forward, suddenly angry again. He knew he should ignore Rice's provocation, should accept the unacceptable, but for now it was too hard, too soon. "You're the one who laughed and egged them on as they lit that poor boy's head on fire, on a day when he needed friends above all else, something you should have known. And I think you did know; that you realized his predicament and did what you could to make it worse. You're a spiteful, lying bastard, and I hold you responsible for Georgie's death!"

Rice met outrage with indignation. "Keep your voice down! This is the officers' mess, and it's just lucky that we're alone, or someone would teach you some manners. What language! To accuse me of causing that poor pathetic whelp's death, you of all people. You're a madman. You're the one who threatened me, or have you forgotten?"

And I'll do it again, Robert thought. *Go a step further, this time, I'll jam my father's sword down your throat!*

But that was the darkness, and he would not surrender to it. That was what he had pledged to overcome, and that was another reason why he had to be the one to compromise, to find peace.

Still, he could not help another dig. "I'm the first person who ever stood up to you, am I not?" he said. "I don't mean just while we were at the Shop, but in your entire life. You've always had your way, haven't you?"

"What has that to do with your improper use of a bayonet?"

"That was a prank," Robert said, though of course that was not true. For a second, he wondered if Rice was right, that he was not trustworthy, that the darkness was too great, too strong for him. But he was aware of the danger, while Rice seemed oblivious to his own darkness, his streak of callous cruelty. Robert reminded himself that Rice had deserved the threat, had deserved to stare death in the face. "That was in retaliation for the time you and your friends decided I was needed a thrashing in the racquet court."

Rice folded his arms and stuck out his bottom lip. "I don't believe you. How can I, when I don't trust you, and never will? And here I am, your second captain. What a company we will be!"

This was the entire purpose of the conversation, as Robert saw it. "We have to follow our orders. We have to make it work."

They sat in silence. From the mantel, a case clock ticked.

The door swung open, and at last a third person entered the mess. He stood blinking around. Rice glanced at him, said, "Ah, and there is our last company officer, Lieutenant Campion."

Robert turned, and his jaw dropped. Campion, of course. He had forgotten his true name.

"Another fine example to the service," Rice grumbled.

The newcomer smiled and said something too quiet to hear. It was Mumbles.

*****

The portrait that hung above the dining table was of Colonel Albert Borgard, father of the Royal Regiment of Artillery. The painted figure stared out from the wall in his powdered wig and tiny, three-corner cocked hat, his right hand gesturing toward

153

the tiny figures of troops and guns in the background, the glint in his eye one of unassuming pride. Or perhaps his spirit, residing in oil and canvas, was showing its satisfaction at the scene below, of the officers in blue, red and gold lace, of the gleaming silver, the sparkling crystal and fine plate, all signs that the regiment had grown and prospered.

This setting, Robert mused, was all his, his by right, as long as he remained a member of this esteemed company. And that, he knew, would be the remainder of his life.

The commander of the new 11th Battalion, Lieutenant Colonel Mudge, sat as senior officer beneath Borgard's portrait. Mudge was of middle age, his remaining hair still worn in the old style, tied back in a tight queue, like the men in the ranks. This was in contrast to the majority of his officers, young men like Robert who preferred the new style of hair—cut short to the collar. They were all merely boys, all fresh to this game, excited with the prospects of what they could achieve in the coming conflicts with Bonaparte. It was a cheerful dinner, and Robert allowed himself to be caught up in the spirit of it all, let himself forget Rice, forget Flashdash for a while. Rice and Flashdash were not the whole of the Royal Artillery, and he would not serve with them forever.

He stared at the wine in his glass, swirled the rich red liquid, red like blood. "Well," he murmured, too quiet for anyone else to hear, "there is only one course, and that's to go on. Fight it out."

Mumbles sat to his left. He leaned over and said, "This is a fine set up (mumble mumble). We shall have to stick together, shan't we? You and me, Robert."

Robert looked at him. Though Mumbles had been the senior gentleman cadet, he had been more than willing to follow Robert's lead. Robert had no doubt that Mumbles would, indeed, stick close to him, and that, he decided, was agreeable enough. Mumbles would probably make a decent, competent officer, if somewhat unspectacular, and he would remain an ally in the struggle against Rice.

"Of course, Mumbles," Robert said. "Or should I call you Lieutenant Campion?"

Mumbles gave him a faint smile. "Mumbles will do."

After the plates had been cleared, the port was served, and then the toasts commenced. The gathered officers raised their glasses to the king, and to the regiment, to the new Eleventh Battalion and for "Confusion to Bonaparte!" By then Robert's head felt packed with cotton, though this was not an unpleasant feeling, and he knew a moment of contentment, of well being, and a sense that things were as they should be, perhaps for the first time in his life.

Colonel Mudge was talking, standing with his glass in hand. Robert struggled to concentrate on his words. "This verges very close to business," the colonel said, "and one should not speak of regimental business in the mess. Nevertheless, this evening I shall make an exception, for this is the first gathering of this body of officers in this new corps of the Royal Artillery. I welcome you all, in particular those who have only just arrived from the other side of the Common. Now we are complete, and soon we will be ready." He knit his brows in an expression of exaggerated fierceness. "Understand, you all, that I do not intend to sit idle while the tyrant remains on the rampage."

New officers were expected to keep their mouths shut, but here, everyone was green and the wine was flowing, so there were cheers at that. Seeming pleased, Mudge went on. "I do not care for rumours as a rule, my boys, but I can tell you, there is truth to the speculation that a detachment of artillery will be required for service soon, somewhere as yet unknown."

He paused, maybe to catch another cheer, but there was an expectant silence. Robert, as alert now as the rest, realized that he was holding his breath.

"I have it that three companies will be required," Mudge continued. This was usual, for artillery battalions did not often operate as single units but sent their companies on detached duties. Each of the detached companies would be linked with a company from the Corps of Drivers, and the resulting artillery "brigade" would be attached to another brigade of infantry and cavalry. "To this end, we must be ready, we must prove our mettle. These men under your command have been with their sergeants for some three months, but that is little more than a beginning. When called upon, I expect we shall not fail—and we will be called upon, gentlemen. I shall be observing your progress. Pray, keep in mind that when I receive my orders, I will be obliged to choose the best of the lot. That is your goal, then."

There were more cheers, though from individuals, a cry of "hear hear" amongst nods and grunts of agreement. Flashdash alone spoke up, crying, "You have set us a contest, sir!"

Robert's stomach leapt. He felt a sudden sense of urgency. If there was to be a contest, he wanted his company to win. To Flashdash, the best company would be that with the shiniest guns, so Robert's duty was clear, and that would be to ensure that their men did not waste their time concentrating on the frivolous, and so be left behind. He did not want to be left behind.

"Do you know where we will be going, sir?" someone else asked, the question everyone wanted answered.

Mudge shook his head. "I do not possess that information, and it is not for me, nor anyone else to speculate. We will follow our orders and do our duty as Englishmen. That is all."

But Robert knew where they would be going, or where some of them would be going: Portugal, Britain's oldest ally. Of that he had no doubt.

*****

The next morning, after breakfast in the mess, Flashdash called his officers to his office. "I mean to have our company selected when the time comes, gentlemen. I am the most senior captain in this new battalion, and I am entitled to it. Entitled! We have been at war with France for more than twelve years, and I have yet to meet the enemy in battle. I mean for that to change."

"We'll (mumble, mumble)," Mumbles said.

"Eh? What did you say, Lieutenant Campion?"

Mumbles lifted his chin and seemed to strain as he said, "I said that we'll do our best, sir."

Flashdash's eyes goggled from his head. "By God, you will! We train on a company level, which means you each have a crack at it. Battalion Parade is for roll call and lights out only. My secretary will draw up a schedule."

Robert was full of nervous energy as he and his fellow officers left the captain's office. "Well, the company will be undergoing gunnery practice drills with the sergeants in about half an hour. I mean to take a look. Care to join me?"

"Actually," Mumbles said, "I thought I would take a nap before dinner. We were rather late... in the mess."

Robert stared at him. Rice said, "I mean to take a turn with Daisy in the park." Daisy was his horse. "Train the men, train the men! What do we have sergeants for? I'm not here to train the men, but to lead them whenever we go into battle. I expect them to already be trained."

"But we should train them to lead them," Robert said.

"They need to know us, and we need to know them."

Rice snorted. "Very well, Saxon, if that's your thing. Maybe I'll find a use for you after all, eh? As your second captain. Report to us what you find, will you?"

Robert was too astonished to be angry. "Certainly. I'll tell you all I can."

"Right then," Rice said, all the time not looking at Robert. "Enjoy your nap, Mumbles."

Mumbles muttered something and moved away. Robert found himself alone on the empty Parade Square.

*****

The men brought the guns out of the storerooms, one piece at a time. It took four to carry each brass barrel, rope slings slung across their shoulders, though one man alone could carry a carriage wheel. The heavy oak trails, limber beds and limber chests all required further cooperation. Finally, everything needed to be assembled, a procedure carried out amid some confusion and a great deal of shouting from about half a dozen corporals.

Robert approached one of the NCOs. The corporal snapped him a salute.

"Where is the senior sergeant?" Robert asked.

"That would be Colour-Sergeant Hunter, sir."

Robert waited for the man to answer his actual question. When he did not, Robert said, "I expect so, but where is he, Corporal?"

"Er... he's there, sir." The corporal pointed to a corner where the storehouse and barracks met at right angles. Leaning up against the brick wall, standing on his head, was the sergeant.

"Thank you," Robert said. He moved toward the strange

figure, curious about the man's actions, though reserving judgement. "Colour Sergeant?" he said, looking down at the fellow's reddening face. There were no colour sergeants in the Royal Artillery, but the term was often used in an informal manner, in reference to the senior company sergeant. "I am Mister Saxon, one of your new officers."

"Ah, hello, sir," Hunter said, and with a groan, he swung down his legs and raised himself to a standing position. There he swayed for a moment before offering a salute, saying, "Ah, now, that's cleared me head, sir."

Robert rubbed his chin. "Ah, so that's why you were doing that, eh?"

"To facilitate blood flow, sir."

Robert had never heard of such a thing. "Standing on your head?"

Hunter's wide ruddy face split into an even wider grin. He had fine teeth, but it was his eyes Robert found most striking. They were merry, intelligent eyes. "Yes, sir. Clears the head, as I say."

Robert nodded. "I'll take your word for it. However, I haven't come to discuss folk remedies so much as to observe the lads at drill."

Hunter's grin did not waver. "Very good, sir. Will you be assuming command of the period, sir?"

"No," Robert said, and he detected the merest hint of relief from Hunter. *I must seem a mere boy to him*, Robert thought. *As I suppose I am.*

"No, I would like to gauge the level of their skills, as they have come to them, with instructors they know and trust."

"Very good, then, sir. I shall be taking them around to the Front Parade. No drivers or teams, just the men and the guns."

"Yes, that's fine. And how are they doing, do you think?

You're a veteran of an older battalion, I presume."

"I transferred from the fifth, sir."

"I see.   And what's your opinion of the skill of these recruits?"

They started walking as they spoke, for the company had assembled the guns, limbered them, and were hauling them into column using drag ropes. "Well, sir, they're fully trained in the basics.   Know their marching and manoeuvres on the Parade Ground. Know their musketry. But when it comes to guns and fuses, projectiles and the like, they're as green as grass." He grinned, eyes twinkling. "Green as grass."

Robert watched as two of the gun carriages ran afoul of each other, the corporals leaping all over both gun crews like a pack of savage dogs.

"As are we all," Robert remarked.

Hunter's grin did not waver, his cheeks like two ruddy apples. "Some of us, sir."

Robert nodded again. Of course, Hunter was a veteran. A proven man, a man of skill and brains, who had risen through the ranks, perhaps even in the field, on campaign. He would know things that men like Flashdash could not even imagine.

"Tell me, Sergeant," Robert said slowly, "what do you consider the most important aspects of gunnery?"

"Accuracy, sir," Hunter said without a pause. "And rate of fire. Rate of fire. It's quite simple, if I may say so, sir."

"And what of the need to preserve ammunition?   You wouldn't want to run out too soon."

"Determined by the situation, sir. Sometimes you need to be slow, sir. But sometimes you need to be quick. So, you need to know how to be quick, sir."

Robert folded his arms. "And what of the safety of the crew, when they move so fast?"

Hunter shrugged. "The crew will be safe when the enemy is dead, sir."

Robert laughed. "My thoughts exactly, Sergeant."

The little column reached the Front Parade, where it arrayed itself in line, facing across the Common. Robert remained in the rear, watching. Hunter took charge as battery commander, with three sergeants commanding the divisions of two guns each. When Hunter gave the command, "Action front!" The crews unlimbered their pieces, turning the barrels to face south. Hunter then cried, "Load!" The recruits went to work, ramming home imaginary cartridges, then firing in dumbshow, each gun in succession.

Robert had taken out his watch and timed the drill. He was disappointed. It had taken the battery a full minute to load and pretend to fire one round.

He approached Hunter. "Sergeant Hunter," he said, keeping his voice low so the men could not hear him, "Can you go any faster?"

Hunter raised himself on his toes and dropped back. "Expect we can, sir. That was not to my liking."

"How much faster?"

Hunter grinned again. "We'll see, sir. As I said, lads are green. But not for long, sir. Not for long."

Robert nodded. He liked this man, liked his confidence and his good humour, though it remained to be seen what quality of instructor he would make. "I won't interfere with what you're doing here today, but I do ask one thing."

"What's that, sir?"

"That in the days and months ahead, you keep me informed, Sergeant Hunter. I suspect I'll be out here with you more often than the other company officers and I think we should work together as much as possible. I want to know your opinions on things, such as speed, drill, ammunition, use of tangent sights, everything to do with our trade."

"Oh, no use for them, sir."

Robert frowned. "What? No use for what?"

Hunter squinted. "Tangent sights, sir. Gunner should know his guns, know how they fly, whether they're true or not. No use for fancy sights. That's for lazy lads, sir."

Robert smiled. He was beginning to like this man very much. "Interesting."

The drills progressed, and Hunter began to push, a little at first, then gradually applying more pressure, barking at the men to move. At the end of an hour, they were firing four aimed rounds a minute.

"Still room for improvement," Robert murmured, but he realized that Hunter had impressed him after all.

He folded his hands behind his back, glancing at the sky, at the brick walls, the brown dust of the Parade, and suddenly he felt more at home than he had for some time. He was at home in the presence of these men, these men that it was his duty to lead. It was a terrifying prospect, for though he understood guns and gunnery, Robert knew he was untried as a leader, untried when it came to command. But now he had an advantage over the others, over Rice, Mumbles, even Flashdash, for none of them had shown an interest in observing this drill today. They had left a void, and Robert had filled it.

I'll train these men, Robert thought. *Train them, push them, perhaps inspire them, with the help of Hunter. They will come to know and trust me, if I do right by them. If I can gain their confidence.*

And soon, he hoped, he would lead them into battle.

Chapter Eleven:

Recital

Rice sat on the bed, not dressed, eyes reddened and sunken within pockets of swollen, darkened flesh. The result of another late night in the mess, Robert presumed, or some other entertainment. That was all Rice seemed to concern himself with.

"Ah, good of you to come," Rice croaked, then cleared his throat. "Ahem. Yes, very good of you."

"You're acting second captain," Robert said, not taken in by Rice's agreeable tone. Rice must want something from him. There could be no other explanation. "I took your summons for an order."

"No, no," Rice continued. "It's just that I'm done in. I would like you to substitute for training this morning. You will be there anyway, after all, won't you? I want to rest up for the live exercise this afternoon."

Flashdash had drawn up a rotating duty schedule for Rice, Robert and Mumbles. At least one of them had to be present for every training period, whether foot and arms drill or gun drill. Robert, nevertheless, attended every period, even those under the command of Rice and Mumbles, as an observer, keeping an eye on the progress of the company.

"Isn't it going to look strange," he said, "if you keep giving me your duty rotation?"

Rice's demeanour changed at once, and he stuck out his lip like a petulant child. It had not taken him long to turn Robert's enthusiasm to his advantage. "You said yourself that you came here in obedience to orders. Now you question them? The orders of your second captain?"

Robert had no patience for Rice's growing tendency to use his newfound rank when it suited him. "You know that I'm not, but if you would like to pretend, why don't you have me on charges, and I can let the colonel know of your late nights, and that I have covered for you three times already? I suppose you're going to the recital at Colonel Mudge's this evening, and after that some other entertainment, so that you'll be done in again tomorrow? Do you think you'll need me then, too?"

Rice looked away. "Damn you, get out of my sight and do as you're told!"

Robert nodded in satisfaction. A little moral victory for him, and the truth was, he did not mind filling in. In fact, he preferred it. He had watched Rice in action, thought him too precise, as usual, too concerned with petty details. He was forever interrupting, stopping the drill to correct the placement of a man's hand or foot. As a result, momentum was lost, the men suffering under the weight of too much control. He was the exact opposite to Mumbles, who stood back and let the sergeants take over.

"I think you'll owe me a favour after this one," Robert added, then added a mocking, "sir," before he left.

This time Rice made no reply, for he had crawled back into bed, head in his hands.

*****

Robert joined Sergeant Hunter and the company on the Front Parade. The orders of the day called for a lesson in ammunition types. Robert drew the men up in three sides of a square, facing a limber that Hunter had brought round and parked in the open end of the formation. The limber chest contained a prepared assortment of projectiles.

"Round shot," Robert said, voice raised to reach every man. He held aloft a solid cast iron ball weighing six pounds. "The basic type of solid shot, used mainly for counter-battery fire, but also against troops in dense columns. Like bowling for ninepins," he added, which elicited a few chuckles.

Next, he held up a canvas bag tied with rope. "Grape shot. This is a quantity of tiny round shot tied together. Upon ignition, the bag breaks apart in a spray of solid iron. Very useful against enemy troop formations." He almost said that he had never seen it in action but decided that the men did not need to be reminded of that fact. They were all, as Hunter had said, as green as grass when it came to the reality of battle, and they needed to have confidence in the abilities and experience of their young officers.

"This is a prepared cartridge," Robert went on, taking out a flannel powder cartridge with a round shot and a wooden disc, known as a sabot, fixed to one end. "Having these on hand means you can load with greater speed and efficiency. You don't need to load cartridge and shot separately, something which will gain you valuable seconds and so spare your lives."

He replaced the cartridge and removed another spherical iron ball, this one with a short fuse protruding from a one-inch hole drilled in its surface. "This is the recent invention of an officer by the name of Thomas Shrapnel. It's known simply as Shrapnel Shell. It resembles common shell, in that it is a hollow iron case filled with powder, but it also contains packed musket balls. The intention is to cut the fuse to such a length that the shell will burst in the air, not on the ground. The resulting explosion will create a rain of bullets and iron fragments. It has been in existence for some ten years, though to my knowledge has never been tested...." He trailed off, for he sensed restlessness in his audience. The faces of the men, he noticed, betrayed a mixture of patience and boredom. They shifted from foot to foot, rubbing their noses, coughing, some staring at the sky.

Robert turned to Hunter and said, "You've taught them these things before, haven't you?"

Hunter's eyes sparkled. "Many times, sir."

Robert sighed, replaced the Shrapnel case, and closed the limber chest with a snap. "Then let's forego the repetition. The best way to know your ammunition is to see it in action. This afternoon we'll act as a battery for the first time, firing shotted guns at fixed targets. We might as well use this time to practice. A little warm up." He turned to Hunter. "What do you think, Sergeant?"

"Men learn by doing, sir. Learn by doing."

"Yes, I agree." Robert grinned. He was not averse to delivering a lecture, but he favoured action. And since coming to Woolwich, he loved nothing so much in the world as a gun well served, to see the power of that gun and the devastation it wrought upon its intended target.

*****

After dinner Number One Company, joined by a company of drivers and teams to make a brigade, formed on the Front Parade with six guns and limbers. The horses stamped in anticipation, as eager as the men. This would be the company's first exercise with live ammunition since the new officers had joined. Robert, Rice, and Mumbles each had charge of a division of the battery, two guns each. When the battery of guns formed in line, Rice's division was on the right, consisting of Number One and Number Two Gun. Robert's position was the centre, and Mumbles was on the left. Flashdash would play his role as brigade commander, in charge of the entire gun battery, with Sergeant Hunter seeing that things got done.

As Robert waited with his two guns, a tall senior artillery officer approached Rice. Robert did not recognize him. The hair that sprouted from beneath his hat was the colour of iron, and he bore himself with a certain nobility. Rice beamed as he saluted, and the two exchanged what seemed like pleasant words. For the briefest of moments, the older man gripped Rice's elbow in an obvious gesture of affection, and it was then that Robert saw the resemblance. This could only be Rice's father, old Colonel Rice.

Father and son laughed together at some private amusement.

They should not make such a display in front of us, in front of the men, Robert thought. A senior officer should not show favouritism, even to his son. The scene added to his belief that Rice was spoiled, overindulged, but even as that thought emerged, it was followed by a sense of bitter envy that verged on outright jealousy. Robert would never know that closeness with his father, had never known it, even when his mother was alive, for he had been too young. Doubtless, Georgie had never known it either, and that, Robert decided, was what had really killed him.

It was then that Flashdash gave the command to start the company moving forward in column. Robert saw Colonel Rice shake his son's hand, and they exchanged salutes again.

Robert faced his front.   He was on foot and marched alongside his guns.   The gunners sat on the limbers and carriages, a few riding the horses in the teams.   They had a few miles to go, south along the Shooter's Hill Road to an open field far from where an errant cannon ball might accidentally damage a house or shop.

Robert fought his emotions as he marched, hoping that reason would overrule the darkness in his heart.   His jealousy was pointless and unjustified, he told himself.   He was his own man now.   He could not change how he had come to be, nor where he had come from.   All that mattered was the road ahead.

*****

The call of "Action Front!" came down from the head of the column.   Division by division wheeled forward from the right in echelon, changing formation from column to line abreast. When Robert's two guns reached their station in the centre of the line, he shouted, "Halt! Unlimber!"

The men leapt into action, unlimbering with fluid efficiency. Robert timed the procedure, and when it was done and the horse teams had been unhitched and pulled even further to the rear, he said, "A company record."

He waited for the command to load.   The burning slow match on the linstocks behind every gun filled the air with the acrid scent of imminent action, and his heart quickened with a rising excitement.   The guns were power, power at his front, and at least partially at his command.   This was what he loved most; and here he could forget about his father, forget about Georgie, his troubles with Rice.

Sergeant Hunter had taken a position in the centre of the battery. This put him nearest Robert's guns. Hunter stood still, his left hand held aloft, palm flat.

"Testing the wind, Sergeant?" Robert asked.

Hunter rotated his shoulders. "Aids the circulation, sir. Cools the blood." He lowered his left arm and raised his right.

"I understand," Robert said, though what he meant was that he understood that Hunter had some odd notions.

A few minutes passed. Wondering at the delay, Robert glanced toward the rear, looking for a sign of the brigade commander. He found him amongst a gathering of officers and civilians who, Robert assumed, had come to watch the exercise. Lieutenant Colonel Mudge was there, doubtless planning to judge the performance of one of his companies, and Colonel Rice, come to see his son in action. With them were gunners and officers from brother companies, and several ladies. One of the latter was Marion Flushing. Robert recognized her from her stance, by the way she held her sun parasol. He almost raised his hand in greeting but caught himself in time. She had not come here to see him.

Mudge and Flashdash at last detached themselves from the gathering and rode toward the battery. Flashdash was a dashing picture on horseback, standing high in his stirrups, one hand propped on his side. Without pausing to rein in, he cried, "Four rounds round shot, load!"

"Four rounds round shot, load," Robert repeated, facing the front and taking out his watch. His men were ready, his gun commanders repeating the command to their crews, who sprang into action without missing a heartbeat. In fifteen seconds, the guns were loaded, the commanders sighting along each barrel at the targets—piles of empty barrels set up two hundred yards away. "Ready," each gun commander called in turn.

"Fire four rounds," Robert commanded.

The guns cracked, recoiling on their trails as the brass tubes spat flame and iron toward the distant casks. Splinters sprayed, the shot true, a good result though not so impressive at this close range. Robert's primary goal was to see his guns fire all four shots in a single minute, and almost twenty-five seconds had already elapsed. "Faster!" he shouted, but the men had already sponged, loaded and primed. Linstocks came down to touchholes, the guns blasted again, and now the ammunition had already been run forward, and the crews sponged and loaded a third time. In their haste, two men lost their shakos, the leather caps sliding from their sweating brows. Robert squinted at his watch and at the targets, jaw clenched and breath held, only half aware that the other four guns in the battery had only fired once.

Two more shakos fell, and the last round blasted out. Robert glanced at his watch. The second hand completed its sweep, the minute having passed. Every gun had fired four rounds. In his front, the targets had been destroyed, blasted to matchwood, mostly by the first two salvos alone.

"Cease firing," Robert shouted, and as the guns were wet sponged and wormed a last time, he waited, satisfied. The guns in the divisions to his right and left fired their final rounds. Smoke drifted, and the sudden silence announced an end to the exercise.

Hoofbeats approached, and Robert turned to find himself facing both Flashdash and Mudge. The battalion commander was smiling.

"Well done, Lieutenant," Mudge said before Flashdash could utter a word. "A truly splendid display! I timed your four rounds in just over a minute."

Robert saluted. "Thank you, sir."

Flashdash's mouth was a firm line, but Mudge said to him, "I reckon this is indeed the best company in the battalion. To this point, none other has managed such a rate of fire.   I congratulate you, Captain Flushing."

"I am most gratified, sir," Flashdash replied, but his smile was forced. "And I am certain we can do better. In fact, we will. I promise you five rounds a minute in two more weeks."

"I shall hold you to it," Mudge said. He leaned forward, almost hanging out of his saddle. "And you, Lieutenant Saxon."

Robert had never expected to be addressed by the colonel, and he beamed, the tension of that single minute having given way to rising elation, almost a light-headedness. It seemed his insistence on speed had paid off in more ways than one. He had not felt such pure satisfaction in a long, long time, and though he knew he should have uttered another simple thank you, he instead declared, "Five rounds a minute is my goal, sir."

Flashdash gave him a sour look. "That will be enough, Lieutenant. I will speak to you later."

"Sir," Robert said, curious about his captain's obvious ill mood, though not overly perturbed. He had just earned the company high praise.

Flashdash and Mudge moved on. When they had completed their rounds of the guns, there was a further pause as a fatigue party removed the shattered casks and set more targets. Robert allowed his men to relax. He was chatting with Hunter when Flashdash returned, reining in at about twenty yards distance. "Lieutenant Saxon, I would have a word."

"Yes, sir," Robert said, approaching.

Flashdash remained erect in his saddle, his face almost contorted with fury, his eyes bulging. "I expect my orders to be obeyed, Lieutenant!"

"Yes, sir," Robert repeated, taken aback. He had no idea what Flashdash was talking about.

"I instructed you not to rush your drills," Flashdash

continued, "and here you are in front of the colonel, the colonel no less, with your men fairly falling over each other, losing their shakos, like some sort of ridiculous farce."

Robert stared in disbelief. Despite what Mudge had said, Flashdash considered the exercise a failure. Because the men had lost their shakos.

Robert folded his hands behind his back, the anger slowly growing deep in the pit of his stomach. "Was the colonel unhappy, sir?"

"Damn you, I am unhappy! I am responsible for this company. I am, and not you. You do not have goals, Lieutenant. I have goals, and you see that they are carried out. Is that clear?"

"Perfectly clear, sir."

Flashdash rode off. Robert did not salute, and watched him go, every muscle in his body now as tight as wet hemp. He had disliked and distrusted Flashdash before, but now he knew the man was both a fool and a poor officer. There was no justification for his admonishment, and Robert was sick of injustice, sick of those in power who abused or did not understand their position. What should have been a moment of triumph for the company had degenerated into a battle of wills, for Flashdash could only be jealous that one of his subordinates had performed so well, which made no sense, for Flashdash would be in his right to claim credit. Perhaps, Robert wondered, it had not been appropriate for him as a junior lieutenant to have mentioned his goal of five rounds a minute, but again he could simply have been agreeing with Flashdash. No, there could be no other explanation, save that perhaps the captain took his love of appearances to a level just short of insane.

But as Robert stood there brooding, another figure

approached, this one on foot, twirling her parasol.

"I have just spoken to Colonel Mudge," she cried, "and he mentioned you by name. It's simply marvellous! So now my personal champion is also the hero of the battalion."

Robert did not want to talk to her now, not after her husband had dealt him such shabby treatment, but he could not be impolite. "Good day, Marion."

She stuck out her lip in mock dejection. "Is that all you have to say? I would have thought you would be aglow with your triumph."

"I should be, but...." He shrugged. He could not tell her that he thought her husband an ass, though as she stood before him, her flawless skin glowing in the sun, he felt his anger lifting. She was happy for him, when she should have been happy for the company commander—for her husband.

"Will you be going to the recital tonight?" she asked him. "At the colonel's? Many of your fellow officers will be there, as they usually are. Yet, we hardly ever have the pleasure of your company!"

Robert had known about the recital, some recent compositions for string quartet, but he avoided such things, even as Rice sought them out. He had not meant to go, and he said so.

"Oh, you must come," Marion insisted, shaking her parasol. "For once, you must."

"All right, then," he said. What was the harm, anyway? He owed himself at least one evening of leisure. "I'll go... if you're going, Marion."

They regarded each other for a moment, not speaking, and then she leaned forward, and he saw her eyes, the clear brown touched with gold. "You should come to celebrate. Your training has borne fruit. After all, do you think the French care if you are wearing hats or not?"

With that she turned away, sparing him just one more glance, one more smile, and he knew he would go to the recital after all. *She knows*, he thought. *She knows what a fool Flashdash can be.* Robert found the contrast strange, almost unfathomable.

"Why did you marry that puffed up shirt?" he murmured, but his only answer came from Flashdash himself, calling his company to stand to, at their guns, to continue the exercise.

*****

The music room at Colonel Mudge's residence was crowded with officers of the artillery and infantry and their guests, an array of deep blue and scarlet, mingling with the pale summer dresses of the ladies. Rows of chairs had been set up, all with dark maroon cushions and gold paint. Robert took a seat third from the back. He had come alone. He spied Rice near the front, two seats away from Flashdash. And there was Marion, on her husband's right.

The recital began. Robert sat with folded arms as the four musicians, each in sky blue livery and powdered wigs, struck up the first movement of Locatelli's "Quartet in C Major." Robert closed his eyes and listened. He had never been terribly interested in music of this sort, though he supposed that was simply an issue of familiarity. Music, for him, had always been a few wooden flutes and fiddles and the raucous singing at the inn, or the martial trill of the fifes and drums. Yet, there was no denying the clear, soothing notes of the strings played together in harmony, even with such a lively piece as this. *Maybe*, he thought after a while, *I should attend these concerts more often, whether Marion invites me or not.*

He opened his eyes, meaning to steal a glance in her

direction. By some trick of timing, she looked back at the same moment. And there was that smile, the same one he had seen at the exercise. One of mischief and anticipation.

He averted his gaze. Suddenly he was unsure of himself, unsure of what he was doing, unsure of why she had insisted that he come tonight. His heart began to race, and as sweat beaded his brow, he closed his eyes again, letting the music wash through him, calming him.

When the piece ended and the applause had died away, he stood with the rest of the audience. He looked for her amid the press of bodies, but she was lost in the sea of colour. When the crowd cleared, she and Flashdash were gone. Robert searched the room, but there was no sign of them.

His shoulders slumped. He had been a fool, mistaken about her intentions. Why had he thought that this was something more than friendship, if it was even that? It was a fantasy, and a dangerous one at that. She had simply been trying to cheer him up in the face of Flashdash's idiotic assessment.

With a sigh, he made to leave, but he had not taken three steps before he found himself facing a footman, dressed very like one of the musicians, in frock coat and wig.

"Lieutenant Saxon?" the footman said.

"Yes."

"A message, sir." The footman held out a silver tray on which rested a single scrap of paper. Robert took it, thanking the man, who bowed and left.

Orders, Robert realized, as he unfolded the note. But the paper smelled faintly of lavender.

The note contained an address in Greenhill. "Meet me here tomorrow, if you can, at three o'clock in the afternoon. If you are not there, I will understand." And the note was signed "M."

He read it over, again and again, to be certain that his eyes were not deceiving him. Three o'clock. The afternoon training would be over at that time. He was not the duty officer, but still, someone would notice if he was not there. Yet, there had to be a way.

The music room was almost empty, and when he realized it, he thrust the note into his breeches pocket and left.

*****

The row of houses was new, each one like the other, red brick with three stories, white window frames, gables in the pitched roofs. Robert hovered on the opposite side of the street. This was not Flashdash's residence, for he lived in quarters closer to the barracks. It must be the house of a friend, or perhaps a relative. That meant at least one other person would know of this liaison, or at least that a liaison has occurred.

He took a series of deep breaths. Why, he asked himself, was he doing this? It was wicked, truly a wicked thing. "Thou shalt not commit adultery," he whispered, but he could no longer control the urgent need, the desire that seemed to drive him on. Though she was not the first woman to catch his eye, he had never known this intense need and had not suspected it existed until this day. But once he had received the note, once Marion had put what was only supposition, a half-imagined dream, into words and deeds, it was as if his passion had become unleashed—growing, doubling and doubling again, so that now he risked his career and his reputation, his sense of what was right. And he did not care.

Flashdash is a damn fool, he told himself. *He doesn't deserve her. He doesn't, and no one will ever know.*

He crossed the street, stepped to the door. A quick glance left and right revealed a few passers-by, including a Royal

Artillery corporal. Robert did not recognize him, but they were close to the Arsenal here, and men from his battalion could be about.

Palms sweating, he grasped the brass lion's head door knocker and rapped three times. He flinched at the unexpected loudness. He had never been so nervous, so sure and unsure of himself at the same time.

The door swung open, though he could not see who opened it. Before him stretched an empty hall, stairs leading up, an open doorway on the right. He stepped inside, sweeping off his cocked hat and thrusting it under his arm.

"I thought you would never cross the street," she said.

He started, head whipping round. There she was, half concealed behind the door, as he should have realized. He gaped at her, catching his breath, for she had never looked so beautiful. Her dress was the pale green of seafoam, the neckline a deep plunging crescent. He wanted to reach out and take her, crush her to him, but not yet, not until he was certain. Absolutely certain.

"I almost didn't cross," he said. "I almost went back to barracks, Mrs. Flushing."

Her soft features clouded. "Don't call me that. Never call me that, Robert."

He nodded, and now he knew that he had been right. He could still stop this, tell her that he could not continue, then simply back out the door and be on his way.

The door swung shut, the latch locking into place. She moved closer, looked up into his eyes. "You're very tall. I have always admired that in you."

"Yes, I inherited my height... from my father."

She placed one hand on his chest, the touch light, but with it, the last shred of Robert's doubt was gone.

"Then won't you come in, my tall young hero?" She led him through the open doorway, and he found himself in a parlour. There were a pair of settees, chairs flanking the cold hearth. The curtains were drawn, the light dim, save for a few candles on the mantel. In the rear of the room a door stood ajar, and beyond it, Robert could see the edge of a full canopy bed.

There was wine and two glasses on a side table. She filled them from a decanter, saying, "This was smuggled through the French lines. Portuguese."

She passed him a glass, and he had to fight to steady his hands as he took it. He almost gulped the smooth liquid down. Madeira.

"There now, you eager thing," she said, her eyes dancing. "Have you ever been alone with a woman before, in her private parlour?"

For some reason her tone made him angry. Did she think him innocent? But he answered with the truth, saying, "Not like this."

"Then we are both in for an adventure," she said, facing him again, and now he saw the light of eagerness there, her cheeks flushed and glowing, and he again, just for a moment, remembered how villainous this was.

But it did not stop him.

*****

Later, the world seemed a different place. He lay on his back, a cool breeze from an open window caressing his skin. She lay close, one arm across his chest. He could smell her hair.

He rolled onto his front, crushing one of the feather pillows. It was perhaps the most comfortable bed he had ever known.

"Does he treat you well?" he asked.

178

She had not wanted to talk about her husband, but her very reluctance had only made him more persistent. He needed to know why this had happened, why she should be so unhappy in marriage, know it in her words rather than from conjecture on his part. At last, she had relented.

"He treats me as he would a piece of furniture," she said, reaching for him and walking her fingers along his spine, toward his neck. "Or one of his family estate's paintings. An attractive vase, or a statue."

"Then you're not happy."

"Oh, but I am! That's what you do not understand. Is that what you wish, for me to be unhappy? I have a rich husband who ignores me, save to do the correct thing by society, and so I am free to engage in... my own pursuits."

"Pursuits," he repeated. He did not like the sound of that—the suggestion that he might not be the only one. "I'm one of your pursuits?"

"Yes, my beautiful boy."

He raised himself on one elbow. "Then I am not special to you. I'm one more adventure? Is that it?"

She touched his nose. "Ah, you are all special to me."

Something turned in his stomach, but he quickly rallied. Perhaps some part of him had dared to think that this might be love, but that was absurd.

But what if I am in love with her? he wondered.

"Do you want to know a secret?" she whispered, her lips close to his right ear.

"Yes," he grunted, swallowing. Deep inside him lay the seeds of anger, anger with her. He struggled to control it. He reminded himself that she had promised him nothing.

"Do you know who my father was?"

"You told me that he was in the cavalry," he said, grateful

for a new topic of conversation. "You said that he was killed in Flanders."

"Ah yes, but did you know that he was a common trooper? A sergeant, for sure, but before that, he had enlisted from the gutter?"

He sat up. "Your father was a sergeant? I had assumed he was an officer."

She shrugged. "Everyone does."

"So how did you... how did you come to know Flashdash? I mean Flushing!"

He coloured at the slip, but she laughed. "Yes, I know what they all call him, and I know his reputation. A hair or line out of place drives him mad. It is a strange compulsion with him, to have perfection. That was what drew him to me, my beauty. His old company, before he began his turn of instruction at the Academy, had been brigaded with the Nineteenth Light Dragoons. My mother had remarried, another sergeant. She had many offers. I was very young when Flashdash first laid eyes on me. He saw a thing of perfection."

She giggled, and he knew that he was frowning. His stomach would not settle.

"Do you think me vain?" she asked him. "It's a simple fact that I am beautiful. It is also a fact that my father believed in the worth of education, for it had been his great salvation. He insisted on respectability, and he doted on us, myself and my sisters. I believe he must have spent every penny he earned on us, determined to make us ladies, or at least to create the illusion, on the surface. And it is the surface my husband adores. I adored him, too, at first, that he took notice, and did not discount me as every other officer in your army had, until then." She sighed. "As I grew to know him better, I discovered that he simply exists on the surface as well. There is very little else to him, or not that I have been able to discover. Even so, he has given me much, comfort and society."

He stared at her. "Whose house is this?"

"One of my sister's. She has come up in the world as well, don't you think? We all three have."

He let his head fall forward onto the pillow. "At least we have one thing in common, Marion."

"And what is that?"

"My father was a sergeant too. In the artillery."

Her eyes widened, then her hand went to her mouth as she laughed, laughed until tears streamed from her eyes and soaked the linen.

*****

"Where have you been?" Mumbles asked that evening when Robert walked into the mess. Robert looked at him, but did not speak. His mind remained elsewhere, burdened with its inability to make sense of the last hours. He could still feel Marion's smooth flesh pressed against his, still breathe her scent, memories that brought nothing but warmth and well being. And yet, as the hours passed, he felt more and more the fool.

How dare I think of love, he thought. *Love is a rare thing, a rare and precious thing.* And he knew that Marion did not love him, that there was no sense in hoping that she ever would, that he had been nothing but one more link in a chain of amusements. Of that he had no doubt, by her own admission.

"I... had an engagement," he told Mumbles, just as the bugle chirped to signal the start of supper.

"What sort of (mumble mumble)?"

"One of a private nature," Robert said as they made their way toward the table. The room was hot, and amidst the blur of blue uniforms, Robert spied Flashdash. The crush of guilt, so sudden and unexpected, almost overpowered him, and he stumbled against his chair.

I have betrayed my captain, he thought, *and perhaps my company.*

But no, he would not pursue such a useless sentiment. The deed was done, and it was too soon to judge how great a mistake it had been, if it were even a mistake at all. He did not regret it, did not regret the memory. He would have to wait and see, and take whatever consequences arose.

The officers took their seats and supper commenced. Robert ate in sullen, self-indulgent silence. The wine had some effect, and the ritual of the proceedings, the serving of the port (smuggled), the Loyal Toasts, toast to the regiment, to their battalion and so on, helped to keep him focused on the immediate. But when there was a pause in the revelry, he was able to only half listen as Mumbles, to his left, did his best to relate some tale of the afternoon's proceedings. Robert supposed the tale was supposed to be funny, for Mumbles concluded with, "Yes, that was a very large fish."

Robert chuckled, as he deemed appropriate.

At the head of the table, Colonel Mudge was rising to his feet, glass in hand. Another toast. Robert took his glass and prepared to join in the chorus of replies.

The colonel did not raise his glass at once but held it in his hand. "Gentlemen," he began, "this battalion has come far in a short time, thanks to your efforts. For that I am truly appreciative, as is our government, and our Army, which as you know, has for some time been preparing an expeditionary force against the enemy."

He paused, and in the expectant hush, Robert gripped his glass in tight fingers, all thoughts of Marion and Flashdash banished for the moment. There was something in the colonel's tone that suggested that such an expeditionary force was in the final stages of planning, and that soon they would join it.

"I have been bursting to relate the contents of orders lately received," Mudge went on, "but the moment is here, and though it will leave most of you disappointed, a select few will rejoice, and all will see that it is an honour for our new battalion to have been considered at all." He cleared his throat, and the assembled officers exchanged glances, some fearful, all hopeful. "I have been ordered to select one company to join a force assembling now in Ireland, originally for the purpose of staging an operation in South America, though the objective has changed. We shall be sending an expeditionary force to Portugal, to assist in the ongoing resistance developing there."

It was as if the room exhaled. There were murmurs, a few men slapped the table. "One company," Rice said, rather too loud, but it was what all of them were thinking, of that Robert had no doubt.

Then a strange calm overtook him, for he knew which company Mudge would select. It would be his, for he had trained his men to fire four rounds a minute; no one else had done that, and the colonel had been impressed.

"I will not keep you in suspense," Mudge added. "That would be the pinnacle of cruelty. I have already made my selection, which was perhaps the most difficult decision of my commission. You are all deserving of a chance to strike a blow at the Corsican tyrant, and in time all of you will have that chance. The operation in Portugal is intended to be long term, for if we are successful there, the liberation of Spain will become our ultimate objective. And I have no doubt that we will be successful."

There were nods and cries of agreement. The temperature

in the room, whether from the candles or the sweat of some forty anxious men, seemed to have increased in the last minutes. If Mudge would stop his pontificating and just tell them....

"Captain Flushing, I congratulate you," Mudge said, at last raising his glass. "Number One Company shall be departing for Ireland at the first opportunity."

The room erupted in cheers, for those not chosen could do nothing else but pretend to be pleased for their comrades who had been.

Robert leaned back and closed his eyes, but Mumbles was slapping his shoulder, and at last Robert faced his comrade and shook his hand. A wide grin lit up Mumbles's face.

Just then, Robert forgot his troubles. He had been in the army for less than a year, and he was going to war.

Chapter Twelve:

Campaign

After that, Marion ignored him. The first time it happened was the morning after Mudge's announcement, when the battalion had been dismissed from Parade and the companies had broken off. Robert was making his way back to his quarters, alone, when he spied her approaching. The grin that burst across his features was involuntary, and he was surprised when she did not return it. In contrast to her usual bright greeting, she looked the other way.

"Good morning," Robert said, stopping and giving his customary salute.

"Good morning, Lieutenant," she said, dipping her eyes as she passed.

He watched her receding back, puzzled. Eventually, he decided that she did not wish to draw attention to their affair. She could not appear too eager in public, he supposed.

Then it happened again. There was a delay of several days, as arrangements were made to transport the company to Ireland, orders and counter-orders flying to and fro, and a supply of new, heavier guns was sought. In that time Robert encountered Marion on the barracks grounds half a dozen times, and each encounter was colder than the last, and with each, the hurt and confusion deepened. Seeing her now never failed to bring that rush of desire, an almost uncontrollable force that left him trembling when she had passed and burning with anger at her sudden indifference.

Finally, the day before the company was scheduled to march down to the Thames and board the transport waiting, he saw her outside his quarters, perhaps on her way to the apartment that she shared with Flashdash. As usual, he touched his hat. She did not acknowledge him.

"Marion," he called, aware that he had raised his voice, that someone might hear and think it odd that a subaltern should so speak to his captain's wife. But he could no longer keep his anger in check.

She stopped, but she did not turn around. Taking a further risk, he moved to plant himself in front of her, stared down into her face. Her eyes remained downcast.

"Why won't you speak to me?" he demanded.

She hesitated, lips working, and at last she said, "Mister Saxon, I do not think it would be wise to continue in this manner."

"Why not?" he cried. "Continue what in what manner?"

"Come now, sir," she murmured, and though there was sympathy in her tone, it was mingled with exasperation. "We have pursued our association to its conclusion, and there is no point in continuing. The thing is done, and that is all. Did you suppose I would leave my husband? I had convinced myself that you understood."

"Did I..." he started to say, then stopped himself. He had been about to ask, "Did I displease you?" But he could not say that, and knew it was not the case anyway. It was exactly as she said. After the long months, the long build-up, the teasing and toying and wondering, they had reached a conclusion.

"It's like a game then," he said. "The common trooper's daughter who wins the officer's affections, again and again?"

Her eyes met his at last, and now they shone like flint. "Please do not accost me again. I would not have your memory sullied by this childish behaviour."

With that she moved on. Her words had stung, and he had no ready reply. He watched until she turned a corner, sensing the darkness, like a black pit at his feet, waiting to swallow him.

"Nothing but a whore," he muttered, but that cruel word tasted bitter, and brought instant remorse. His father had hurled such insults, and Robert had vowed that he never would, that he would never be cruel to anyone. Though it was hard, hard to forgive sometimes.

"I had thought," he began to say, and wondered what he had thought.

Maybe it was a simple matter. He was too easily taken with things of beauty, a smile, a laugh. He had not had enough of such things as a child. Not since the death of his mother.

*****

A steady June rain fell as the company, at last, set out for the Thames. The vanguard marched in a column of fours, while the remainder manned dragropes to transport the guns. The guns were new. Gone were the old six-pounders, replaced by three brass nine-pounders and three five-and-a-half inch howitzers from the Arsenal. There were no draft horses, for those stabled at the barracks would remain there for use by others. Horses would be had in Ireland, along with a company of Royal Artillery drivers.

The single transport vessel, a fat bodied merchantman, was moored hard against the quay, and the troops boarded by a long gangway. The men carried all they needed, muskets and full knapsacks, wooden drum canteens, linen haversacks and wool blankets. The officers had brought a great deal more, including servants and extra baggage. Robert brought his trunk with his good uniforms and his old cadet coat, which he had modified for field service.

The guns were brought on board in pieces, wheels, trails, and barrels disassembled for ease of storage. Sergeant Hunter oversaw the operation, and Robert went to the starboard rail to watch. Amid the melee of shouting, cursing, and straining men, he spied Flashdash still on the quay. Facing the captain was his wife, and the sight of her almost made Robert turn away. Almost—for he had never run from what made him uncomfortable, and he did not see how this was different from anything he had faced at home, school or at the Academy. He made himself look, saw Flashdash take Marion's hands in his. Their smiles spoke of love, though a love Robert knew to be false, at least where Marion was concerned. And if what she had said about her husband was true, then in Flashdash's case his love was the same as that one might have for a fine painting or some other beautiful object.

The couple embraced. As they did, Marion glanced over Flashdash's shoulder, toward the ship. Robert met her eye. She betrayed no recognition, simply stared through him. *This could be the last time I see her*, Robert thought, and for some reason, his heart softened a little, enough for him to say farewell by touching his hat in salute.

She ignored the gesture, turning back to her husband, flicking at the drops of rainwater on the front of his cloak.

Robert was still at the rail when Flashdash came aboard. "Well, a quick and efficient march," the captain said, flashing a smile so cheerful and genuine that, for a moment, Robert could not dislike him. "Let's hope we sail soon."

Robert saluted quickly, then averted his eyes, for his sudden sympathy for Flashdash also brought another wave of shame. He knew that whatever Marion had done, it was he who had also played the villain here, and that would not do, for Robert had always hoped to be something greater, something far greater, than the misguided, frustrated, and brutal man who had raised him.

"Yes, sir," he said, after clearing his throat. "The sooner the better."

It had been a mistake, and one he would not repeat. He could not demand perfection of himself, but he would learn, and he vowed to spare no more time with thoughts of Marion Flushing, especially now that the long-looked-for campaign was underway at last.

*****

A day out from England, and the air was brisk, clean after the summer heat on land. This was the first time Robert had been to sea, the first time he had set foot on the heaving deck of a ship, the first time he had felt the salt wind in his face. He had heard and read much about the supposed music of the sails and rigging, of the freedom of being far from land, romantic notions he supposed, for he found it all made little impression on him. He was not seasick, and for that he was thankful, but otherwise the journey was a means to an end. The quicker they arrived in Ireland the better.

Below him in the waist, the company had just dismissed, the men sweating despite being garbed only in shirts and breeches. Sergeant Hunter had taken them through a series of physical exercises of his own devising. Another of the sergeant's notions, though having witnessed it, Robert decided that it had been a useful way to pass the time.

"Let me guess, Sergeant," he said, as Hunter came toward the larboard gangway. "This sort of evolution is good for their circulation."

Hunter squinted up at him. "Can't have the men cooped up below all day, sir. Not healthy, sir."

Robert sighed. "I have to agree with you."

Hunter said nothing more, but remained at attention, grinning his strangely foolish grin. Of course, he could not go until Robert dismissed him, but Robert folded his hands behind his back, searching for something else to say. He had grown to like Hunter, or rather respect him for his opinions and his competence, his experience. They seemed to work well together, but even so, Robert did not feel he truly knew the man. Not beyond his obvious eccentricities.

"What do you think of our new ordnance, Sergeant?" he finally asked.

Hunter shrugged. "Nine-pounders are first rate, sir. I like a heavier weight of metal than six pounds. Although the howitzers trouble me. Would have appreciated some time training with them, sir."

Robert nodded, for he also did not know what to think of the howitzers. Their principal use was to fire explosive shells in an arching trajectory, and he had not had much experience with them at the Academy. They were strange looking little things, no more than two feet in length, and mounted on the old double-bracket carriage, which was heavier and less moveable than the new carriage with the single block trail.

"They may come in handy with the Shrapnel shell," Robert suggested.

"True, sir, true, but that's not what worries me, you see. It takes some knowing to place a shell on target. Our lads will have to learn the hard way."

That was correct, and the core of the worry. It made no sense, on the eve of war, to give the company a weapon they had never used before. "Hopefully we'll have some time to work on the things in Cork."

"I hope so, sir. I hope so. Now here's Lieutenant Campion, sir."

Hunter saluted as Mumbles approached along the gangway. Robert almost said, "Hello Mumbles," but checked himself in time, offering just the word of greeting instead.

"May I be dismissed, sir?" Hunter said. "Would like to get aloft. Good for my joints. The altitude, you see, sir."

Robert hid his disappointment, for he had hoped to continue the conversation. "Of course."

A moment later, Robert watched as Hunter scrambled up the ratlines like a born sailor. "Like he's done this a thousand times," he remarked to Mumbles.

"Seeking to get closer to heaven," Mumbles said.

Robert looked at him. "What?"

Mumbles shrugged and looked uncomfortable. "Those men in the rigging. Seeking (mumble mumble) to God."

Robert leaned on the railing as the ship began to heel leeward. "I had not taken you for a religious sort, Mumbles. Not more so than the rest of us, that is."

Mumbles brushed a strand of hair from his broad forehead, tucking it under the brim of his cocked hat. "Actually, my parents greatest wish was for me to enter the clergy, but (mumble mumble), and perhaps I was not cut out to be an orator, or one who gives sermons."

Robert suppressed a chuckle. "Then it would have been the Reverend Mumbles."

The run of water along the hull of the ship gurgled and hissed. Gulls followed in their passage, and Mumbles pointed.

"There's a black back, and a few herring gulls.   They ply between here and North America.   I believe I should do some sketches." He grunted. "Well, here comes our supposed second captain."

Now, Rice was coming toward them along the gangway. Mumbles locked his fingers together and studied the gulls. Robert touched his hat and said, "Good morning, Lieutenant Rice," keeping his tone respectful if not welcoming.

"Good morning," Rice said. There was a hint of a smile on his lips.   "I have just learned that we shall most likely be quartered in tents when we get to Cork. We're to stay in camp outside the city.   Not nearly enough barracks space for an army."

"Tents," Robert repeated, a little suspicious, for this was small talk, something Rice did not engage in with either himself or Mumbles. "I suppose that will be something to put in a letter home."

Rice's smile became a smirk.   "I'm surprised you write letters home, Saxon."

"Oh, and why is that?"

Rice waved his hand, and the smirk did not leave his face. "Oh, things you have said."

Robert leaned back on the rail. Even when he tried to be agreeable, Rice was insulting. "And who do you write to, Rice?"

Rice shrugged. "Well, the king, of course. To whom do you think? I write to my sisters and my parents."

"And I trust they enjoy your letters."

"Yes, yes, of course they do. I say, Mumbles, do you mind if I have a word with Lieutenant Saxon here?"

Mumbles eyed him, and Robert thought he saw the briefest flicker of malice, of pure hatred. Then he simply gave one curt shake of his chin and strolled away along the gangway, hands still locked in front of him.

"What's this, then?" Robert said, for now he knew that Rice was up to something. Robert had no doubt that he could deal with it, though, whatever it might be.

Rice folded his arms and turned his gaze toward the blue horizon. "I observed something curious last week. Something curious indeed. Are you well acquainted with Captain Flushing's wife?"

Robert felt his muscles stiffen. "Of course."

Rice was stroking his chin. "They say she is low born, that she came from the gutter, and old Flashdash passes her off as a lady." He lowered his voice to a whisper. "They even say that she is altogether too friendly with some of the other officers on the station."

Robert did not hide his disgust. He had no use for this sort of talk, and even though everything Rice had said was true, it was still gossip, and too close to home. "Who says these things? And why are you repeating them to me, insulting our captain's wife? I swear you're trying to bait me into something."

"Not me, old chum. It's just that I wondered if you knew."

"And why should it matter if she's low born? We're Royal Artillery officers, and we don't purchase our commissions. Some of us are, no doubt, low born as well."

Rice chuckled. "Yes, that's true. Very true indeed, and it reminds me of my next point, which you will find interesting. I was strolling along a street in Greenhill one day, when I happened to see a door open, and a certain low born officer emerge onto the step. I recognized him and recognized the woman hovering in the doorway."

Rice paused, as if waiting for a reaction. Robert struggled to control his shock, to keep his face impassive, but he felt the blood rushing in his ears. Suddenly he found himself on the verge of panic. Had he been found out, or was Rice bluffing? And if the latter, how did he know enough to bluff? Robert thought back quickly, trying to remember if anyone had been in the street when he had left Marion's sister's. He had been careful on entering the house, but on leaving, his head had been a whirl. It was possible that he did not even look. He may even have kissed her on the doorstep.

"What are you talking about?" he said.

Rice sneered. "Oh, come now, Saxon. I saw you, standing there with her. I've seen how you moon after her around the barracks."

"Half the lads in our academy mooned after her!"

"But not like you, stopping and taking off your hat at every chance. I know what you're up to, and I know that she is capable, as well. It's true, what I said, at least according to my father. The Royal Artillery is still a small corps, and secrets are not easily kept. Flashdash may not see what his peach of a bride gets up to, but everyone else does."

Robert's hands balled into fists. "You disgust me."

"You disgust me more! Just remember that I know, and all it will take is an interview with our captain, who, I suspect, is not as ignorant as he pretends, and you will be out of this battalion."

"Ah, so now you're threatening me?"

Rice grinned. "I would wait for an appropriate time, of course. I won't jeopardize the operations of the brigade. Not in theatre. Though one never knows what can happen."

Robert leaned close to speak almost into Rice's ear. "You've already jeopardized the operations of this brigade. I've done everything I can to work with you, to forget about our past. This isn't the schoolyard, you bloody bastard. I've offered olive branch after olive branch, and you have refused to take them.

Now this! And we're supposed to work together as brother officers? You're a treacherous dog. I should kill you after all, call you out and put a pistol ball through your brain."

Rice recoiled slightly, but quickly mastered himself. "I would fight you, and gladly, if it were possible, but I'm your second captain, and you cannot challenge me."

"How convenient for you, to have your rank to hide behind."

At that Rice flushed red. "I'll have you up on charges, any more talk like that!"

"My word against yours," Robert said. "Not enough evidence, sir. Not enough."

He would listen to no more of this, would not continue this conversation. He turned his back, pivoting on his heel, remembering to salute before he did, the briefest touch of his hat. Rice did not try to stop him, only chuckled, and Robert suddenly felt his knees weaken. He walked a few paces, but in an instant, the world had changed again. All it took was a moment. Rice had found his revenge, had placed a bayonet of another kind to Robert's throat, and Robert had given him the means. He had made a mistake, committed a sin, joining the ranks of the fools and bastards that he condemned.

I could kill him anyway, Robert thought. *Beat him senseless. Put a pistol to his head. Toss him overboard.* Yes, he could throw him overboard, and it would appear an accident.

He was sweating, almost shivering, his teeth grinding together. One sin did not require another, he reminded himself. He was no murderer. He would find a way to deal with this as a soldier, as a gentleman. Rice had no proof, and Robert had admitted nothing. Rice was simply trying to provoke him.

He would not rise to it, would do nothing more to endanger

himself.

One day, he vowed, he would be out of the reach of tyrants and fools who had control over him. One day, he would be a colonel, a general, and return to England a man to be reckoned with. Promotion in the artillery was slow, but not so slow in war.

Rice would not win this game.

*****

They made Cork the following day. Theirs was one of the last units to join the growing army, an army cobbled together from the four winds. As Rice had predicted, there was no accommodation left in town, and there were only enough tents for the officers. Most of the men were required to bivouac in the open. The battery of six guns was placed on the edge of the camp line, silent and still, without means of transport.

"We will receive our horses tomorrow morning," Flashdash told his assembled officers. "I have been to see Colonel Robe, and he tells me that he has had some trouble with the procurement, but the Irish commissaries have found suitable numbers. Our horses are to arrive with Captain's Tunge's company from the Drivers. I am familiar with Captain Tunge, and consider him more reliable than most officers of that much maligned corps. We must have patience, gentlemen."

"Any word on when we are to depart for Portugal, sir?" Rice asked. "Are we to remain here long?"

Flashdash sat back in his canvas camp chair, the wood creaking under his spare weight. His face was in shadow, for the walls of his marquee tent were turned down, and no lantern was lit, despite the gloom of the day. "That, at least, I am able to tell you. It will be days, gentlemen, not weeks. We have arrived here at the last minute, with this army ready to embark at a word. Tomorrow morning, before the horses are due to arrive, we Parade with Colonel Robe and the other three brigades that make up the artillery contingent. It may be our only Parade together before we again take ship."

"Who is the commanding officer?" Robert asked. "The general in command, that is, sir?"

"Fellow named Wellesley. Arthur Wellesley." Flashdash made a sour face. "An Irishman, and one of these Indian officers, made his name fighting half naked savages, though I understand he also commanded the recent land operations outside Copenhagen." He sighed. "We shall see."

Officers who had made their name campaigning in India were for some reason despised in the Army, though the thought gave Robert some comfort. "He will have seen action, sir. No doubt handled troops in battle."

"That is so. We must remain hopeful, mustn't we?" The captain brushed at his right knee, then looked at Robert. He pursed his lips. "Well, I will see you all at tomorrow's Parade, gentlemen. Till then, you are dismissed, though if you would be so good to remain for a moment, Lieutenant Saxon?"

The others shuffled away, ducking through the tent flap. Robert remained in place.

Flashdash stood, folding his hands behind his back, and glared down his long nose. "I will not have you appear in my quarters again with such filthy boots. Of my three subalterns, you were the only one who had not bothered to tidy himself. It is not acceptable."

Robert had spent the morning seeing to the placement of the camp while the others had busied themselves solely with their own baggage. He had still been engaged in his duties when the officer's call had sounded. Flashdash knew that, and yet... this.

"Yes, sir," Robert said slowly. There was no other response possible. An excuse would only make him appear weak or petulant. "I understand."

Flashdash brightened. "Good, then. I strongly suggest you find yourself a personal servant. You are the only officer I know without one. It's expected, you realize, and necessary."

"I've been looking, sir," Robert said, which was an exaggeration. He had been reluctant to hire a servant, for he did not know the men well enough and did not have time to undertake interviews, so engrossed was he in gun drill and training. And there was also the fact that he would have to pay the man.

"I'm glad to hear it. That was the main point I wished to make, actually. Yes. That is all."

"Thank you, sir," Robert said.

He left the tent shaking his head. "That bloody fool," he muttered, though in truth he was puzzled. There had been no point to Flashdash's admonishment.

Mumbles was waiting for him, standing with one foot forward, his sword dangling at a crooked angle. He looked ridiculous with his slouched, unmilitary figure, the cocked hat seeming far too large for his small, round head. Yet his shoes were clean, so to Flashdash he must have looked the very picture of neatness.

"I have a good bottle of port," Mumbles said. "Proper Portuguese, too."

Robert did not feel much like celebrating. "I still have some work to do, Mumbles."

"What work? You (mumble mumble) and we won't be here long enough for it to matter!"

Robert hesitated. He stared about him, but what he saw did nothing to dispel his ill mood. This was the greatest number of men he had ever seen together in one place, and it should have been something to behold, but instead it seemed motley, a confused tangle of disparate units, fraught with supply problems, such as the delay in the arrival of the artillery's horses.

"We have to be better prepared," he said.

"What more can you do? You (mumble) work harder than any of us. I think you're trying to prove something, that you're better than Rice, better than everyone. The company is in good hands; we're ready for whatever orders we receive, at least for the time being. Forget your worries and have a drink."

Robert had never heard such a speech out of Mumbles, nor his voice raised to such a steady pitch, and that, at last, was enough to make him smile. Perhaps Mumbles was feeling it too, the sense of impending disaster. He seemed in desperate need of company and good cheer.

"All right. All right, I'll have that drink."

Their quarters were a bell tent they shared. Once there, Robert sat on his trunk and said nothing as Mumbles busied himself with the bottle and a pair of glasses. When the dark liquid was in his hand, he sipped. It was warm and very smooth.

"What sort of company are we?" he said after a minute. "I mean the officers, not the other ranks. You're a good sort, Mumbles. You take things as they come and do your duty without complaint. You're not like Rice, in other words. I've tried my best, but he keeps at it like we're still at the Academy, and here we are, on the eve of war, and we're supposed to rely on each other."

Mumbles drained his glass and poured another. "Rice is an idiot."

"Yes, and our captain is weak, which may be worse. He

doesn't see the danger. All he cares about is shiny guns and shiny boots."

"You should not say such things."

Robert knew that was so, that to question his commander was to undermine his authority and thus erode discipline, but he did not think his words would make the situation any worse. "It's true, and you know it. Luckily, we have good NCOs."

He drained his glass. The wine was sweet but burned a little going down. He fought a deeper swell of melancholy, a sense of dashed hopes. Nothing was how he had wanted it, and now he was about to leave the British Isles and sail to a foreign land, perhaps never to return.

"We have to trust in men like Hunter," he murmured. "... and men like this General Wellesley, whoever he is. There may be opportunities ahead. I have to believe that."

Mumbles refilled Robert's glass. "I never worry about the future. There's no point."

Outside the tent there sounded the rumbling of wagon wheels, and the marching feet of many men, a company of infantry passing.

"Yes, that's right," Robert said. "That's good advice."

The future, he supposed, could only be an improvement on the past.

Chapter Thirteen:

Powder

An army on the move. Some fifteen thousand British troops and twenty-five guns, a long baggage train of mules and wagons. Robert was a part of it, part of this machine of war, this column of redcoats, blue coats, green jacketed riflemen, and drab civilians. It was small, as armies go, but still the column stretched for miles along the dusty strip of road, winding south between low, sloping hills that were clad in green and dotted with houses and outbuildings of white plaster. The guns rolled along in front of each infantry brigade, each led by two horses but drawn mainly by lumbering oxen. Many, if not most, of the Irish horses, broken down and sick, had perished on the voyage to Portugal, so Colonel Robe had been forced to purchase whatever was available locally. He reserved the best horses for the artillery officers to ride.

Robert shaded his eyes as he gazed at the seared blue of the sky. He would not have thought such a sky possible and could not keep from staring. Though he suspected that, if he stared too long, he would go blind from the glare.

"Damn this dust," Rice said, slapping at his breeches. "And damn this heat."

Robert said nothing, though for him, the heat was as

unexpected and unfamiliar as the sky. Sweat had already stained his collar and the band of his cocked hat, and he was covered in dust. This was a land of dust, dust coating everything, and a dry heat he had never thought possible, like the inside of an oven. It was a land unfit for Englishmen, but even so, the army was pushing south with all possible speed. The fleet from Cork had bypassed Biscay and its storms, landing on August 9 at a place called Figueira da Foz. The guns and remaining horses had come ashore on rafts, an operation supervised by the sailors and sergeants and done with smooth efficiency. Once the army had assembled, they had at once headed south for Lisbon. That was their objective, as Robert understood it, for once the capital city of Portugal was safe in British hands, the liberation of the entire country would not be far off.

They had made good progress. This General Wellesley intended to waste no time, it seemed.

*****

Batalha was a small town—little more than a village—a cluster of simple white houses surrounding a massive medieval abbey. The abbey was a tangle of sharpened turrets and steeples, rows of towering Gothic windows, a more ornate place of worship than any found in England, even in the great cities. St. Paul's in London seemed a simple church by comparison.

"The French have only just left," Flashdash said, his saddle creaking as he turned to face his subalterns. The brigade had just turned off the road, having found a suitable place to bivouac. Already Captain Tunge's drivers were parking the guns and unhitching the snorting, groaning oxen. Here and there on the ground were circular black patches of ash, some still smouldering, evidence of another army's recent occupation. "The fires are still hot."

"Frightened of us, no doubt," Rice said. "They're too used to fighting a rabble, not a disciplined force, such as ours."

He glanced at Robert with a mocking grin as he spoke, as if to suggest that Robert was undisciplined, reckless, an opinion Rice had held for some time. But it was discipline alone that prevented Robert from smashing Rice's face that very instant, just as it was discipline that prevented him from smashing Rice's face, every waking minute they were together. The darkness was hovering, whispering in his ear, exhorting him to destroy his enemy – for that was what Rice had become – and have done with it. Still Robert resisted, though he hated Rice all the more for bringing this inner struggle, for forcing him to face and acknowledge this part of his nature.

Did my father, he wondered, *struggle with this all his life? Did he suffer the command of fools while he was a sergeant, giving in only years later, when mother died?*

Robert would never give in.

The men had marched beside the guns, a few riding on the limbers, on the carriages and oxen, and now they were breaking into their messes, small groups who piled arms and started searching for firewood. The tents had not caught up, and they would sleep in the open, but the air would be warm and there was no danger of rain. On the road, a regiment of cavalry in blue and yellow cantered past, a Portuguese regiment, one of several that had joined Wellesley's force. The Portuguese troops were an assortment of patched together units, the remnants of an army defeated in the winter, which had held on and risen again to score some small victories against French outposts. Robert had no idea how many they were, nor to what use Wellesley would put them. That was not his concern, for his duty lay with his guns, and his men.

Captain Tunge's drivers had established a picket line for the horses. Robert dismounted, handing his reins to a farrier, who led the horse away. Flashdash had also dismounted, and said, "Lieutenant Saxon, I require an accounting of our ammunition after the march. We shouldn't wish to have lost anything since landing. I also wish to have a fatigue party polish the guns. They are beginning to tarnish after all this exposure to the sea air."

Robert hesitated. "Shouldn't we let them tarnish, sir?"

The captain looked horrified. "Why should we do that?"

"They'll make less obvious targets for the enemy, sir, in the sunshine."

Flashdash recoiled as if from a bad smell. "We will not hide ourselves! We will announce our presence, Lieutenant, to these damned Frogs. Dazzle the enemy. As Mister Rice has said, we are no rabble."

Robert chewed his lip. Flashdash already thought him reckless, and that meant the captain was less inclined to listen to his suggestions. Yet, this was simply too important an issue. This was their lives at stake. "With respect, sir, the other artillery brigades have not polished their new guns. Ours will be the only ones visible in the sun, and the ones most likely to draw fire and to take casualties, sir."

"I don't care what the other brigades are doing. We must look respectable." Flashdash waved his hand. "The smoke of battle will conceal us from the enemy."

That was possible, but not if there was any sort of wind. "Why risk it, sir? If our duty is to destroy the enemy, why make it easier for them to destroy us?"

"Do you preach duty to me, Lieutenant?" Flashdash snapped. "Need I remind you that until recent months, you were a gentleman cadet under my command? My orders stand,

and any more protest from you, I will consider insubordinate."

Robert opened his mouth, but quickly shut it, knowing that further argument would do no good. The anger rose in him, and with no outlet, he simply boiled. It was an effort to speak two simple words: "Yes, sir."

Flashdash slapped at the arms of his coat with a glove that had once been white. "There must be something we can do about this dust," he said, changing the subject as a means to let Robert know the previous matter was closed. "I shall have to have all my kit brushed down tonight."

"I'll have the men brush their coats, sir," Robert suggested, with just a hint of mockery.

Flashdash suddenly smiled, as if gratified that Robert was finally learning. "Yes, yes. They must do their best to keep up proper appearances."

As the captain rode off, Robert could only look at the surrounding trappings of war, of men and guns, horses, oxen, mules. He could smell the animals, and the dust. This would prove to be a great deal of work, and dirty work at that.

In the road, a battalion of redcoat infantry were marching, muskets sloped on their left shoulders. The white lace around the buttons on the front of their coats resembled exposed ribs, like some harbinger of their doom.

*****

The brigade ammunition wagons were parked next to the guns. There were a dozen vehicles piled high with barrels of powder and stacks of shot, wooden crates of grape and the new Shrapnel bursting shell. Robert held a stub of pencil as he counted powder barrels, checking them against his manifest. He was halfway through when he stopped, leaning against one of the wagons. The smell of wood smoke was heavy around him, for the men had begun to cook their rations. Robert wondered if the ammunition had been stored far enough away from the campfires, and if not, what could be done about it.

He started pounding one fist against the side of the wagon. Frustration seamed to spill from every pore, and there was nothing he could do to stop it. Damn Rice and his games! Damn Flashdash! Damn him and his hatred of dirty boots, his dust and his shiny guns!

"Something wrong, sir?" a voice said, and he turned to see Hunter standing there, leaning on his sergeant's spontoon—a short polearm that was the symbol of a senior non-commissioned officer. The three white chevrons on the sergeant's right arm seemed to glow in the dying light of evening.

"No," Robert said, speaking around clenched teeth. How could he tell a sergeant that most of his officers were bloody fools?

"Powder all accounted for, sir?"

"Yes," Robert said. It was an automatic response, for he had not actually finished his account. He looked back at the wagon he had just passed and added, "No, Sergeant. Not yet."

He resumed the task, counting powder barrels, the simple act of concentration helping him forget his troubles for a moment. When he was done, he started counting shot. With that finished, he stared at his manifest. There were discrepancies.

"This doesn't match," he said to Hunter. "We're twenty barrels short of powder." Twenty barrels, almost two thousand pounds of powder. "And two crates of Shrapnel." He checked his manifest again and reread some of the notes he had made the previous day. No, they definitely did not add up.

Hunter showed his teeth. "Drivers, sir."

Robert counted the number of transport wagons. They were all there, so it could not be that he had missed one. He faced Hunter. "The drivers?"

Hunter seemed more amused than concerned. "Drivers look after the wagons, mount sentries on them. They will be skimming it off, sir. Selling it to the Portugee, more than likely."

Robert had heard talk that the Corps of Royal Artillery Drivers lacked discipline, but to undermine the capabilities of one's own army seemed tantamount to sabotage and treason, and he would not believe it without proof. "Are you saying our drivers are stealing our ammunition and selling it for personal profit?"

Hunter made that little chuckle deep in his throat. "No doubt, sir. Seen it before. They ought to be investigated, if you say there's discrepancies, sir. Find the culprits, teach 'em a lesson, if need be, sir."

Robert sighed. It was one more thing, one more thing to deal with. Could anyone in this army be trusted?

He made a quick count of barrels and Shrapnel again, but the result was the same. "Well," he said. "Then I'll investigate."

Hunter jutted one thumb toward a single tent at the end of the row of wagons. At the moment, it was the only tent in the camp. "Captain Tunge had that set himself, sir. Now, what's he need a tent for? Stores are kept in the wagons."

Robert studied the tent. It was a small marquee.

"I'll take this to Captain Flushing," he said. He would do this properly, through the chain of command. The military system was a good one in his estimate, and only failed when its people failed it. He would give it a chance. "Then he can address this with Captain Tunge."

Hunter nodded, but something in his face fell. It was just for an instant, but Robert saw it, and he realized that Hunter had the measure of Flashdash, and he did not trust him either. "It's the proper thing to do," Robert added. "The captain ordered the manifest check, and doubtless, he will have a solution to this problem."

"Of course, sir."

Robert sighed. "One more thing, Sergeant. Have the men polish the gun barrels. Captain's orders. However, see that they don't do their best job. Just have them at it and have them dust off their clothing as best they can."

Hunter put his hands behind his back. "We'll be the smartest brigade in the army, sir. Do you think the French will ask us to dance?"

Robert stared at the sergeant, for this was not proper talk. But somehow, he found himself smiling, and some of his frustration ebbed. Hunter knew. He understood, and he was letting Robert in on it.

"I hope not," he said. "I hope the French find us plain, and so pass us by."

*****

Flashdash had found a billet in an airy cube of a house with white plastered walls and a red tile roof. There were other officers there, scarlet and gold infantry from Brigadier General Fane's brigade, cramming the rooms and hallways. Flashdash had a small chamber to himself. The room had been a study, its walls lined with books. There was a wooden chair and a desk, but no bed.

"How may I be of service, Lieutenant?" Flashdash said.

Robert lingered in the doorway. The smell of the study was

so like his father's that the old memories came flooding back, just for an instant. Then he remembered his purpose.

"Sir, there is an issue with the ammunition manifest," he said. "Twenty barrels of gun powder are unaccounted for, and two crates of Shrapnel's shells, sir."

Flashdash was sitting in the single chair, and he suddenly braced himself with his feet, wide planted on the floor, his hands gripping his knees. His face seemed to expand in his astonishment. "Well, that won't do. That won't do at all!"

Robert explained his suspicions concerning the drivers, and their strange tent. "Colour Sergeant Hunter seems certain," he added, for Hunter's experience carried weight. Or so Robert thought.

Flashdash looked at the floor and twisted his hands together. "Colour Sergeant Hunter? A good man, Lieutenant, but hardly one to judge the integrity of an officer! No, no, this is completely out of order. I have been brigaded with Captain Tunge before, prior to my appointment to the Academy, and he is most reliable."

Robert supposed he should have been surprised by this reaction, but he was not. He was also prepared to defend his case, to not give up so quickly. "Maybe it's not the fault of Captain Tunge, but one of his sergeants."

"No, no. We cannot pursue such a line of thinking. We have had trouble with the drivers in the past; that is true, but I cannot accuse Mister Tunge or anyone under his command of corruption. Not without proof, and we are not here to be catching thieves, Mister Saxon. We are here to fight the French. We must have cooperation amongst ourselves."

"However, the fact remains...."

"The fact remains that we are responsible for our ammunition, not the drivers. We cannot go blaming others."

Flashdash drummed his fingers on the desk, and Robert saw pain there behind his eyes. Disappointment, perhaps self blame. "Yes, we are responsible. I am responsible, and I will deal with it, Lieutenant. Thank you. That will be all."

As before, Robert started to say something more, but again he stopped. There was no use. Flashdash would do nothing, so Robert would have to solve the problem himself. If proof was all that was required, he would find it.

"Right, then, sir," he said, "I've taken up enough of your time."

Flashdash stood. "Not at all. This is an important matter. I will see you in the morning, Lieutenant."

*****

"When I was a boy at school," Robert said, "and we were having trouble with another boy, it was generally no use to go fetch a teacher or the headmaster. You dealt with it yourself, discreetly."

"Now, I never went to school, sir," Hunter said, "but that sounds like a good lesson."

Hunter had assembled a guard of six men. They had halted outside the store tent at the end of the line of wagons, muskets at the port, bayonets fixed. The sky was rapidly growing dark, and Robert had not brought a torch. Not near the ammunition.

He turned to the corporal who was right marker of the guard. "Corporal Foster?"

"Fosten, sir," the man said.

Damn, Robert thought. *I have to get to know the names of the men.* Why did he not know their names by now? "Corporal Fosten, have your men secure this tent. The sergeant and I are going to have a look."

The corporal brought his firelock to the advance and

slapped the whitened sling in salute. "Sir."

The gunners surrounded the tent, facing outward. Over amongst the line of campfires where the drivers had bivouacked, Robert thought he saw a stirring, a few heads turned toward his party.

"Come on, Sergeant," he said.

He threw back the tent flap. There was little light, just the filtered glow of twilight through the canvas, but it was enough to make out the bulk of barrels and crates. To one side of the tent flap was a small camp desk, covered in papers, and a folding stool.

Robert crouched by the barrels, and when his eyes had adjusted, he saw that Hunter had been right. The markings on the barrel heads were distinct. "FG," fine grain powder, in red lettering. High quality cannon grade. And the crates contained the missing Shrapnel shells.

"The brazen bastards," he said. To steal from their own men and hide it in plain sight. It was either brilliant or clumsy. Maybe the former, if Captain Tunge was behind it and had guessed that Flashdash would not confront him.

"Let's tear down this tent," Robert snarled. "Then secure this in the wagons."

Someone shouted outside, "Get out of my way, who do you think you are?" Robert rose to his feet, hand straying to the hilt of his sword. When the tent flap opened, the figure that entered was all shadow, but Robert recognized Tunge by his stubby build, much like a barrel himself.

"What is the meaning of this?" the driver captain shouted. "Who has placed a guard on my tent?"

"There will be worse in a moment, sir," Robert said with unconcealed contempt. The rage in him was building, and no thought of caution entered his head. Tunge was a superior officer, but save for Hunter, they were alone together.

Tunge stepped forward. Behind him, Hunter moved to block the tent entrance. "Who are you, you damned subby?" Tunge cried. "I'll have you out of the Army for this!"

Robert did not hesitate. Surprise was key here. He drew his slim sword, his father's gift, with a hiss, at the same time grabbing Tunge by the front of his coat. Tunge had no time to react, and just let himself be forced back to collide with the camp desk, knocking it flying with a crash and a spill of papers. Tunge stumbled over the wreckage, tripping and falling. Robert was on top of him, pressing his blade against the man's neck.

"You're a traitor, sir! A traitor to the men of this army! How dare you threaten me?"

Tunge gurgled something, then said, "Damn you for a madman, I'll have you arrested...."

"I am a madman, sir, and I'll slit your throat if you give me the opportunity." He put more pressure on the blade, slowly squeezing. Tunge made a squeaking sound in his throat, like a frightened child. It would be easy, so easy, to rid the world of this disgusting creature. Robert could hear the man's heart beat, smell the fear, the sweat. The fellow was a coward at heart, a sneak and a cheat. "I'll speak and you'll listen. You'll listen. My men are going to place this stolen material back in the wagons where it belongs, and they are going to stand guard day and night. You will not object or interfere, unless you wish to face a court martial. Is that understood, sir?"

The other officer slowly nodded. Under the tent flap, Hunter chuckled.

"I won't bother to report you to the brigade headquarters," Robert added, "because I dislike the thought of having to bear witness. I prefer direct action, sir. From now on, if you or any of your men so much as touches a handspike, or if so much as a tompion goes missing, I still won't report it. I'll simply kill you, because it will have been your doing. I'll kill you and find some way to blame it on the enemy. Do you understand me?"

Again, the nod. Robert released the pressure on the sword; sat back. "Now get out," he commanded.

Tunge scrambled to his feet. In the darkness, Robert imagined a flash of crooked teeth, like fangs. Then Tunge was brushing past Hunter and into the night.

"No doubt, he'll cooperate," Robert said.

Hunter was nodding. "That should do the trick. You're a quick study, then, sir."

The remark should have been an insult, coming from a sergeant to an officer, but Robert said, "I'll take that as a compliment."

He sheathed his sword but let his hand rest upon the bone grip. The act was done, finished, and suddenly he was weary and sick to his stomach. He had not planned this; had just seized the opportunity upon Tunge's entrance, but it had been dangerous. The darkness had loomed large, and with it had come the rage, the need to strike, to press home the attack. He had so wanted to kill Tunge.

"Maybe this is war," he murmured. Maybe he was not the only one who struggled. "Will it make savages of us all?"

He had not meant for Hunter to hear him, but the sergeant said, "War just brings out who we are, sir. Brings out what's always there."

That was no comfort, but Robert could not argue with the sergeant's assessment. "Let's hope that we remember that we're men."

Then he was moving off, barking at Corporal Fosten. Within minutes, the tent was struck and the barrels were rolling across the stony ground, back to the wagons.

214

Chapter Fourteen:

Pursuit

Somewhere, battle was joined. From the green hazy hills came a distinct pop-popping, the telltale sound of musketry, although sharper, higher pitched than Robert had heard before. Perhaps it was the dry air but whatever the cause, the sound could only mean that the enemy was close. The British advance guard must have engaged elements of the French rearguard.

"So soon," Robert whispered. It seemed that the army had just landed, and here fighting had already commenced. A larger engagement seemed imminent.

He turned in his saddle to look back along the column, back at the guns with their fresh coating of that day's dust, dampening the hated gleam of bronze. Behind the guns rumbled the train of wagons filled with ammunition, fodder for the horses and oxen, officer's baggage, the mobile forge and farrier's stores, spare carriages and wheels, a wagon of tools. Most of the wagons bore gunners who did not wish to march, reclining on the crates and barrels, though a few squads still trudged along the verge of the road. Following the wagons was a brigade of infantry, three battalions of redcoats marching in fours, snaking back along the road. Robert knew it would take time to deploy this strung-out force into a line of battle.

The distant popping came again. Robert shaded his eyes, but he could see nothing, just more redcoats, these ones snaking forward, their vanguard disappearing into clouds of dust and heat haze. Somewhere up there was General Wellesley, riding at the head of his army. Robert had caught only a few glimpses of him, a slim, upright figure in a plain blue coat and unadorned hat. Now and then, it was said, he would ride ahead of the cavalry scouts to see the lay of the land himself. Robert liked that, a general who did not hide in the rear behind his troops. He hoped the rumours were true.

The sky was that vivid blue again, the few mares' tail clouds a reminder that there was such a thing as rain. Sweat trickled down Robert's face from the brim of his shako, which he wore in place of his cocked hat, the bill offering better shade for the eyes. Mumbles was beside him, sitting at ease in the saddle, more at home with horses than humans. Rice and Flashdash were just ahead.

"I wonder who is shooting?" Mumbles said.

"Rifles," Robert suggested, referring to the new specialist corps of Riflemen, troops who ranged ahead in loose skirmish order, forming a screen in front of the main army. They carried the Baker rifle, a far more accurate and longer ranging weapon than the standard smoothbore musket. It was the job of the Rifles to harass the enemy, to choose targets of opportunity such as enemy officers, opposing Light Infantry, even artillerymen. Rifles fought in pairs and utilized what cover they could, which was why they wore green and black instead of the more conspicuous scarlet and white.

"The Rifles are in front of the army," Robert added, "so it must be them. Or cavalry scouts, or both."

The firing seemed to have built to a crescendo, but then it suddenly ceased. Neither Robert nor Mumbles spoke. Robert listened to the creak and rumble of wheels, the jangle of trace chains, snorting of horses, lowing of the ridiculous oxen, and the rattle of the accoutrements dangling from every marching man.

After a few minutes, an officer came riding back along the column from the front, his horse weaving in and out of the traffic. Robert recognized the blue of the artillery and realized that the man was Colonel Robe himself, commander of General Wellesley's artillery. The Colonel made for Flashdash and turned his horse to ride beside him.

"Good morning, sir," Flashdash said, raising his cocked hat.

Robe looked to be about fifty years old, his face hard and weathered, his hair pulled into a queue at his neck. He also wore his cocked hat the old way, athwart ships instead of fore and aft. He touched its brim and said, "Our forward skirmishers have engaged a French rearguard. The Ninety-fifth Rifles have met resistance at a windmill in a town call Obidos."

Robert nodded to himself in satisfaction. Of course it had been the Rifles. Perhaps that even explained the sharper pitch of the firing.

"They rather overextended themselves, unfortunately," Robe continued. "They were struck by a fierce counterattack and could not disengage until our main column reached them. They suffered about thirty casualties. Too eager by half."

"Well, that's unfortunate," Flashdash said.

"It doesn't matter. General Wellesley believes the enemy will make a stand in force, sometime today. Perhaps just a rearguard, but a stand, nonetheless. I want your brigade in reserve, Flushing. The other three batteries will go ahead with the three infantry brigades."

Robert saw Flashdash's shoulders slump. If there was to be a battle today, they would miss it. Robert shared the captain's disappointment.

"Never fear, Captain," Robe added. "Nothing will be decided today. Another opportunity will present itself."

"Yes, sir," Flashdash said.

Robe nodded, then reined about and continued toward the rear of the column. Robert watched his receding back. It made sense, he supposed, to place the youngest unit in reserve. Their company had not yet proven their mettle. Though they would, before this campaign was over. Of that he was certain.

*****

The infantry had split, deploying into three attack columns, each with an attached artillery brigade in support. As Robe had explained, Robert's brigade alone remained unattached and rumbled along in the rear. The central attack column, with Wellesley at the head, continued along the road. The two flanking columns plunged through the countryside, snaking across the flat fields. They made for a village of brown and tan coloured houses, surrounded by what looked to be hedgerows of brown shrubs. In the distance rose a range of piled, dusty green hills.

"We shall certainly be left behind at this pace," Flashdash complained. He swept off his cocked hat and mopped his brow with a white handkerchief. "If the French do not stand and fight."

"They are there in the village, aren't they, sir?" Robert asked.

"Yes, yes. Rolica, my maps call the place. The question is whether they will remain there long. I doubt very much a reserve will be called upon today."

Today, Robert repeated in his mind. The seventeenth of August. Perhaps a day to go down in history, perhaps not.

The British infantry changed formation, and from their position in the rear, Robert had an outstanding view as a spectator to a grand play. As if arrayed on a vast stage, the redcoat columns turned and wheeled forward into line, swinging like a series of vast human doors. The guns halted and unlimbered, while green clad riflemen moved out in the front, some dropping to their knees and aiming at unseen targets. Small puffs of smoke appeared at the muzzles of their rifles, and a second later came the sharp reports.

"What are they shooting at?" Robert wondered aloud. He wanted to rush forward, to leap into the thick of it. He felt no fear, just a building excitement, although whether that excitement would remain when the casualties began to flow back from the battle front, he could not say. He strained to catch a glimpse of the French and wondered, perhaps, if the riflemen were simply being overcautious, firing into the houses.

Then he realized that what he had taken for hedgerows were, in fact, lines of men, and he started in astonishment. He had expected the French to wear blue. Yet there they stood, arrayed in tight square columns, each man clad in a long, dust coloured coat. Not brown hedgerows. Blocks of brown coated men.

"Not wool, surely?" he said to himself, for no sane general would dress his men in wool overcoats for the Portuguese summer. Maybe the coats were linen, something more practical for the climate and terrain.

The long lines of redcoats swept forward. On their flanks, smoke appeared as the gun batteries opened fire. Robert saw the arching smoke trails of howitzer shells. A second later came the piercing shriek as the shells plunged toward the earth, then the fierce bang as they burst in the air.

"Too short!" Robert cried, for the shells had exploded far

from their intended targets. But they must have had some affect, for the French columns began to move back, facing about and withdrawing.

"They won't stand," Flashdash growled, and Robert saw that this was true. Every French column was moving away, retreating. Not as a scared rabble, but in good order, just turning their backs, raising more dust to mingle with the smoke from the curtailed artillery barrage.

It had not been much of a battle after all. The British lines again formed their three columns, while the artillery limbered up and moved forward. Robert's brigade continued to roll along in the rear, and after about a quarter of an hour they reached the battlefield. The village proved smaller than Robert had at first thought; just a small collection of houses, most of two storeys, the windows in the upper floors arched, those on the lower levels cut square. The walls of each little structure were white or the colour of dust, the rooftops made of striking red clay tiles. In the center of the village, next to the road, rose the square tower of a church. Beyond the village, the terrain sagged and broke into a series of gullies, running parallel to the road. And further on, past the broken ground, the French had reformed, lining the crest of a ridge. The rising mountains lay piled at their back.

"Not over, then," Robert murmured, for the British columns had already plunged into the gullies, using them to cover their advance. Smoke suddenly blossomed on the ridge, followed by a deep thud. The French were firing, no doubt sending round shot down into the advancing redcoats.

"Do you see the fall of the shot?" Robert asked of no one in particular, and no one answered. He ground his teeth in his impatience, for the brigade and its interminable train of wagons seemed to crawl, crawl along as the infantry formed lines again, halted halfway up the ridge, and at last, opened a controlled storm of musketry at the enemy position. Smoke rose in dense clouds, completely obscuring the field within seconds.

Robert sighed in frustration at his inability to understand what was happening. On his left, a squadron of Portuguese cavalry thundered by. The horsemen disappeared into the smoke. Muskets and cannon continued to roar, and a deep-throated cheer went up. Suddenly, the Portuguese cavalry appeared again, thundering back, though now their formation was ragged, the troopers whipping their mounts.

"What, is it defeat?" Flashdash cried.

But no aides came back to order a retreat, so the battery continued forward, and there was no sign of any more of Wellesley's troops having been forced to withdraw. Then, just as the road started ascending the ridge, the sound of firing stopped.

The smoke cleared quickly, and there, sprawled in the dust, as Robert and his fellow officers rode past, were the bodies of French soldiers. Some were still and lifeless, while others writhed from the pain of their wounds. Sight of them left Robert unmoved. He did not see any fallen redcoats, and that was a relief. There was no defeat then, and he wondered what had so alarmed the Portuguese horsemen. Perhaps nothing but the screening smoke and the noise.

His eyes met those of one of the French, a man lying on his stomach, trying to raise himself with his arms. One hand reached out, and Robert saw that it was soaked crimson. The man called something in French that Robert could not make out. He noticed the fellow's black shako, the brass badge of the eagle, and the collar of his blue and white coatee peering out from under the long coat.

The coat was made of linen, as Robert had guessed.

*****

The British advance wound through a narrow pass in the hills, a canyon that lay deep in shadow. When the land widened and opened again, the sun was setting. The battle of Rolica had ended, and Robert's guns had not been engaged. It had been a running action, an attempt by the French to delay the British advance. And, perhaps, they had succeeded in that.

The army bivouacked in the hills. The air was warm still, and speculation circulated that the French were massing their forces and would make a stand somewhere and some time soon.

"They won't simply let us march into Lisbon," Flashdash said as the brigade officers gathered around their mess fire, sitting on crates and barrels. They had dined on plain rations, the same as the men, salt pork and biscuits. "Thus, I suggest you all make a night of it, as I intend to do." He rose to his feet. "Good night, gentlemen."

Robert found himself alone with Mumbles and Rice. For a moment, none of them spoke. Mumbles produced another bottle of port. "A local sutler," he explained, pouring a measure into three tin soldier's cups. Keeping one cup, he passed the others to his comrades.

"To our endeavour here," Mumbles said.

"Confusion to the enemy," Robert echoed.

They drank, the three of them, though Rice said nothing.

"Odd, isn't it?" Mumbles continued. "To think of how we were all in the Academy together (mumble mumble) about to fight the French."

Robert smiled, for this was so very close to his own thoughts. "Yes. It's a pity—." He stopped himself. He had been about to say that it was a pity that Georgie was not here with them. And that was so. He wondered how Georgie would have fared, how he would have behaved here now that the war was real. Put on a brave face and bumbled his way through, he supposed, the same as the rest of them.

He looked at Rice. Perhaps the war would have a healing effect. Perhaps it would reveal the true absurdity of the conflict between them. Robert knew that Mumbles wished for solidarity among the three of them, and that was why he had raised the toast. Rice had not refused the offered cup, and that seemed a hopeful sign. He had not carried through with his threats. Maybe there was a chance that he would not.

"We'll risk our lives together soon," Robert said. "Maybe even tomorrow. We need to trust each other."

"Hear hear," said Mumbles.

Rice looked from one to the other, his expression inscrutable. Robert paused, wondering exactly what he wished to say. It was not his intent to provoke, but to mend fences. After all this time, he wanted to put things right. It was important that he succeed here and now, that he not bungle this, for his very life could depend on it. Surely, Rice understood that, as well?

"We're fellow officers in a new brigade," he went on. "We have much to prove, but we know each other well, and we're more than capable of meeting whatever the enemy can send our way. Our own honour, and the honour of our battalion is at stake." He raised his cup. "I propose a toast to what we can achieve together."

"Yes," Mumbles said, also raising his cup.

Rice did not join them. He scowled at Robert, then drained his cup and tossed it down with a dull clang.

"Spare me your sentiments, Saxon," he said. "When the time comes, we'll follow our orders, and that will be that. You can't appease me, and you can't escape from the consequences of your own actions so easily." He looked at Mumbles. "You'd best do as the captain says and seek your bed. I know I am."

He strode off to where the officers' baggage wagons were parked. Robert's knuckles were white where he gripped his cup. Mumbles looked struck, his face drooping.

"The bastard," Robert muttered. Something inside him twisted, coiling like a steel spring. A voice told him to forget it, to shrug this off as nothing more than childishness or pride, but that voice grew fainter and fainter by the second, drowned out by a more powerful force that grew a roar within his skull.

This was it. This was Rice's final insult. Robert would never again try to appease him. He was sick of trying, and there was no point. Rice's threats still stood, and that made him Robert's enemy, a more present and dangerous enemy than the French.

It was time to put an end to this, once and for all.

The darkness howled. And this time Robert was listening.

*****

At Morning Parade, the four Royal Artillery brigades of Wellesley's force assembled as one, the gunners forming ranks in front of their twenty-four cannon. After roll call and inspection, Colonel Robe made an announcement. Two fresh infantry brigades had arrived in Portugal from England, their transports anchoring off Peniche. The troops would land at Porto Novo, near the village of Vimeiro. "This makes our eventual success all the more probable," Robe stated. "The army will move to the heights of Vimeiro to protect these fresh troops from possible attack from the French forces, which have halted a few leagues from there."

The artillery commander then reached into his coatee pocket and drew out a folded piece of paper. "General orders have arrived with the reinforcements, having come ashore with the despatch vessel." He paused, studying the paper, his lips pursed. He cleared his throat. "From Horse Guards, dated the tenth of July, the year eighteen hundred and eight. The practice of powdering the hair and tying it in a queue is . . . hereby abolished. The men will wear their hair cut short, away from the coat collar, and in its natural colour."

The colonel lowered the order. His face was strangely bleak. "We will comply at once, before the commencement of today's march."

Neither Robert nor any of his comrades at the Royal Military Academy had ever worn their hair long, for the new style had already been in effect for the cadets. But the men had still been expected to adhere to eighteenth century tradition. Now a curious scene was repeated throughout the camp, in the infantry and cavalry lines and amongst the gunners of the artillery. Robert watched as the men dunked their heads in buckets, then had their best mates hack off the hated queues. There was something both unsettling and encouraging about the relish with which they approached the task.

"This is the start of a new era in warfare," he said to Mumbles.

About an hour later, the march resumed. The army passed through the village of Vimeiro, which seemed a larger version of Rolica. Next to the road stood the most imposing building in the village: the church, an enormous, whitewashed plaster block with a tall square clock tower in its south-eastern corner. A curving whitewashed stone wall surrounded most the churchyard, save for a small graveyard of white stones.

As he rode past, Robert stared up at the brass weathercock perched at the tower's summit. It sat still, unmoving, like the close and heated air.

Once through the village, the column turned right, leaving the road to file along the crest of another low ridge. The ground sloped downward from there, toward a river valley, and there, the land was greener, the river making a brownish trace on its westward journey to the sea. Further on stood another range of low, tree-covered hills. Objects in the distance shimmered in the heat, including the rising smoke of many campfires. Enemy campfires. For there sat the retreating French army, bivouacked within sight.

From column, the British troops again swung into line of battle, but there, they halted. "We will bivouac here," Flashdash said, reining about and trotting his horse along the waiting, sweating, ranks of his men. "We will remain in our lines in case the French attempt an attack while our fresh brigades are landing."

Robert's brigade had halted a few yards in front of a vineyard that hid much of the village behind them, save for the tall church tower. They were near the left of the line, with the three infantry battalions of General Fane's brigade on their right. Flashdash ordered the guns unlimbered to the front, and the silent muzzles gazed over the heads of the dispersed skirmish line, thirty yards forward, a company of the 95th Rifles. General Fane's infantry included another rifle regiment, the 60th Royal American Rifles, which had deployed in a standard, close-order line of two ranks, as had the redcoat 50th Foot, the last of Fane's units.

The afternoon ebbed. A breeze ruffled the vines, and bees hummed. Robert sat on a limber chest, facing the French lines and chewing a biscuit. Away to the west, he could see the glimmer of the sea, revealed in the apex of two hills. The reinforcements would come from there.

The infantry troops nearby were lounging in the grass. They

had piled arms in stacks of four, fixed bayonets interlocking. Robert looked at the muskets and wondered at their effectiveness. It would take a dozen of them to destroy one or two of the enemy, while his weapon of choice was the great gun that could destroy a dozen men at one shot. The guns could turn the tide of a battle.

I'm a gunner, Robert thought. *If the French should not retreat again, but should attack, our guns will be heard.*

Mumbles came to sit beside him. "There are rumours that a more senior commander has arrived with the new troops," he said. "That he will replace Wellesley."

"Where did you hear such rumours?"

Before Mumbles could reply, a drum began to chatter the officer's call. The drummer boy stood not more than twenty yards away, near the centre of the first line of ammunition wagons. Flashdash was with him. Robert slid from the limber chest, and he and Mumbles made their way toward the captain. A moment later, Rice joined them.

"Gentlemen," Flashdash said, "I have received our orders from Colonel Robe's headquarters. General Wellesley plans to remain here tomorrow, and not to resume the march."

Mumbles nodded and gave Robert a knowing look, as if this bit of information confirmed Wellesley's imminent replacement. Flashdash went on, "The men are, nevertheless, to sleep tonight, wearing their accoutrements and will be under arms at three o'clock in the morning."

"Three o'clock!" Rice complained.

Flashdash frowned. "That is what I said. Be sure to make it so. That is all."

Flashdash left them there, moving off with the drummer to where he had made his headquarters, a patch of ground between two wagons. Robert turned to Mumbles and said,

"That means the general expects the French to attack. Maybe he has intelligence."

"Saxon," Rice interjected, "I'd like a word with you."

Robert fixed Rice with an icy glare. "Say what you like. I'm right here."

Rice glanced at Mumbles, then shrugged. "Very well. I simply want to remind you that the imminence of battle does nothing to change things between us. To be frank, I have no doubt that the French will continue on their way, and we will march into Lisbon unopposed. Then there will be weeks of idleness, as each side plots it next move."

"What is he talking about?" Mumbles asked.

Robert ignored the question, just faced Rice with an icy calm. "What are you planning to do, then?"

Rice smiled. "I plan to pass certain information to our captain. That is, if you don't listen to good sense, come to understand that you are a disruptive force in this brigade."

"*I'm* a disruptive force...?"

"Yes, and you know it! Perhaps after we reach Lisbon, it will be time for you to move on. I'll write to my father. Perhaps he can arrange for your transfer, for he has influence over such things. Or maybe you should simply resign your commission. After all, you have demonstrated that you're not fit to command."

Robert smiled and folded his arms. "You've said enough. I won't listen anymore."

Rice snorted. "Suit yourself. For now. I simply wish to let you know that I do not think of us as Shakespeare's band of brothers, and I haven't forgotten your sins. That's all."

Robert turned on his heel. "Do your worst, you damned blackguard."

Rice did not follow. Robert suspected that he was bluffing,

that he would do nothing, but it was certainly feasible that old Colonel Rice could have Robert transferred, taken away from the company he had worked so hard to train. Perhaps that would not be so bad, because he would escape Rice, escape Flashdash. But it would not be fair. The night passed slowly. When three o'clock came, and the fifes and drums jarred the men from sleep, sputtering and cursing, Robert was already wide awake. He had tea and local bread for breakfast. Mumbles joined him, and asked, "What was that (mumble mumble) about resigning?"

"Nothing," Robert said. "Rice is just a spoiled brat. A dangerous spoiled brat."

The sun rose, and the air grew hot. The troops remained in their lines, facing the smudge of enemy smoke amongst the hills. Robert walked along behind the guns, greeting the few men he knew by name, hoping the others he did not know did not notice. When he came upon Hunter, the sergeant was standing on his right leg, the left leg raised and stretched before him. As Robert approached, Hunter shifted position, standing on his left leg and raising his right. He grinned. "Have to be well oiled to face the Froggies, sir."

"You think they will make a move against us here?" Robert asked.

"Oh, yes sir. We must be a mighty tempting morsel."

Robert was not so sure, but a few hours later, as he examined the enemy line, he saw it begin to move. It was, by now, almost seven o'clock. The French were not moving south, away from the British, but north. Raising a cloud of early morning dust, they advanced, a screen of cavalry in their van, followed by three heavy columns of infantry, one to the west, one to the east, and one directly to the south. The artillery lumbered in the rear.

As both General Wellesley and Sergeant Hunter had predicted, the French were attacking.

Chapter Fifteen:
Battle

The enemy advanced from the hills in a great, spreading wave, marching in full view of the British, for the valley was an open plain below Vimeiro; fields criss-crossed with lanes and stone fences like chalk marks on a green slate. Robert counted nine French infantry battalions, each arrayed in attack column, the same formation that had broken every army on the European continent. The sun glinted from their shako plates and bayonets, sparkling and dancing in rippling lines.

Over on the right of Wellesley's line, the redcoat infantry was re-deploying amidst a great deal of shouting and beating of drums, shifting their front to meet the angle of the French attack. On the left, Robert's artillery brigade held its position, as did Fane's entire brigade, the riflemen and redcoats waiting in dressed lines of two ranks, colours fluttering above their heads.

"Strange that they should just come at us in this frontal assault," Robert said when the French were still about a mile away. "It's an uphill march the entire distance."

"Think they frighten us, sir," said Sergeant Hunter. "As they have frightened everyone else."

Flashdash was trotting along the line of his guns, the only officer still on horseback. Bringing his mount to a halt, he pressed a spyglass to his right eye. A few seconds later he cried, "Stand to your guns!" An unnecessary order, for the officers and crews of his brigade were already in position, the slow match already smouldering on the linstocks. Robert waited with his division, the centre two guns, one nine-pounder and one howitzer.

The French columns drew closer, moving with ponderous inevitability to the distant pounding of their drums. Robert thought it curious that he still felt no fear. There before him was death, coming for him, but he was having no trouble facing it without flinching, without wanting to run. He supposed this was because he had faced death before, at least in his mind. He had faced it every time his father had struck him a blow, every time he had wondered if his father would kill him, either by design or accident. In time, he had become immune to the possibility, resigned to it.

"At three degrees elevation, guns load with round shot," Flashdash said, lowering his little telescope. "Howitzers with Shrapnel."

A drummer on the ground near the captain beat out the appropriate call. "Load," Robert shouted to his crews. The men reacted as they should, as they had on the Parade Ground in Woolwich, sponging the barrels, ramming home prepared rounds of cartridge and shot, then the wadding. When the guns were loaded, Robert stepped in to sight along the long barrel of the nine-pounder, adjusting the elevation screw to enable him to drop a round shot into an enemy column at about twelve hundred yards. This was the so called "first graze" range, the distance at which the ball first struck the ground. After that it would continue to roll, continue to destroy, maim, and kill. He gave quiet commands of, "Trail right," and "Trail left," to the man on the trail handspike, shifting the gleaming, polished muzzle until it bore on the second enemy column from the left.

"The howitzers will hold their fire," Flashdash said, again riding back and forth. "We will wait for our skirmishers to come in." Then he repeated, "Nine-pounders at three degrees elevation."

Out on the green plain, the crack of rifles rose as the skirmishers of the 95th opened fire, trying to shoot down officers, sergeants and other key personnel within the French ranks. Robert could detect no damage to the enemy from this distance, but he was certain at least some of the accurate rifle shots were telling.

"Guns only will open fire on my command," Flashdash cried, and his voice broke. He was speaking too much, giving the same or similar orders over and over. Clearing his throat, he added, "Long shots to find the range."

"Ready," Robert said, stepping back, away from his nine-pounder. One of the crew members brought the linstock forward, holding it aloft and waiting for the word.

"Number One Gun, fire," Flashdash said. Rice's nine-pounder blasted smoke, but Robert's attention was on his own gun. Then the word came as Flashdash cried, "Number Three Gun, fire!"

"Fire!" Robert repeated. The linstock came down, the quill in the vent jetted flame, and the gun lurched backward as it recoiled, a perfect smoke ring billowing out from its muzzle. Robert saw the shot, a black speck, hurtling down into the valley. It struck with a spray of earth, fifteen yards short of the advancing column. But it was on target, and as it bounced, it hit the column dead centre, ploughing a dark groove through the dense formation of men.

It was the first time Robert had seen men killed—men killed at his word.

"Load and fire," Flashdash called, the start of a new command, but his next words were drowned by the roaring of the other three artillery batteries on the ridge. Only the company drummer was audible as he beat the call for divisions to load and fire at their discretion. "Load!" Robert shouted at the sergeant in charge of his gun. The men worked quickly, and when the gun fired a second time, they leapt into action at once, as Robert had taught them, sponging and loading, then firing again, sending round after round into the same advancing column. Dense smoke began to settle at the edge of the plateau. The shape of the enemy slowly grew more and more dim, a shadow advancing through a fog.

"Depress to two degrees," Robert cried after five rounds. The muzzle velocity, and thus the range, would increase as the gun barrel heated, and he did not want the gun to overshoot. No one was certain why this was so, though Robert wondered if, perhaps, the gun expended energy heating itself, and once heated, all the force behind an ignited cartridge was directed to throwing the projectile.

"Cease firing," Flashdash called, and the drummer beat the call. "Cease firing!"

The guns fell silent. The smoke drifted, clearing, and there were the skirmishers from the 95th, running back to form lines within Wellesley's main position. The French attack columns were still coming on, no more than a hundred yards away now. For some reason, they had not deployed their own skirmishers to counter the British riflemen. Instead, they were hurling their main attack at the ridge, like a great battering ram. It was pure arrogance, Robert decided. They expected the British to run. French drums pounded, and a great shout went up, a cry of, "*Vive l'Empereur!*" It was the cry that had shaken every other nation in Europe.

It will not shake us, Robert thought. He could see that the artillery had told, for the enemy formations were already ragged and had left a distant trail of fallen, broken bodies like discarded dolls.

"Load and fire, grape shot," Flashdash shouted, his voice rising to a shriek. The guns opened again, and a moment later they were joined by another sound, the ripping, tearing roar of musketry. Robert saw his nine-pounder tear a gaping hole in the nearest French battalion. All around that gap, other men were falling, struck by musket balls, while others edged back, back. The French advance had slowed, then stopped, stalled at about fifty yards from the British line.

Then the French began to go back.

"Cease firing!" Flashdash cried again, his voice just audible over the cheering from Fane's infantry, as they suddenly charged forward, down the slope toward the remnants of the nearest enemy.   Fane dashed in amongst them, shouting, "Don't be so eager! Reform, men! Reform!"

It took some time to bring the infantry under control. Despite the humming and aching in his ears from the noise of the guns, Robert watched, with a strange elation, the French streaming back across the valley, even though he knew they were not finished, that they would rally and come again. Still, this was an inkling of what victory must be like, how it must feel.

It felt good.

*****

The French columns reformed at their starting point, drums rattling and trumpets blaring.   Fresh infantry battalions arrived, taking up positions in front of those who had withdrawn.

"Who are they?" Robert asked Hunter. "They have red epaulettes on their shoulders."

"Grenadiers, sir," Hunter said. "Elite troops. Won't run quite so quick, sir."

The columns began a second advance as ponderous as the first, but this time they were accompanied by a battery of eight guns. The guns rolled across the plain behind their horse teams, and when they were within a thousand yards, they suddenly swung into action, unlimbering with swift precision.

"Target the infantry," Flashdash commanded. "We will use the Shrapnel now that we no longer have fear of striking our own skirmishers."

"Load for eight hundred yards," Robert said to the sergeant in charge of his howitzer, Number Four gun. "Two rounds at that distance, two at six hundred, two at five hundred, two at four hundred, and so on until cease firing is called."

"Sir," the sergeant acknowledged.

The nine-pounders opened fire again, hurling round shot toward the French grenadiers, knocking down rows of men just as a football might crash through a field of wheat. The howitzers waited until the distance closed.

"Number Four Gun ready, sir," the sergeant said.

"Steady," Robert said. On the right, a few howitzers had fired from the other batteries, and Mumbles's leftmost gun rang out, the shell whining as it arched into the sky. Robert had judged the distance and knew the shells would fall short, wasted. He waited.

"That's it," he said at last. "Number Four Gun, fire!"

The linstock came down, the heavy oak carriage lurching back about three feet as flame stabbed upwards. Robert kept his eye on the smoke trail from the shell. It plunged, screaming like a skyrocket. About twenty yards short of the first French rank, it burst in the air with a flash. A crater appeared in the French column. Robert had judged the distance exactly, taking into account the forward momentum of the shell fragments and musket balls after the shell burst. A dozen men had been knocked flat.

The blood started to rush in Robert's veins. "Load!"

Shells shrieked and whistled as every British battery began a steady, continuous fire. Soon archways of hanging smoke connected the two armies, though still the French closed their diminishing ranks and came on. They would not get far, could not press this attack home. This was systematic destruction, killing from a distance. The gun crews sweated as they worked, but they performed as they would on Woolwich Common, their movements quick but calm, as if the enemy were nothing more than an array of empty casks. All the while, Sergeant Hunter moved from gun to gun, yelling encouragement to the gunners, making sure the guns were on target, that the men did not forget to run the carriages forward after every shot, and that ammunition flowed from the limbers and ammunition wagons.

The ground suddenly shook, and a great spray of dry earth and small stones shot from the slope, just in front of Rice's guns. A second explosion burst forward of Robert's position, showering his gunners with dust. Robert understood at once what was happening. The French battery was targeting the British artillery, and they had chosen Flashdash's company.

Hunter was next to Robert, peering down into the valley. "The have the measure of us, sir," the sergeant said.

Flashdash must have seen it too, for he suddenly cried, "Counter battery fire with the guns, troops with the howitzers!"

"Number Three Gun target the battery," Robert ordered. "Number Four the infantry!"

More earth showered down, and something hummed past

on Robert's left. A round shot. A scream rose behind him, a high-pitched screech. He turned at the sound, at the unexpected terror and horror contained within it, and saw that Flashdash's horse had been hit. The poor beast was on the ground, its intestines spilling out of its ruptured belly. Flashdash was in the dust, struggling to both rise and avoid the horse's thrashing hooves.

The next incoming shot also struck home. Rice's nine-pounder gun rang like a bell as it leapt backwards from its carriage, the long gleaming barrel spinning in the air like a toy. Next, a howitzer carriage wheel exploded, spraying splinters and steel fragments from its shattered tire. Three men fell, not screaming, but simply dropping dead. At the same moment, it seemed as if an invisible hand pushed Robert backward, a force he could not resist. The ground came up to meet him.

He lay for what seemed like several minutes. His ears seemed to have shut off, closed over. He could not even hear his own heart beat. Smoke drifted by, and for the first time, he noticed the heavy stench of the sulphur. Then, perception returned, noises striking almost like a blow to the head, and he winced at continued screaming of horses. He tried to sit, managed only to roll onto his side, fighting sudden nausea, drawing in deep breaths. Then he noticed the spatter of blood dotting his right wrist and hand. His eyes followed its trace, expecting to find a deep gash in his arm, or worse, that his arm was no longer there.

What he saw was not an arm, but a severed leg lying in the grass. Just the lower part, with the booted foot attached. Next to it, crawling forward on his elbows, was Flashdash.

Flashdash's eyes were wide and staring, his hat gone, his face caked in sweat and the pale Portuguese dust. He pulled himself to within a few feet of where Robert lay, leaving a scarlet trail behind him, like the trace of some strange bleeding slug.

"Saxon," he croaked.

"Sir!" Robert shouted, certain now that the blood on his arm was the captain's. "Sir, can you hear me?" Behind him, the remaining guns still fired on, and someone was shouting commands in a loud, unshakable voice. Hunter.

"Keep firing," Flashdash said. "We... will hold... our position...."

Robert could see the life fading behind the captain's eyes, but all he could think was, *You and your damned, stupid polished, gleaming guns.*

"Of course we'll hold, sir," he said. "Of course."

And suddenly he and Flashdash were surrounded by men stooping to help, to staunch the flow of blood from the captain's severed leg. The firing had stopped, and the air was full of cheers. Robert no longer felt sick, but he accepted a hand, offered to help him stand. Once on his feet, he swayed a moment as he looked around. There was Mumbles, coming toward him.

"Are you all right?" Mumbles cried.

Robert did not answer. He was transfixed by the sight of two gunners, lifting Flashdash and placing him in the bed of a wagon. The captain still lived. They would take him to the rear.

"You don't appear to be wounded," Mumbles said.

Robert at last came to his senses. "The force of a blow nearby, I think. Yes, that must have been it."

"Was the captain killed?" Mumbles shouted. Robert had never heard him raise his voice before.

"Not yet," Robert said. Then Rice was there, too, his face as white as letter paper. He met Robert's eye.

Robert rested his hand on his sword hilt. "Well, it looks like you have command of the brigade, Second Captain Rice."

*****

Hunter had taken charge after Flashdash and Robert had fallen. Under the sergeant's steady eye, the undamaged guns had remained in action and had driven off the enemy battery with a rapid and accurate fire that the French had been unable to match. The sergeant had also detailed men to remove the wounded to the rear, then had ordered a spare wheel brought forward for the damaged howitzer.   The howitzer was remounted and back in action in time for a third French attack. The French grenadiers got about halfway up the hill toward the British lines, but that was the crest of their wave, a wave that broke and streamed for the rear, leaving behind piles of the fallen, where the Shrapnel had rained death.

"Very good, Sergeant Hunter," Rice was repeating as Hunter made his report. "Very good."

"Ammunition restocked from the wagons, sir," Hunter added.

Rice nodded. "Very good, Sergeant. Very good." He drew in a breath and puffed himself up. "Perhaps they won't come a fourth time."

Robert had found Flashdash's telescope discarded in the sparse grass, and he trained it on the enemy lines. The French were still in position, though they had taken heavy casualties in their attempts to capture Vimeiro Ridge. Foolish attempts, in Robert's estimate, foolishly contemptuous of the British soldier. Did the Frogs think they could be frightened so easily, made to run away at the mere sight of the vaunted French column?

"No sign of another advance," he said, sweeping the glass to and fro. The lanes and fences and fields were strewn with the unmoving dead, the groping wounded. He supposed it was a horrible sight, but it left him unaffected. His sense of compassion seemed to have retreated, if it existed at all under such circumstances. He had no way of knowing if it would return until this had all ended.

"Wait a minute," he said, for he had spied movement on the center right. Three more columns of infantry were moving forward from the flank of the French line, marching along the road to Vimeiro itself. "Yes, there's probably going to be another attack, but not against our position. It's going to come further to our left."

"Good, then," Rice said. "Good. We will have a rest."

Robert lowered the telescope. "Trying to outflank us," he suggested. There were very few British troops in the village of Vimeiro itself, and unless British troops intervened to cut the road, that was where the French attack would fall. "If the French should get into the village...."

Random rifle shots cracked from within the valley, the greencoat skirmishers returning to harass the enemy line from long range. The British infantry dressed their lines amidst the barking of their sergeants, preparing for further action. A horseman rode along the ridge, making his way through the vineyard, then entering the battery before halting in the space between the guns and their limbers. The horse stamped and tossed its head, and the rider doffed his massive cocked hat. It was Colonel Robe, hair still in a queue despite the new regulations.

"Captain Flushing," he said. "Where is Captain Flushing?"

Rice strode forward. "Captain Flushing was wounded, sir. I have taken command."

Robe squinted at him. "And you are?"

Rice's mouth twisted. "Lieutenant Rice, sir. My father is

Colonel Rice?"

"You sound uncertain of that, Lieutenant," Robe said, face a dark mask. "This is no time for uncertainty. General Wellesley is concerned that the village is vulnerable, and that the French are preparing to make an attack there. You will re-deploy your guns eastward, placing them in the village, close to the road, near the church."

Rice hesitated. "By ourselves, sir?"

Robe looked irritated. "There is a battalion of infantry there in reserve, in the churchyard. The Forty-Third Regiment, I believe. Take a position on their right. General Wellesley expects you to hold there until he can muster more infantry reinforcements without robbing them from this position on the plateau."

Rice again looked dumbstruck. Robert stepped forward, declaring, "We'll hold it, sir." Rice shot him a withering look, but Robe nodded. "Good, then. You had best move off at once."

The colonel crammed his hat back on and pulled his horse around, not waiting for a salute. As he thundered off, Rice turned and said, "Don't you ever interrupt me again!"

"I didn't interrupt you. You weren't saying anything."

"I was about to!"

Robert was not listening. He spied Hunter and said, "Left limber up!"

"Left limber up, sir!" Hunter cried, then repeated, "Left limber up!"

Rice leaned on his sword, a sour look on his face, as the drivers brought the horses and snorting oxen forward. In the whirl and rush of limbering the guns, Robert caught a glimpse of Captain Tunge, their eyes meeting for a fraction of a second. But then, Tunge had moved on, doing his duty, and in no time the five guns were hitched and rolling east, following a slender track back toward Vimeiro.

*****

The brigade unlimbered its five remaining cannon in the yard of a one-story house. The house was typical of those Robert had seen in this country, whitewashed stone walls, a red clay tile roof, wooden shutters painted a bright blue. Surrounding the yard on three sides was a wall little more than knee high. The wall was the only available cover for the guns. The house itself enclosed the yard on the north side, in the rear of the battery. Adjacent to the house stood the village church with its higher wall and towering steeple.

On the east side of these structures ran the main road to Lisbon. The view along the road was un-obscured, the fields and hills beyond laid out in a wide vista. Crossing those fields, in and on either side of the road, were the three columns of French infantry that Robert had seen. Drums beat out the monotonous cadence, growing ever closer.

"Place the three howitzers facing south," Robert said, "with the two nine-pounders east, obliquely across the road. Double shot the guns with grape and round shot. You lads on the howitzers," he shouted, cupping his hand. "This is the time for your training. Rapid fire is a must!"

Mumbles was beside him. "Feel rather (mumble mumble) exposed and on our own."

"We're not on our own," Robert stated. But he thought, *they could outflank our battery here, if they wanted to. If they leave the road and take to the yards and gardens to the west, get between us and the rest of the army, they could cut us off.* However, he did not believe they would. The road was the easiest and most obvious route, probably the only route the

French knew of, for they could not have had time to make a thorough observation of the terrain. If they kept to the road, Robert's guns would stop them. It was a gamble, but he thought it would work. And more British troops were coming. All they had to do was hold on here.

He pointed behind them to the church. "Look, there's the infantry Colonel Robe mentioned." The redcoats were there, the tops of their shakos just visible along the lip of the high wall, and they had a lookout on top of the church tower. "Mumbles, go and make contact with their colonel, let them know we're here. although, unless they're blind, they've already seen us."

Mumbles nodded and scurried out of the yard through a low wooden gate, disappearing around one corner of the house. Robert found himself with Rice.

Rice had done nothing to stop Robert issuing orders, and he was sweating. "This is a terrible position," he muttered. "Terrible."

Robert gripped his hands behind his back. The men had loaded the guns, and now they waited. A horse snorted and stamped, and the French drums grew closer. The road curved around to the right here, which placed his guns roughly on the right of the infantry in the churchyard, with an incline to the left. Together, they could stop the enemy, if they could load and fire fast enough.

"I think this is a good position."

"Good?" Rice whined. "Everything depends on the enemy doing what we want. What if they form lines and spread out to envelope us on both sides?"

"The French don't like to form lines. Their aim is to punch through our position in column, like a battering ram."

Rice was shaking his head. "Yes, or three battering rams.

We can't fight them all. Colonel Robe or this damned Wellesley don't understand. It was a simple matter to break the frontal assaults when we were well positioned on a hill, but not here. This is a trap."

Robert's smile was grim. Rice was a coward after all, just as he had always expected, and now he had nowhere to hide. He had never had to face a hopeless situation, never in his life. Robert had faced countless such situations, every time his father had raised his hand. He had not given up then, and he saw no reason to now.

"Rice, we have our orders, so your worrying is pointless. Look, here comes Mumbles. We have the support of the infantry, and we have these walls for cover."

Rice sighed in exasperation. "Damn you, Saxon, have you forgotten that I'm in command? You're very good at taking care of routine orders, but I have the final say. This is a mistake, and I mean to correct it. We're pulling back, and that's an order."

Robert stared at him. "If we leave, we go against superior orders, and we endanger the army."

"If we stay, we'll be slaughtered. Our ammunition is almost spent."

"We only need what we have. We fire rapidly, break their front ranks, use up the grape, depress the howitzers and fire the Shrapnel into them—"

"No! We only have five guns. We'll retrace our steps, redeploy to the west, toward the vineyard where the ground begins to rise. We can still target the enemy columns from there."

The French drums were rattling, closer and closer. There was no time for such a re-deployment, no time to hitch the lumbering oxen, to pull the guns back five hundred yards. "If we do that, we'll be caught while still limbered, and the enemy will cut us to pieces."

Rice rounded in fury. "I won't repeat my order, Lieutenant!"

Robert did not move, did not speak. Rice was wrong, completely wrong. He would lead them to ruin with his cowardice, just as Flashdash had nearly had them all killed with his ridiculous obsession with Parade order.

And then Robert realized that this was the moment. He could not allow Rice to disobey orders, but most of all, he could not allow them all to be killed. This was the moment he had long looked for, the opportunity to strike, and so end this feud.

"Rice, you're a damned fool."

Rice's eyes bugged. "What? What did you say?"

Robert ignored him. "Sergeant Hunter!"

Hunter was facing the enemy, and he turned on a pivot. "Sir."

"Sergeant Hunter, our Acting Second Captain Rice has been knocked on the head, and is not thinking straight. I am assuming command."

"What?" Rice cried. "What did you say?"

Robert's hand shot out, gripping the front of Rice's coat. He pulled, felt the fabric tear. Rice screamed as he lost his balance and toppled into the dust. Robert was upon him, taking hold of Rice's epaulettes and dragging him toward the house, where the door stood ajar, swinging on its hinges. He shoved Rice inside, sending him sprawling across the clay tile floor of the little central hallway.

"Stay here and shut your mouth," Robert said.

Rice's face contorted in fury. His hand went to his sword hilt, and he drew the blade as he pushed himself to his feet. "I'll have you in irons for this! I'll see you bloody hanged!"

Robert drew his sword in one fluid motion, the slim,

inadequate blade his father had given him. He dropped into the guard in time to parry Rice's first blow, the swords ringing in the confined space. Rice drew back and struck again, then again, his thrusts wild, unfocused, but full of murderous intent. Robert danced back, slid along the wall, and kicked with his left foot. He landed a blow against Rice's left knee, and Rice cried out in pain and rage as he staggered. Robert then snapped his sword like a whip, aiming for Rice's wrist, but Rice recovered in time to parry, the two blades scraping together. Rice howled, striking with his left fist, aiming for Robert's face. Robert dodged aside, but the blow landed on his shoulder, swinging him round. He hit the wall with a grunt. Rice cried out in triumph, aiming a sharp thrust with his keen blade, but Robert rolled out of the way. Rice's sword stabbed into the plaster and stuck. He tugged at the blade in desperation, unable to free it. Robert again fell into the guard, fully intending to thrust his steel into the soft flesh of Rice's neck, but at the last second, he diverted his aim. The tip of his sword scored across Rice's forehead.

Rice screamed, letting go of his sword hilt, both hands coming up to cover his face. Dark blood streamed down into his eyes, over his nose and lips. Robert raised his right foot, gave his adversary's stomach a hard shove, enough to knock him over. Rice hit the wall and rolled onto the floor, where he gasped and whimpered.

Robert knelt beside him. Rice's injury was minor, but it had blinded him with blood and pain. "Stay here, and stay out of my way," Robert said, "or I'll make good on that old threat to slit your throat."

Sheathing his sword, Robert stalked out into the yard.

*****

The first gun opened fire.

The head of the French column had just capped a rise in the road, grenadiers in tall shakos, linen coats, and red epaulettes. They seemed to rise from the ground, like the vengeful dead returning to earth. Their pounding drums reverberated, but Robert's howitzers were louder, each going off in succession. One of the Shrapnel shells failed to detonate, but those that did burst on target, and the entire front two ranks of the lead column seemed to melt. But there were more coming up behind, and they were no more than two hundred yards away and closing.

"Load and fire, load and fire!" Robert shouted. He had taken charge of the howitzers, while Mumbles had the two nine-pounders. "This is the time for rapid fire, lads! Load and fire!"

The howitzers blasted as one, recoiling away from the wall. The shells screamed as the gunners leapt in, taking hold of trails and wheels, running the guns forward, sponging the stubby barrels, bringing forth the shells with their short fuses. Shells flew and burst, and men fell, were blasted away, bits of bodies and kit cast into the air. Still more infantry came up, striding over the bodies of the fallen. They began to run, doubling forward, shouting as they charged up the road.

The howitzers crashed again, fired almost at a flat trajectory. The shells plunged through the column like round shot, tearing down men, then exploding deep within their ranks. Robert could do nothing but watch, watch as his men reloaded. It took no more than ten seconds, then the linstocks came down again, three more shells stabbing into the dust and smoke.

Still, the French did not stop. Not all of them. The

survivors were there, not forty yards away. They had no formation, were just a screaming mob, and some had left the road and were coming across the open ground beyond the little wall, making straight for the howitzers with levelled bayonets.

"Trail left!" Robert said, which meant to turn the carriage trails to the left, thus sweeping the muzzles to the right to meet the new threat. The guns went off as one, two of the shells seeming to burst on contact with human flesh, and the grenadiers disappeared. Almost at the same time, Mumbles's two nine-pounders bellowed their deeper note, sending a wall of solid iron straight down the road. A spray of blood rose like red mist, and the enemy column divided into two, the survivors hugging the verges, but coming on, those in the rear stumbling over bodies and parts of bodies, but no longer a column, just a blackened and half mad mob.

From behind the churchyard wall, a rolling crash of musketry poured out from the Forty-third. The nine-pounders fired again, cut more men down, and still more came to take their place. Meanwhile the howitzers continued to plough shells into the rearmost column, which had come up last and was, until now, unscathed.

That was when the redcoats charged. Some still fired from behind their cover, but at least half the battalion must have crept around to the north in secret, and they poured up the road, a dense line of bayonets rushing straight into the remains of the French reserve. For a moment there was chaos, a mingling of redcoats and French greatcoats, a melee of men stabbing, thrusting, striking with musket butts and fists.

"Cease firing!" Robert cried, hoping to be heard, for the guns now might kill friend as well as foe. "Cease firing!" Whether his men heard or not he could not say, or maybe they realized that the enemy was too close, for they threw down their rammer staves and sponges and grabbed their carbines, adding their small arms fire to that of the infantry.

To Robert, the fight seemed to carry on in a strange and silent world, for with the guns no longer firing, he could no longer perceive a normal level of sound. He could only hear the pumping of his blood, as the enemy began to go the other way, to break and flee, stumbling along the road, and see the redcoats going after them, a single British battalion putting flight to what had been a French division.

"Cease firing," he said again, though there was no point. He noticed then that his sword was again in his hand. He did not remember drawing it. Its tip was still stained with Rice's blood.

"Let's hope that's the last of them, sir," Sergeant Hunter said, coming to stand beside him. "We just used the last of the Shrapnel."

Robert thought of Captain Tunge's attempted theft. If the theft had succeeded, the battery would have run out sooner, before the last push. "Thank you, Sergeant."

"And might I say congratulations, sir? We held 'em, sir."

Few officers would accept such presumption from a sergeant, but to Robert, it was welcome, and a reminder that, though Hunter knew about Rice, knew what had happened, his only concern was for the outcome of the battle.

"It's congratulations to you and the men that are in order, Sergeant. I think we may have managed five rounds a minute toward the end."

"Maybe, sir."

Robert looked around. "Is that drums I hear?"

Hunter cocked his head. "My ears are still ringing, sir. I'll need some hot tea to clear them. Always hot tea for the ears, sir."

Robert listened. No, it was not drums. It was hooves. As he

turned, he saw them. British cavalry, thundering from the rear, and now pouring through the village in attack column. They had seen the French grenadiers routed, and now charged. The gunners in Robert's battery were cheering, as were the infantry in the road and those still in position behind the church wall.

"I don't think we need to worry about our Shrapnel, Sergeant," Robert sad. "I think we'll have a rest now."

Chapter Sixteen:

Dust

Robert made his way to the rear, where a field hospital had been established in a stone barn. The day was dying, yet the smoke lingered, the last rays of the setting sunbathing Vimeiro and the battlefield in an eerie, brownish light. With a sense of unreality, almost as of a dream, Robert entered the barn, finding himself in a vast space filled with wounded men laid out in rows. They huddled on blankets and on the ground, men wrapped in crimsoned bandages, men who chatted quietly, or stared at the ceiling, or screamed in terror behind the screen where the surgeon worked. The place stank of blood and shit and the beginning of gangrene. It was a scene from hell, but it was not the particular hell Robert was looking for.

"Private," he said to the infantryman posted at the door. "Where have they taken the officers?"

The soldier stiffened to attention. "Farmhouse, sir."

The farmhouse was adjacent to the barn. It was small, too small to serve more than a dozen wounded, in Robert's estimate. He had heard that almost forty officers had been injured in the battle, but most of those had been in the effort to break another major French flank attack, far to the east of Vimeiro. Those fellows would not have been carted all the way back here, and doubtless, remained where they were, on the field where they fell.

Like the barn, there was a guard at the door to the farmhouse. The man shouldered arms as Robert drew closer. Robert idly touched his shako brim in response, then pushed open the door, ducking into an entry hall with a low ceiling. The dingy light from a few candles illuminated cracked plaster and the shapes of several uninjured officers milling about. The air was stifling and stank of blood and vomit. Robert's stomach clenched, though not so much from the stench as the general atmosphere of gloom about the place. This gloom, like a mantle of melancholy, had settled over the entire army, despite the victory, despite the light casualties. Robert supposed that one reason for this, perhaps the primary reason, was that the British were to remain on the ridge, squandering their victory and letting the French escape. This was because General Wellesley had been superseded at the last minute, just as Mumbles had predicted. Reinforcements from Britain, landing a short distance down the coast, had brought with them a senior commander, in the form of Sir Harry Burrard. Burrard wished to wait before continuing on to Lisbon. So, they would wait.

"Is there someone I can speak to here?" Robert said, doffing his shako. "I'm looking for a Royal Artillery officer. Captain Flushing, wounded in the leg."

A few faces turned to him, blinking like stupid sheep. Someone said, "One of the surgeons will know."

Robert found two surgeons within, both conferring in the parlour. He repeated his question, and one of the surgeons took him aside, leading him by the elbow to a dim corner.

"Ah, yes, Captain Flushing," the surgeon said. "A shame, that, a real shame. I'm afraid the wound was mortal. We did what we could, but the shock and loss of blood were too great. Losing a leg is no small thing."

Robert could only nod. For some reason, the news of Flashdash's death came as a surprise. Somehow, he had convinced himself that the captain would pull through.

"I suppose we should bury him then," he said, not meaning to sound heartless. He was simply considering the practicalities, and after a moment's reflection he discovered that Flashdash's death seemed not so tragic. He had not liked the man, and there was death in war. Flashdash had been stupid, and he had paid for it. "The body is still here?"

"In the kitchen. There are three officers there."

"I'll send a fatigue party to deal with it, once I learn where the cemetery is to be established."

After that, Robert did not linger. It was growing darker when he emerged from the house, and for a few seconds, he did not recognize the stout figure that was crossing the yard toward him. Then he realized that it was Captain Tunge. Tunge was probably also wondering what had happened to Flashdash.

Robert had no wish for further unpleasantries amongst the officers of his brigade. Saluting, he said, "Good evening, Captain."

Tunge stopped to return the gesture. Robert paused, assuming that the driver was about to say something nasty, but instead, he asked, "Have you news of Captain Flushing?"

"I have just made inquiries. I'm afraid that he died of his wounds." He let that sink in, then added, "That means that until Lieutenant Rice recovers from his injury, I'm retaining command of the company. Lieutenant Campion has no objections."

Tunge nodded slowly. He cleared his throat. "Well then. Well then, we must work together."

Robert tried to gauge the man's tone, searching for signs of hostility, but as he studied the driver captain, he noticed the soft flesh under the man's eyes, the drooping chin, the tightness of his waistcoat. Tunge was a thief, no doubt corrupt to the core, and Robert saw now that he was all fat and no fibre. This was an officer who liked his comforts, one who stole to pad his income. Robert decided that he would have no more trouble from him.

"We will work together, Captain," he said. "I look forward to it."

Then he touched his hat again, and with a final, "Good evening," he continued on his way.

*****

Rice had not gone to the officer's hospital but remained in the little house in Vimeiro. The artillery brigade's two drummers, upon discovering him bleeding in the hallway, had carried him to the only bedroom. There, a surgeon from General Fane's brigade had at last seen to him, stitching and bandaging the wound.

"Get out," he whispered when Robert strode into the room.

"Shut up and listen to me," Robert snapped, dragging a stool to the side of the bed and sitting. "Flashdash is dead, died not long after his wounding. So, your threats to me now mean nothing. Do you understand? No one is going to care what I did with his wife."

Rice said nothing. His breathing was steady, but already he was showing signs of fever. The bandage on his forehead was brown with dried and crusted blood.

"I'll have you cashiered," he finally murmured. "You struck a superior in front of witnesses. You disobeyed my orders. You committed mutiny, Saxon, and you'll hang for it. I swear you'll hang for it."

Robert remained calm. Rice could no longer threaten him. "Actually, you disobeyed orders, or tried to. I reminded you of your duty, but you wouldn't listen. If anyone is a mutineer, it's you. As for witnesses, I challenge you to produce them. Sergeant Hunter claims to have seen nothing, as does our friend Mumbles, who was with the nine-pounders the entire time. Captain Tunge was not in the yard, but with the limbers and wagons on the north side of this house. So, you see, everything stands in my favour."

Rice sat up, grimacing from the pain. "No, it doesn't, you blackguard! When I recover, the company is mine. You're still under my command and bound to follow my orders."

Robert balanced the tip of his sword scabbard on the floor and closed his hands over the hilt. "That's what I've come to see you about. You see, I think it best if you don't return to the company. Would you like to know my reasoning? I'm not the only one who heard you ordering us to withdraw. Unlike you, I have willing witnesses who know that you would have left a gap in our line that the French could have exploited. You displayed cowardice under fire. It would be a pity if that became common knowledge. If your father were to find out, for instance."

For a moment, Rice was speechless with rage. Then he managed to bleat, "How dare you threaten me!"

Robert resisted the urge to slap this spoiled brat across his ruined face. "Oh, it's all right for you to threaten me, or for you to threaten anyone, but as soon as they strike back, it's an outrage. That's how it's always been with you, Rice, and I've had enough. You may learn to be a useful officer some day, but not yet, and I won't have you around me anymore. There's something you need to understand. As a result of the fact that I did not panic, that I held the ground as ordered and helped put the French to flight, I'm very much in Colonel Robe's good books. He was pleased with our performance, impressed that we had fired all our ammunition, and told me himself that he will mention my name in his report to General Wellesley. This means I have a great deal of credibility, whereas you," and he shrugged, "are just another officer who was wounded."

"You wounded me, you bastard!"

"No, no, no, it doesn't have to be so. Listen carefully. Here's what I propose." Robert leaned in close, lowering his voice and grinning, just as if he and Rice were clever friends and conspirators. "Rather than have everyone know that you panicked and wanted to run, you will claim that your wound was inflicted by the French. Perhaps by a musket ball, or a plaster splinter thrown up from the wall. I'll back you up, if anyone asks. This way you avoid the shame of everyone knowing that I beat you, and you can also avoid the humiliation of anyone else ever knowing that you ordered a withdrawal against orders. You can save your reputation and probably your commission, Rice."

Rice's mouth worked, and he spluttered something unintelligible. Robert folded his arms.

"I am disposed to show mercy, Rice, though God alone knows why. I want you to write your father, as you threatened to do before, but instead of asking him to pull strings to have me transferred, you'll ask that he find you a new assignment. There will be more new Royal Artillery brigades coming out to Portugal, and maybe, as an officer with some battle experience, they'll give you one. We've just scored a victory against one of Bonaparte's marshals, and I have no doubt this is the start of a long and fruitful war. However, if you decide to remain with me, I'll spill everything and make your life hell."

Rice had settled back into his bed and stared at the ceiling.

"You can't blackmail me. You can't tell anyone what happened without also revealing that you struck me, a superior officer—"

"Not true. You wanted to withdraw, but luckily for us, a stray French musket ball cut a furrow in your head at that moment, and I took command. At least, that's how I remember it. That's how Mumbles will remember it, and Sergeant Hunter, if needed."

Rice closed his eyes.

"Damn it, Rice, I'm giving you a chance here. You can start over again and forget this ridiculous feud."

"Go away," Rice said. "You can have this cursed company. I don't care. Just go away."

Robert stood. "Thank you. I believe I will."

* * * * *

The army remained in camp and Robert remained in nominal command of the company. Colonel Robe warned him not to grow comfortable with the position, not to presume too much. Robert had only just left the Academy, was still a boy in the eyes of many, and like General Wellesley, it was likely that he would soon be replaced by a senior officer.

"The campaign against the French in Iberia is just beginning," Robe said. "Every officer who wants to make a name for himself will be clamouring for a place here in Portugal. Unless you have particular influence, you will soon have to share your company again."

A few days after the battle, another general arrived to take command from Burrard. Sir Hew Dalrymple brought with him still more troops, more ammunition, more horses, and some officers' wives and other auxiliaries. He did not order a resumption of the advance to Lisbon. Instead, on August 22, he negotiated an armistice with the enemy, allowing the French to evacuate Portugal with all their men and arms. Under the terms of the armistice, the French would not be paroled nor treated as prisoners but would simply be shipped back to France at Britain's expense. It was said that General Wellesley, who had advocated a plan to capture the entire French army, was outraged.

Robert was not surprised at the news. The problems he had encountered at the Academy and in his company could not be unique. The British Army, he suspected, was filled with well placed fools.

"The world," he said to Mumbles one evening, "is truly a dark and gloomy place, for the men who inhabit it make it so."

Yet, that was not the end of it. Still more troops arrived, including a fourth general to command the army, a fellow named Sir John Moore. "The king himself will be next," Robert had quipped when he heard this latest. Though perhaps, he decided, this was an improvement, for it was rumoured that Moore had plans to retrain the Portuguese army, then advance his combined forces into Spain.

"I hope that the king and Parliament see us through this time," Robert told Mumbles. "The other British land operations against Bonaparte have been either failures or pinpricks. I want us to stay here, rout the bastards from Portugal, then fight them across Spain and so on, up into the underbelly of France. I want us to beat them. I want us to show them that they have no right to do this thing, this evil, terrible, criminal thing."

The bully and tyrant of Europe had to be given a taste of his own medicine. He had to be beaten, routed, utterly destroyed. Robert could conceive of no other ambition now, than to see that done.

*****

"The world is a dark and gloomy place," Robert repeated to himself one evening as he sat alone in his makeshift company headquarters, a house in Vimeiro. A single candle burned on the top of his writing desk. Outside in the yard, an ox lowed. Robert sifted through a series of reports, records of company punishment, of their new ammunition supplies. There was much for a company commander to keep track of, but Robert found it a simple task, if tedious. A small price to pay for command, and he meant to do the most, to work as hard as he could, to keep the company sharp. If he was to be replaced by a superior, he would give his new captain the best artillery company in the British Army.

Until that time, they would spend their days in drill. They were good, had proved themselves, but they could be better. They could always be better, and he suspected there would not be as much idle time as many believed. The army would, again, be on the move.

He took a fresh sheet of writing paper from a pigeonhole. The desk was fully stocked with quills, ink and paper. The house was across the street from the church, and its owners had fled in apparent haste, leaving all their furniture, bedding, clothing, dishes and cutlery.

He dipped his quill in the ink bottle and scratched, "My dear sister," at the top of the fresh page.

There was a sharp rap at the study door. He paused, quill poised. The rapping sounded again. This time he rose to his feet. The chair creaked as his weight left it.

"Yes?" he said, opening the door.

He had expected Mumbles or Hunter, but Marion Flushing stood in the hall. They faced each other in silence. Her face was composed, expressionless, and as soft and beautiful as he remembered. Her gown was a pale yellow. She held a straw bonnet in her hands.

"Marion," he said at length. She was like a ghost, something that should not be.

"Is he here?" she said.

"Is who here?"

"They told me this was your company headquarters."

"It is," he said, and then he understood. She must have arrived with General Moore's contingent, probably had landed and asked directions to her husband's brigade. She had been directed to their position, but no one had told her that her husband was no longer in command. No one had told her that he had not survived the battle. "I... please, come in."

There were two chairs in the room, one at the desk and the other in the corner. He gestured toward the latter. "Maybe you should sit. I think it would be best."

She walked with a strange stiffness he had never seen before, as if she were struggling to keep her balance. She obeyed his suggestion, dropping onto the chair, her features hardening. "What has happened? Why are you here alone?"

"Because I command the company. Listen, do you want a drink?" There was a bottle of something in the desk and a pair of small wine glasses.

A flicker of a smile touched her lips, just for a fraction of a second. "No. No, I want to know where my... where Captain Flushing is."

"Captain Flushing," he repeated. She would not refer to him as her husband. Robert set down his quill, keeping the nib away from his sister's letter. "They should have told you. Someone should have told you. Your husband was killed in the action."

He knew he could have softened the blow, been more tactful, more understanding, but perhaps there was no point. She claimed not to have loved the man, so what did it matter? Robert had little fear of her erupting in tears and rage.

And she did not. What Robert saw, just for a brief flash, was triumph. Then the grim mask returned, but he had seen it. Seen the spark within her eyes.

"I see," she said.

"I'm sorry," he tried, the words sounding ridiculous.

"No, you're not, and neither am I. He died doing his duty. That's all that mattered to him."

She let the silence between them stand for a moment, then Robert asked, "And what matters to you?"

Her sudden anger was fierce, contained and perfectly genuine. "Don't question me, Robert."

He met her with the same. "Fine, I won't." He bowed. "Good luck, then, Mrs. Flushing."

She stared at him, and now there was something lost about her. "I came all the way from England to be with him."

Robert shrugged. "And he's not here, but I can have someone show you where the grave is."

"Yes, please do..." She rose to her feet, slowly, carefully, "... in the morning. For now, I must... find somewhere to stay. This is not what I had expected. Not at all."

Robert held his hands behind his back, a force of habit. "The village and surrounding farms are crowded, and you won't find anything. It would be best if you took my quarters, here in this house. I'll sleep in one of the wagons. The nights here are too warm to be inside, anyway."

She looked away. "Thank you."

"It's the least I can do," he said, making for the door. "I'll fetch an orderly to help you with your things."

"Thank you, Robert," she called after him.

He pulled open the door, but something made him pause. Glancing back, he watched as she sat still in her chair. The light from the candle played across one cheek, across her lips. She was smiling.

"I won't be long," he said.

"Yes, thank you," she said again.

With a nod, he left the study and moved out into the Portuguese night.

THE END

It may seem astonishing and even unbelievable that gun detachments of the Royal Artillery could achieve a rate of fire of five rounds a minute with a muzzle-loading gun, but they could and they did, and there are reports of even higher rates. For example, in 1802 the British Army authorized a series of military experiments in Hyde Park, London, in which they conducted simulated attacks of cavalry and infantry against artillery. In the cavalry attack, the artillery was able to fire thirteen rounds in 115 seconds, which is almost seven rounds per minute. In the infantry attack, they fired thirteen rounds in 102 seconds, which is close to eight rounds per minute.

Of course, this rate of fire was difficult to sustain for long, and could exhaust both the gun crew and the ammunition supply. An extreme rate of fire was also unsafe. Having worked with historic artillery for many years, I have seen attempts at "speed drill" and can say that it can only be achieved by cutting a few corners. This may have been acceptable in a moment when French cavalry was bearing down on your position, but in a present-day ceremonial or re-enactment context, it is not worth the risk. So if anyone reading is thinking about trying it, I strongly recommend you do not (at least not with ammunition)!

Robert Saxon had no such concerns and seems drawn to extremes. I have only just begun to explore his career, and as the Peninsular War has also only just begun (from his perspective), that career may be a long one – if he survives. Will his passions lead to success, or his undoing?

—Harold R Thompson

ABOUT THE AUTHOR

HAROLD R THOMPSON

Harold R. Thompson is the author of a bestselling series of historical novels which include *Dudley's Fusiliers*, *Guns of Sevastopol* and *Sword of the Mogul*. His standalone novel, *The End of the Tether*, is a dramatization of the siege of Yorktown during the American Revolution. He has also written short science fiction and fantasy for a variety of print and online magazines. He lives in Nova Scotia and, when not writing or spending time with his family, works for Parks Canada in the field of public history. For several years he was the senior instructor of artillery for the living history program at the Halifax Citadel National Historic Site, and is a national historic weapons instructor for Parks Canada.

Lieutenant James Lockwood

By

Mark Bois

"Captain Barr desperately wanted to kill Lieutenant Lockwood. He thought constantly of doing so, though he had long since given up any consideration of a formal duel. Lockwood, after all, was a good shot and a fine swordsman; a knife in the back would do. And then Barr dreamt of going back to Ireland, and of taking Brigid Lockwood for his own."

So begins the story of Lieutenant James Lockwood, his wife Brigid, and his deadly rivalry – professional and romantic – with Charles Barr. Lockwood and Barr hold each other's honor hostage, at a time when a man's honor meant more than his life. But can a man as treacherous as Charles Barr be trusted to keep secret the disgrace that could irrevocably ruin Lockwood and his family?

Against a backdrop of famine and uprising in Ireland, and the war between Napoleon and Wellington, showing the famous Inniskilling Regiment in historically accurate detail, here is a romance for the ages, and for all time.

"… Bois' meticulous research and command of historical detail makes this novel a must read. He sets the standard for research and understanding… and the audience will demand more novels from this new author. Historical fiction welcomes Mark Bois with open arms." – Lt. Col. Brad Luebbert, US Army

PENMORE PRESS
www.penmorepress.com

Capital's Punishment
by
John Danielski

The White House is in flames, the Capitol a gutted shell. President Madison is in hiding. Organized resistance has collapsed, and British soldiers prowl the streets of Washington.

Two islands of fortitude rise above the sea of chaos—one scarlet, one blue. Royal Marine Captain Thomas Pennywhistle has no wish to see the young American republic destroyed; he must strike a balance between his humanity and his passion for absolute victory. Captain John Tracy of the United States Marines hazards his life on the battlefield, but he must also fight a powerful conspiracy that threatens the country from within.

Pennywhistle and Tracy are forced into an uneasy alliance that will try the resolve of both. Together, they will question the depth of their loyalties as heads and hearts argue for the fate of a nation

PENMORE PRESS
www.penmorepress.com

THE AMERICAN CAPTAIN

BY

JAMES KEFFER

The war was going poorly for the US Navy in 1814. Despite some early successes in single-ship engagements, Britain's Royal Navy ruled the waters off the American coast. All the major ports were closed by British blockade squadrons, and the British Army captured and burned the capitol city of Washington. Even in this darkest hour, there is a glimmer of hope. Two new warships are about to take to the seas for the Americans, the 44-gun frigate *Columbia* and the sloop of war *Argus*. To command them, the navy turns to its most experienced officer, Captain Hezekiah Albritton. Albritton is ordered to go to sea and raid the British sea lanes, but he has many obstacles to overcome.

PENMORE PRESS
www.penmorepress.com

Midshipman Graham and the Battle of Abukir

By

James Boschert

It is midsummer of 1799 and the British Navy in the Mediterranean Theater of operations. Napoleon has brought the best soldiers and scientists from France to claim Egypt and replace the Turkish empire with one of his own making, but the debacle at Acre has caused the brilliant general to retreat to Cairo.

Commodore Sir Sidney Smith and the Turkish army land at the strategically critical fortress of Abukir, on the northern coast of Egypt. Here Smith plans to further the reversal of Napoleon's fortunes. Unfortunately, the Turks badly underestimate the speed, strength, and resolve of the French Army, and the ensuing battle becomes one of the worst defeats in Arab history.

Young Midshipman Duncan Graham is anxious to get ahead in the British Navy, but has many hurdles to overcome. Without any familial privileges to smooth his way, he can only advance through merit. The fires of war prove his mettle, but during an expedition to obtain desperately needed fresh water – and an illegal duel – a French patrol drives off the boats, and Graham is left stranded on shore. It now becomes a question of evasion and survival with the help of a British spy. Graham has to become very adaptable in order to avoid detection by the French police, and he must help the spy facilitate a daring escape by sea in order to get back to the British squadron.

"Midshipman Graham and The Battle of Abukir is both a rousing Napoleonic naval yarn and a convincing coming of age story. The battle scenes are riveting and powerful, the exotic Egyptian locales colorfully rendered." – John Danielski, author of *Capital's Punishment*

PENMORE PRESS
www.penmorepress.com